THE THIRD CRAFT

THE THIRD CRAFT

JAMES T. HARRIS

THE THIRD CRAFT TRILOGY 1

BPS books

Published in 2008 by
BPS Books
Toronto, Canada
www.bpsbooks.net
A division of Bastian Publishing Services Ltd.

ISBN 978-0-9809231-2-4

Cataloguing in Publication Data available from Library and Archives Canada.

Cover, text design, and typesetting: Greg Devitt Design

Cover image: istockphoto

This is a work of fiction. Names, characters, places, and events are either the product of the author's imagination or are used fictitiously.

This book is dedicated to the ones I love

CHAPTER 1

Elliot Lake, Ontario, July 1982

It is said that the difference between an adventure and a tragedy lies in the outcome. Young Joe Grayer was about to discover that difference.

Joe grasped the Suzuki's black rubber handle grips with his weathered leather gloves. He wore a grin like a wraith. His motocross bike wobbled and shuddered in an effort to fling him off the worn black-vinyl seat into the trees that lined the path. But Joe guided the Suzuki with an expert grip, and his bike responded as if alive to his wishes.

He twisted the throttle sharply and lifted off the seat for balance, ready for the thrust to come. The soles of his scuffed leather boots gripped the foot pegs. The ring-ding-ding of the motor burst into a throaty growl as a gush of fuel jetted into the carburetor. Staccato fire rang out from both cylinders. With a burst of energy, the Suzuki was airborne, clearing a rotted log blocking the path. The rear wheel grazed the bark on the way down, throwing up a cascade of splinters.

The knobby tires expelled chunks of tree like a grinder's wheel.

Evergreen, maple, and elm trees became a soup of blurred green as the bike dashed its way through the forest like a deer. The mosaic of the sun's rays on the forest floor flew past in pencil-straight lines.

God, it was great to be eighteen and feel so alive! The air was fresh, the sun was new, and the throbbing power beneath his body was intoxicating.

Joe knew no fear. Barely past the peach-fuzz stage of maturity, he was lean and rugged. While there was not an ounce of fat on him, he was not Hollywood-hard or chiseled. He had the beauty of youth that most males share for a short period. Not a boy, yet not fully a man, Joe had one particularly outstanding feature—his eyes. They were an intense brown, so deep and dark that they often appeared black. Yet at times they seemed to catch the light and become almost luminescent, a hint of green buried deep within. This trick of the light was a startling offset to his tousled light brown hair and devil-may-care attitude.

An effortless A student, he had found little to challenge him at school. No, to be honest, he struggled to find any real purpose for scholastic academics. He felt his destiny lay somewhere other than sitting in a lecture hall, even though he and his twin brother, Hawk had been promoted two grades in advance of their age, leaving high school at fifteen. Now in the final year of his three year course at university, Joe pondered his future.

Joe raced his bike mercilessly along the overgrown footpath, failing to gauge the path ahead for danger. The thrill of motocross is to push the limits, to explore and learn on the go. Plunging headfirst into the unknown was just part of the adrenalin rush. Throw some youthful inexperience into the mix, and you've got a dangerous cocktail of pleasure and adventure.

It had rained heavily the previous day. The surface of the ground appeared dry, but underneath, the pebbly soil was unstable. Joe rounded a cluster of thick bushes, only to discover that the path had abruptly disappeared. Actually, the entire side of the hill had disappeared. Joe stared into a void as he and the bike became airborne.

"Oh crap," he hissed through his teeth. He twisted in mid-air to regain control, but to no avail.

The bike nosed down and plowed into gravelly, loose dirt. The front wheel dug in first, then the bike began to tumble nose over tail. *Ass over teakettle* was the expression that jumped into Joe's mind. At this point, he and the bike parted company. His feet left the pegs, his boots pointing upwards, parallel to the seat. Then he experienced a brief arching handstand as his face was buried in the speedometer gauge. His body was at right angles to the bike, face down, feet high above the seat. The handstand continued for a split second until he finalized his forward arch over the handlebars, feet flailing. He went spinning cartwheel-style down the hill, followed closely by his bike, which flipped from side to side like a fish arching to work free of a hook.

The machine twisted and turned in a dance of agony as it tumbled down the slope. Then, forty feet down the hill, it stopped abruptly. So did Joe. The hill, however, did not—the disruption had caused a sort of mudslide. The hill began to move. Joe was lying on his back when he felt the earth give way beneath him with a whispering groan. Like a lazy surfer, he rode the tons of muddy, pebbly earth flexing and rolling beneath him, oozing and burping like porridge down the hillside. He fought to stay on top of the flowing mass. His fiberglass helmet took several sidelong blows from falling stones. His black nylon Suzuki jumpsuit was a mess of orange and brown mud, but it didn't rip. He cried out in pain as rocks pummeled his shoulders and back. He could feel the crush of rock through his knees and legs, despite the fact that they were well padded.

Miraculously, though a massive section of the hill had broken away, neither he nor his bike was buried. As the dust cleared and settled, he lay on his back still staring up at the cloudless pale blue sky. He began gingerly flexing various parts of his body to determine the damages. He would be bruised, he concluded, but there was no serious injury. He lay back and rested, gathering his strength.

His heart rate finally returned to normal, but he had received a good scare. He was amazed that he hadn't broken any bones. Like a wounded soldier on a battlefield, he crawled over to the bike.

The Suzuki was lodged in a most unusual manner. It was resting perfectly perpendicular to the ground. Its front wheel, pointing straight up at the sky, turned slowly. Gas was trickling from the fuel cap into the soil, creating a small but growing puddle. The bike had stalled during the crash. The only sounds were the ticking of the exhaust pipes and the engine fins as they cooled down at different rates.

Wincing with pain, Joe hauled on the frame of the bike to roll it over and free it. The bike rocked laboriously from side to side, but returned to the center point each time, like one of those old clown punching bags with sand in the bottom.

Joe just stood there and stared at it. Since when did motorbikes balance perfectly upside down? He tried to tip the bike over, but once again it simply bounced back.

A mysterious force seemed to be keeping the bike in this very strange position. Try as he might, Joe could not dislodge it. It was as if the bike had a mind of its own and had chosen not to move. Joe sensed a strange buzzing sensation beneath his feet, but all he could see was mud.

Damn it, he thought. The mud's not deep enough to embed the bike. Why won't it move?

After a few more attempts to topple the bike, he gave up. Kicking out at the yellow bike frame, he resigned himself to getting some help. He muttered and grumbled as he clawed his way up the hill.

It was dusk by the time his walk was over. His twin brother Harry, whom people always called Hawk because of his penetrating eyes, met him at the door with a concerned look.

"God, you look awful. What happened?"

Joe winced. "I wiped out on the hill out back. I lost it on the top trail. Some kind of slide. I couldn't stop. I went over, big time."

"You OK?"

"I'm hurting, but nothing is busted. Helmet took most of the hit."

"Lucky you were wearing your gear."

"You're right there."

Hawk ushered Joe inside. Joe plunked himself down at the kitchen table.

"The bike is stuck. It's upside down. I couldn't move it. There's something weird —"

Hawk cut him off. "Yeah, with you there's always something weird. Let's get you cleaned off and you can tell me more of your tale of woe. Did you total the bike?"

"Nope, don't think so. But it won't budge. Like I said, there's something weird —"

"Everything's a mystery with you, Joe. Let's worry about your weirdness later, OK?"

The two boys were fraternal twins. Yet there was something about them that made people say they might as well have been identical. They had grown up near Los Alamos Air Force Base in New Mexico. They were considered military brats because their father, Frank Grayer, was a career man with the U.S. Air Force. Their mother had died in child-birth, and Grayer had struggled to raise the twins on his own.

Grayer was in a special branch of military intelligence known as the Air Intelligence Agency. He was an assistant to the Secretary of Defense in the U.S. Department of Defense. The twins ended up spending a lot of time with Grayer's trusted friend and only confidant,

David Bohr, and his family. The Bohrs unofficially adopted the twins because of Grayer's impossible travel schedule. They were no trouble. Joe and Hawk nicknamed David "Da Bore" because he of his extreme preoccupation with his work.

Several years ago, after some big security issue, their father went into deep cover and the twins were sent to live with their aunt and uncle in Toronto.

Joe had wanted to leave Toronto for the summer. His girlfriend was studying over in Europe. He had no job. His friends were at camp or simply away for the summer doing family stuff. The prospect of a lonely, boring summer in the city did not appeal to him. And he got the feeling that his aunt and uncle felt likewise. That's why he had jumped at the opportunity to join Hawk at his job site just north of Sudbury, Ontario, for the summer holidays.

And what a summer it had turned out to be! Joe had nothing but time on his hands. It was too late to find a job for the summer and, to be honest, he hadn't been trying too hard to find one. He chose instead to ride his motorcycle through the woods near Elliot Lake to hone his biking skills. The time flew by.

Hawk's job site was near Blind River, about five miles west of Elliot Lake on Highway 17. Elliot Lake had an interesting past. It was originally mined for uranium, but it had been abandoned for several years. There was a four-lane highway, now empty, off the main Trans-Canada route into the downtown area. The highway was in surprisingly good shape after ten years of neglect, though grass now grew between its cracks.

Elliot Lake was a modern ghost town. The town's single employer had been the mine. Its closure in the early 1970s caused a huge migration out of town. Property values tumbled overnight. Families and miners left quickly in search of new employment opportunities. Unsold homes and unusable items were left behind. Anything portable was packed into cars, vans, or trucks and moved away. Even ten years later, a few abandoned luxury cars—a Cadillac Eldorado and an Olds 98, among others—were visible in the fields beside the highway as you drove into town. With no local mechanics available, they were too costly to repair, so their owners had just pushed them to the side of the highway. Eventually obscured by tall grass, windows cloudy with age, these depressing monoliths greeted anyone driving into town, mere hints of the glory days of uranium mining.

The old mine entrance, rigging, and equipment were situated a quarter of a mile from the center of town. The primary processing had been done on site, with the ore then sent directly to the processing plant via a narrow-guage siding line. The mining administration offices were in the center of town. The demand for that particular ore grade of uranium had diminished almost overnight. The arms race was in full swing, but the U.S. had a massive stockpile of nuclear materials.

There was a growing concern about how to safely dispose of the arsenal once a nuclear weapon became obsolete. As demand evaporated, the cost to mine the ore exceeded the value of the uranium.

Businesses closed soon after the mine shut down. The town's lone shopping mall ceased management operations after losing its main tenant, the IGA supermarket. It had been the "anchor" store drawing the shopping traffic that fed the other retailers. What few shoppers were left were greeted by a cheerless expanse of floor-to-ceiling windows covered on the inside with sheets of brown paper.

Elliot Lake achieved official ghost-town status after the telephone crews came in and disconnected the main PBX. Thereafter, there was no phone service to any homes or businesses. Some clear Plexiglas Bell call boxes remained intact. There were four working pay phones in the entire town. To alleviate the threat of fire, the main Hydro power grid had been cut off.

That was then. In the last few years, utilities had been restored to small sections of the area as new people—mostly pensioners and retirees on fixed income—began to migrate north to the region. It was cheap living, and a bargain if you factored in the breathtaking Canadian wilderness at your doorstep. Joe and Hawk lived in one of the abandoned homes. Cheap, but clean and in pristine shape, frozen in time.

Frowning at the thought that his reckless brother might have been killed, Hawk dragged Joe into the bathroom to clean up and then back into the kitchen. "Sit. I'll get you a drink. What do you want? Coffee? Beer?"

"Just a soda, thanks. Anyway, my bike's still there. It's upside down and stuck. It shouldn't be stuck, but it is. Something's holding it, and it isn't the mud."

Hawk raised an eyebrow.

Joe hated asking anyone for help, but he was in a jam. "Can you help me get it back home?"

Hawk shrugged. "Sure. Why not? After work tomorrow. I'll borrow the ATV. We'll go see what's so weird." He grinned at his brother. "You sure you didn't hit your head?"

CHAPTER 2

Elliot Lake

The next day was overcast but mild. Summers in this part of Canada were usually hot and humid, with swarms of deer flies and mosquitoes. Not this day. There was a constant, determined wind off the lake that drove the insects inland to the deep woods beyond the town.

When Hawk returned home from work in the late afternoon, the sun was still high. He had a small trailer hooked to the back of his Corvette. On the trailer was a Mean Green John Deere 4x4 ATV, strapped down on all four sides to the black trailer frame. The trailer had a steel mesh flip-down ramp at the rear, slightly rusted from wear.

It was unusual to see a Corvette being used to haul a trailer. The car's body was fabricated primarily of fiberglass, which, like glass, tends to shatter. The vehicle was also too light to make a very good truck. None of this stopped Hawk from having a trailer hitch welded to the car's wishbone frame. The Corvette's 427 engine—once one of

GM's truck engine blocks—was very powerful, and its steel frame was certainly strong enough to haul around a light trailer.

Hawk honked the horn as he pulled up to the house. Seconds later Joe came out and met him in the driveway. He had just pulled on a fresh gray T-shirt.

Hawk was grinning. "The boss let me use the ATV," he said. He jumped out of the Vette and lowered the ramp, then backed the ATV off the trailer. The Corvette's rear lurched appreciatively upwards when the burden was lifted off the trailer.

"Nice machine" Joe said, he looked at the John Deere. "Nothing like traveling in style. Let's bring some tow rope." He went to the carport and fished two rust-yellowed half-inch white nylon ropes out of a wooden bin at the back. Like a range cowboy, he slung the ropes over his shoulder and mounted the ATV behind his brother.

The vehicle drove handily down the cracked paved roads of their small subdivision and roared along the same trails that Joe had taken yesterday. Dust snakes skittered away from the balloon wheels as the vehicle charged along the trail. Joe tapped Hawk on the shoulder as they approached the slide area. He signaled Hawk to slow down. Hawk nodded and slowed the vehicle to a crawl. He stopped the ATV on the edge of the washout and looked over the fifty-foot edge.

"Quite a slide," Hawk said, shaking his head. "It's a wonder you weren't killed."

Hawk began the descent down the hill in a crisscross pattern, like a skier coming down a steep mountain. He managed to direct the ATV to the spot where the Suzuki balanced upside down. It was a curious sight.

Hawk killed the engine, jumped off the ATV, and walked up to the bike. Joe was right behind, rope in hand. Hawk bent down on one knee to examine the bike. He braced himself and shoved hard. The bike wobbled and returned to the same position. He tried pushing it several more times, finally glancing up with a puzzled look.

"Strangest thing I've ever seen. What do you think, Joe?"

"Something is holding the bike upright. I told you, this is so weird. Let's use the rope and see if we can pull her free with the ATV. You drive."

Joe wound the rope around the frame to distribute the load, then hooked the ends to the ATV ball hitch.

"Gently. Gently," he told Hawk as the ATV pulled the rope taut.

The ATV wheels struggled for a foothold in the soggy dirt and skidded a bit in the loose gravel. The John Deere slowly pulled away from the bike. You could see the strap begin to stretch. Then, suddenly, the bike broke free with a strange popping noise and was dragged sideways toward the ATV.

"Like pulling a tooth," Joe said. He walked toward the prone motorbike lying undignified on the ground. "Hey! Hawk, look at this."

Hawk unhooked the rope from the ATV and stowed it in the vehicle's storage compartment. He walked over to Joe and looked where Joe was staring. Where the bike had been, the dirt was roughed up, revealing a tiny metallic surface. Joe bent down and brushed the dirt away, exposing more gray-silver metal. Looking at each other in excitement, the two of them began to claw away at the ground.

"Something big is buried here," Joe said. "It's not a car. I wonder if it's an airplane wing?"

"Could be. Maybe an old crash site."

"Maybe there are bodies inside," Joe said. "Let's dig some more and find out."

Hawk rubbed his chin thoughtfully. "Why not? There's still time to go back and get some shovels before nightfall. Maybe we'll figure out what it is tonight."

"You go and get the shovels. I'll stay and see if I can get my bike going. Don't be long."

Joe always seemed to have an innate ability to understand things mechanical. So Hawk wasn't surprised, when he drove up a half hour later, to hear the motorbike idling noisily, its throaty exhaust gurgling away.

"Got her going, I see."

"There was some flooding in the carb because she was upside down, but yeah, I got her going." Joe looked over at Hawk, then at the bike. "I had to be careful. You don't want to fire up the engine without purging the gas. It could blow out the cylinder wall."

Joe's face screwed up as he watched Hawk unload the gear from the ATV. "Nice shovels," he said. "Who gets the *snow* shovel?"

"Hold on now," Hawk said. "I have been giving our little mystery some thought. I came up with a theory. Observe and learn, little bro."

He pulled a metal spade from the ATV. Walking over to the object, he began a digging motion with the metal spade. He aimed the spade at a mound of dirt covering the silver surface. As the blade arched downwards, it attached itself to the metal surface. The shovel seemed glued to the metal. It took their combined strength to wrestle the shovel free.

"So we now know that our airplane here is magnetic," Hawk said.

"That's weird. Since when are airplanes magnets?"

"Beats me, but this one sure as hell is." Hawk grinned directly at Joe and arched his eyebrows. "I have just the thing." He nodded toward the other shovels. "These snow shovels are made of fiberglass. They aren't metallic. They won't stick. I say we use them for the close-in work and maybe save the spade for the other stuff." He repeated the shoveling action with the other fiberglass shovel.

The fiberglass shovel worked. "Then this thing does have some sort of magnetic field," Joe said.

"Exactly," Hawk replied with a smile. "Here you go, start digging." He tossed a shovel to Joe.

"Hey Hawk," Joe said a few minutes later, talking as he shoveled. "Did you notice something strange when you hit the metal wing with the regular metal shovel? What did you hear?"

Hawk paused a minute, blue plastic shovel arched in mid-air. "Nothing. I heard nothing."

"Right! That's the point. There was no sound, no clanging noise. How can that be?"

Joe walked over, picked up the metal shovel, and swung it at the object. There was perhaps a whisper of a thudding sound, as if from very far away. Absent was the familiar clang of metal on metal.

"Now that's just plain spooky, isn't it?" Joe said.

Hawk leaned on his shovel, looking back at Joe. "It's a genuine mystery, Joe. It must defy all the laws of normal science. Well, any laws that I know. Let's dig and find out what the hell this thing is."

They toiled for almost three hours before the light finally failed. Hawk mopped his brow with the sleeve of his T-shirt. "I'm done for now. Let's call it a night."

Hawk jumped up onto the ATV horseback style and turned the starter. The machine coughed to life. He flicked on the headlamp and observed their work. They had excavated a patch of ground roughly ten feet by ten feet, exposing a shiny metallic surface that reflected the light from the headlamp. It was still only a shallow hole, less than three feet deep. The mudslide had done most of the heavy uncovering for them.

"How big is this damn thing?" Hawk asked.

"Don't know, Hawk. But life just got a whole lot more interesting."

Joe kicked down on the starter. The Suzuki engine gave a tenor roar. His right toe nudged downward and the bike clicked into first gear.

Holding in the clutch with his left hand and the brake with the other, Joe leaned toward Hawk and shouted, "Let's leave the shovels. I'm coming back tomorrow." With that he let the clutch go and the bike leapt away, spraying dirt and stones behind it. The engine screamed like an angry hornet's nest and the bike flew straight up the side of the hill.

Watching his brother go, Hawk's eyes narrowed. He did not have a good feeling about this place. His eyes focused on the digging, but there was nothing to see except a silver reflection like that of a frozen pond. Frowning, he coaxed the ATV back up the hill away from this mysterious place.

CHAPTER 3

Crash site, Elliot Lake

The next morning, Joe ambled into the kitchen and read the note Hawk had left for him: "Joe. Am going to check into any records of plane crashes in this area. Keep away from the dig. Please."

Joe half smiled. "Like I'm nine years old."

He wolfed down a decent breakfast of Shredded Wheat and blueberries and exited by the side door that led to the carport that served as their garage. He halted in front of the Suzuki.

"OK." He closed his eyes and said, half out loud, "Here's the deal. If the bike starts, it was meant to be that I go to the site. If not … well …"

It was a silly game because the outcome was never in doubt.

The Suzuki sputtered to life on the second thrust of the starter pedal. After a few cranks of the throttle, Joe knew the bike was good to go. "Meant to be," he muttered as he adjusted his gloves and helmet.

No full suit today. Only gray workout sweat shorts because there was work ahead. Digging and exploring. He pictured the newspaper caption: "JOE GRAYER DISCOVERS CRASH SITE." Joe was ready for something big to happen to him.

Like one of the seven dwarfs heading to the mine, Joe was off to the dig. He guided the bike to the crash site. *Hi ho, hi ho, it's off to work we go …*

The day of digging and pushing away debris went by fast. Joe was proud of his work but a little unnerved by the lack of progress. There was no "find" yet, just more exposed silvery-gray metal. He worked until dusk, then rode home, careful to arrive before Hawk.

Cleaning up after supper, Joe asked Hawk, "Anything on the plane crashes?"

"Nothing yet. I asked around, even phoned the *Sudbury Herald.* No outstanding missing aircraft near this area."

"What next?"

"We go to the RCMP. There's a local detachment in Sudbury. I can ask there."

"When?"

"It's got to be early next week. They've got me working overtime for the rest of the week. How did you spend your time today?"

Joe considered lying for a second, then said, "Went to the site. Dug some more."

"Figured as much. Look Joe, be careful. That place creeps me out a bit. Can't put my finger on it. Something about it doesn't feel right."

Joe shrugged. "Just a big patch of shiny metal so far."

"Let me know how it's going. If you uncover something, you know, weird, don't be a hero, come and get me." Hawk smiled and added with a hint of sarcasm, "Especially any bodies or little green men."

The next day, Hawk was up at 5:30 and gone by 6:00. Joe was not far behind. He left immediately for the crash site. He worked again from dawn to dusk, digging continuously, making slow, frustrating progress. The next day was the same. And the next.

On the fourth day after the discovery, Joe skidded the Suzuki to a halt several feet above the wreck site. A damp, earthy smell accompanied the early morning chill. He slowly removed his helmet and looked down. The early morning fog swirled around the dig site below.

The sight of the uncovered craft took his breath away.

It was definitely an aircraft of some sort. Even with only about one third uncovered, the shape was becoming apparent. It looked like a rounded boomerang. The exposed span of the single wing, which Joe guessed was about thirty feet long, caught the sun and gleamed perfectly silver in the dewy fog. In the young sunlight it looked like it was alive.

The depth of the belly of the craft was still unknown, because Joe had not dug around the fuselage yet. He would today.

He leaned the bike down gently against a rock and gathered up his tools. He used the metal spade sparingly because of its affinity for certain sections of the metallic surface. Joe had discovered that the metallic attraction was only on a small portion of the craft, not all over as they had first thought. If he kept the metal blade a foot or so away from the craft, there was little attraction. He preferred working with the metal spade because it was heavier and more efficient than the fiberglass shovel.

Joe took a break for lunch and liquids as the need arose, but on this particular day, he was like a man possessed. His enthusiasm had evolved into fanaticism. He moved a lot of soil. It had become lighter and lighter because the soil under the surface was relatively dry. Joe's digging became more efficient, and his yield increased.

By dusk he had cleared an important part of the fuselage away. Still, there was no evidence of a hatchway or entrance to the craft. The body of the fuselage was identical to the wing—velvety smooth, and cool to the touch. Strange, but it *felt good* to be in physical contact with the object. He found himself running his bare hand over the metal as if stroking a thoroughbred horse. He could almost feel a reactive quivering from the craft.

He took a break from digging. He leaned forward against the craft with both hands above his head in the standard police "spread 'em" mode. His skull rested comfortably against the skin of the craft, framed by his hands on either side. He felt a sense of longing for something. No. Not that. Joe felt a sense of comfort. It was pleasing and positive. He longed to know what was inside this object. He had a feeling that it was inexplicably linked to him personally, and he felt a nagging compulsion to continue digging. This compulsion caused him to ignore his instinct to return home before dark. He decided to keep digging until he found *something*. What that was, he had no idea.

He didn't know where he found the energy to keep digging, but he unearthed more of the ship that night than seemed humanly possible. At around 11:00 p.m., his physical energy gave out. He had his Home Hardware magnetic flashlight trained on his work area, but the light was poor. He picked it up and placed it on the metallic-looking skin of the craft, to give him more light for packing up his tools. But instead of the expected soft clank of magnet to metal, there was only silence. Dead silence. Then, in the stillness of the forest night, came the whispering hiss of air escaping.

Joe's heart skipped a beat and his eardrums pounded as blood rushed to his head. His eyes swung toward the sound. Inches from where he had placed the magnetic flashlight, the smooth gray metal was slowly but steadily spreading apart.

Humans, like all animals, have a fight-or-flight instinct. Adrenalin rushes through the body, carried along by a rapid increase in heart rate, which in turn creates more blood flow. Senses become sharply alert. Time slows down.

Joe's body began to shake uncontrollably. He stared, mesmerized, at the black opening. His pupils widened involuntarily. His eyes sucked up all the available ambient light as he strained to see inside the growing pitch black hole. He was ready to run in an instant.

The outer skin of the object widened fully to reveal a hatchway and utter blackness within. The hatch opened with a soft gust of air and a whoosh of fog as air in the craft met the moist warm air outside. Patches of dirt and pebbles burst away from the craft. A soft click sounded as the mechanism finished its work. Then silence.

Spitting out the dust, Joe Grayer coughed and stared in shock and disbelief. He stood like a statue slightly bent over, peering into the dark opening. With a start, it occurred to him that something could come screaming out of the hole and attack him. He gained some composure and took a breath. He took a few steps backwards. His eyes never left the black opening.

He retreated cautiously and sat down with an abrupt thump as his energy suddenly left him. His hand combed through his dusty hair as he tried to get his mind around the idea that he might have unearthed something not from this planet, something from outer space. If that were true ... The significance of the discovery began to dawn on him. Joe had read reports of downed spacecraft before, but he always felt they were science fiction stories made up by people with overactive imaginations.

But what *was* this thing lodged in the wilderness near Elliot Lake? How long had it been here? Who sent it? Were they still aboard? Were they dead or alive?

Alive! No. They couldn't be. They would have attacked him. Wouldn't they? Or maybe they are waiting and watching.

CHAPTER 4

The New Mexican desert, 1944

The year 1944 is one that stands out as a pivotal year for the planet Earth, yet few are aware of its true importance.

It started off on a gloomy note, as war raged on every continent of the planet. Mankind was in the throes of a massive culling. It had been like this for years. The entire herd of civilized people would reduce their ranks by 25 percent before the insanity came to an end.

Nineteen forty-four was the beginning of the end. In the summer of that year, the Allies landed a massive collective force of army and navy on the shores of Normandy in France. Called D-Day, it was a savage slaughter of mankind's finest youth on both sides. It was a collective effort—some say a last-ditch effort—on the part of the Allies, because the resources of Britain, Canada, and the U.S. were critically low. In the end, however, a beachhead was established, and the Allies moved east from there.

This moment was the turning point of World War II, which was fought in order to rid the Earth of the Nazi scourge.

In 1944 the Polish Home Army rose up against the Germans. The Poles had meager weapons and suffered some of the worst atrocities meted out by the merciless German army. But what they lacked in weapons, they made up for in spirit. They attacked the demoralized Germans, captured their weapons, and attacked again with these renewed resources.

There were various other milestones for the Allies in 1944. They liberated Rome. And they fought the important Battle of the Bulge against the Germans in the Ardennes. There was a huge loss of life, but the Allies won. In the South Pacific, the Americans successfully invaded the Philippines.

But 1944 also brought with it an event of far greater magnitude to human history than any of the above. Some time in August 1944, before the end of World War II, a strange aircraft crashed in some part of continental North America. To this day, no one knows with certainty where exactly the craft went down. It is of little importance anyway, because the remains were carefully moved to Los Alamos Air Force Base under a cloak of military secrecy. Allied military advisors believed the craft to be of German origin—on a spy mission or a test flight to gather technical information about the aircraft's capabilities. This theory made sense because Germany was at war with Britain and her allies.

Under the U.S. War Act, no mention of this discovery was tolerated. Any intelligence leaks could tip the Allies' hand, so the discovery was kept under close wraps.

On discovering this strange aircraft, as the war was in its final throes, the Allies believed that the Germans, whose scientific prowess was renowned around the world, had perfected a Doomsday weapon or a super-advanced military aircraft or rocket. The crashed aircraft was unlike any production or prototype craft the Allies had ever seen. Was it on a bombing mission? What was its range? Where was it launched? Was it capable of carrying nuclear warheads and delivering a nuclear attack from Germany? Could Germany be planning an H-bomb attack on Britain and America?

If this was indeed a German aircraft, the Air Force would be forced to acknowledge that the Germans had the technology to develop an aircraft so far advanced that they would win the war. Nazi Germany would be victorious. All hope for a civilized mankind would be lost. Investigators from the newly formed National Security Agency and Britain's formidable MI7 were sent to nearby Albuquerque to assess vital intelligence. Little was known about the details of that investigation beyond the conclusion that the origins of the craft were not German. Nor was the ship American—or the product any other military power on earth. It was unquestionably extraterrestrial.

Days later, a second spacecraft plowed into planet Earth. Its trajectory was almost identical to that of the first vessel. It crash-landed less than two hundred miles east of the first craft. The fate of this ship was different, however. The second vessel smacked into the desert, dug out a sizable crater, became airborne again, then skidded, spinning like a top, across the barren desert floor. A huge plume of dust rose into the air. It would have been visible from miles away. But no one was there to see it.

Compared with the first vessel, which had crashed into the side of a mountain, this one landed relatively unscathed. The fuselage cooled quickly, but not before a substantial amount of silica sand from the desert floor had melted to a molten glob around it. The ship looked like an island shimmering in the middle of a light brown lake. At one end, where the craft had come to rest, was a twenty-foot-high wall of transparent reddish-gold glass where the sand and rock had plowed ahead of the ship as it slid to a stop. There had been a huge wall of sandy rock there, which had melted instantly on contact with the craft. Golden plumes were frozen in the air as the hot silica cooled from liquid back to solid in milliseconds. Six strands of quick-cooled molten silica took on the uncanny look of a hand with fingers outstretched, reaching up from the desert. The hand is still visible today.

That same evening, after a glorious desert sunset, the ship's silver fuselage popped open like a winking eye. Seconds later, a surveillance/ recovery Bot emerged rather tentatively. It was a round, silver device three feet wide, with eight spider-like limbs. It stopped about twenty feet away from the craft and hovered, perfectly silent, a few feet off the surface. Its appendages retracted for a moment. The fading desert light reflected dull orange off its round body. Its sensors confirmed the ship's location of a living human about ten miles away. The multi-functional Bot was programmed to retrieve hosts for the occupants of the craft. In a blink, the Bot looked onto its target and disappeared.

The target's name was Corey Wixon. Wixon was a thin but otherwise physically fit young Caucasian male with a permanently sunburned face. He was a twenty-one-year-old geophysics grad student working on his doctorate. He was studying the various strata of rock formations along the cliff walls of the desert. He was alone in his tent, examining his latest findings. A single Coleman high-intensity gas lamp hung from the center post, its hiss the only sound in the quiet desert. Wixon loved the solitude. He relished the opportunity to work in quiet concentration without distractions. He was a focused and intense youth with a bright future ahead of him. But that future would change tonight.

The Bot arrived at the camp in less than two minutes. There was no urgency in its movements. It hovered at five feet and silently circled the tent. The host was inside and actively awake. The Bot advanced toward the closed nylon door flap, hovering at chest height. Wixon looked up with a start. His eyes darted all about him. Nothing.

Then, out of the corner of his eye, he caught the faint rustling of the tent flap as if something had brushed up against it. Always mindful of the danger of being alone in the desert, he reached over, lifted his pillow, and extracted his Russian-made pistol. Cocking the weapon, he walked to the door and flung open the flap.

There, observing him at face level, was a strange silver globe with tentacles flailing about. It looked like a bloated spider. Wixon screamed and fell over backwards. Fumbling like an upside-down crab, he fired off two rounds. The bullets ricocheted soundlessly off the little machine. The machine stayed rigid. Then, three lights came on, catching him in a three-dimensional scan. It checked out his heart and other internal organs for disease or deterioration. Next it scanned the brain for similar afflictions. It checked out mental bioelectrical strength. Finally, it scanned for general radiation, rot, or terminal disease of the human's whole body.

The machine found that the human was young, strong, and as uncorrupted as flesh and bone could be. This host was suitable. The scan lights were replaced by a green glow that expanded outward from the Bot and enveloped both the device and Wixon. That was the last moment that Corey Wixon would ever be truly himself. He was now the host of another Being.

The Bot projected an ultrasonic tone that rendered the victim incapacitated. The frequency of the sound wave worked on the human brain to cancel out functional processing thought, while permitting cognitive observation and recognition of the subject's surroundings. His brain could watch, but it could not think. Wixon's brain had gone numb. His body was completely relaxed and he slumped over backwards as if in a swoon. His pistol slipped from his fingers. Rather than fall, he actually rose a few feet. His head bent back at an acute angle, so that it looked as if surely his back must have broken. His body, limp as a rag doll, was slowly extracted from the tent. The intensity of the green glow increased. The machine and the host organism began to rise in unison, held together like two dancers by this globe of silvery green. They rose to a height of about twenty feet. Then, in the blink of an eye, both were gone.

In deference to the human's inability to withstand sudden high velocity, the Bot took four minutes to return to the vessel, roughly half speed. A portal opened and the two entered. The ship's ambient light helped make the passageways visible to Wixon as he was carried to a small room the size of a shower stall. Wixon was deposited inside. He never lost consciousness. He never protested. The whole event was so surreal that—with help from the sonic control exerted by the Bot—his mind had gone into a kind of sensory overload.

Wixon watched the stall door flick shut. The Bot's control over his body ceased. He shook his head and blinked. His mind reactivated. He stared down toward his feet at a thick green goop that snaked up his legs as the stall flooded. Wixon pushed against the door, pounding first with his fist, then with his shoulder. The liquid rose so quickly that he had no time to assess or react to the situation. He cried out in horror just before his entire body was submerged.

CHAPTER 5

Crash site, Elliot Lake

Joe had never felt so alone. It was almost dark. He was sitting beside the aircraft upright but slumped from exhaustion. A door or porthole had opened. As yet, nothing had slithered out to greet him or eat him. The ship could be some Air Force prototype, or it could be from outer space. Outer space! Think of it.

The human body reacts to shock with careless disregard for the human who may happen to occupy the body. In other words, no matter how cool you would like to appear to the rest of the world, your body will betray you. Your body happens to be identical to the bodies of billions of other humans, and you will have the identical physiological reactions to stress and shock.

Thus, Joe Grayer, tough, fit, and young, suddenly felt tired and weak. He was confused. His thoughts were frozen in some higher plateau that he could not access. His brain was unable to process this astounding new information. It was searching for known experiences so that it could label this new experience. It found nothing and was thus paralyzed.

Joe's body was ready for fight or flight. Huge quantities of adrenalin pumped into his bloodstream. He was ready for action. Except there was no action available, at least not yet. The inevitable result of the underutilized adrenalin was visible shaking. Still seated, Joe stared at his hands, willing the shaking to stop. Eventually it did. Then he began to feel very tired and chilled at the same time. Since there was no fight happening, nor was there any flight required, it was decision time. What should he do?

He looked over at the craft and its dark gaping entranceway once again. I'm not ready, he thought. There would be no brave exploration today.

He was torn between the excitement of exploring further and the security of waiting for his brother. Maybe he should just pack it in and turn this over to more senior adults, he thought. One of his eyes began to twitch and become itchy. He rubbed it absently and began to rise. He wobbled to his bike and headed home.

At the crest of the hill, he seemed to regain his energy. The farther he was from the object, the stronger he became. He charged back to his house in a shower of flying stones that flew away from the tires of his bike like live cinders from a fire. He roared up to the house in high expectation and excitement. He didn't see the Corvette. Not a good sign. He burst into the house. It was absolutely quiet. Disappointed, he settled in to wait for Hawk.

He paced around the property. Where the hell is he? He wondered as the minutes wore on.

Then he remembered the little check-in procedure that he and Hawk had devised in case they missed each other during the day. He dashed down the road to the phone booth two blocks away. He checked his watch. He and Hawk had set up a time of day that Hawk would call in if he was going to pull an all-nighter: 11:00 p.m. It was now 11:30 p.m. The allotted time had passed, but Joe hoped that Hawk would try calling again. He skidded to a halt in front of the Plexiglas Bell Telephone pay booth. The phone was ringing. Joe snatched it from the cradle.

"Hawk?" he said breathlessly.

"Yeah. What happened to you? I called about half an hour ago." Hawk sounded irritated. The call had taken him away from other business.

"Got tied up. Where are you?"

"Out with the boys."

"Hawk, I—"

Hawk interrupted. "Almost forgot. Talked to an RCMP cop called Hunter this afternoon. Told him about the crash site. He was cool about it and took my name, address, ya know, the usual stuff. Wanted to know where the thing was. He asked a lot of questions. He seemed seriously interested. Didn't think it was a hoax or nothing."

"Hawk, what did you tell him, exactly?"

"I told him the part about how we dug up part of this airplane, or something. I described what we had found so far. How we figured it was either a crashed airplane or even a UFO. Told him where it was in the hills behind the subdivision."

Joe paused, then said in an authoritative tone, "It's definitely a UFO, Hawk."

"Whatever, bro. It's now officially reported. Don't wait up for me. Out with friends, if you know what I mean. Might not be back tonight … if I'm lucky. If you know what I mean!"

Joe could hear some loud laughter in the background. Some girls were yelling Hawk's name. Hawk was giggling as if he was being tickled. The phone had slipped from his hand and rattled against something amid squealing laughter.

A girl's voice came on the line. "Joe! Joe, I hear you are really cute! Why don't you come to Casey's and have a beer with us?"

Joe's face flushed hot for a moment. "Thanks, but no thanks. I got stuff to do."

"Don't be such a party pooper! We need more cute guys!"

Joe was stammering, thinking of something to say, when he heard a muffled sound on the phone line. "Joe? You still there?"

Joe hid his disappointment. He had wanted to talk to the girl who thought he was cute sight unseen. "Hawk, put the girl back on."

Hawk yelled into the phone. "What? Can't hear you! The band just came back on stage. Too noisy!"

"Put the—" Joe yelled into the phone over the screech of a guitar. "Oh, never mind."

"What? Sorry, can't hear. Gotta go. Wish me luck. I am getting some tonight! Oh yeah! See ya, Joe. Don't wait up."

"Don't hang up. I have to—" Joe stared at the dead line. "Talk to you."

Joe slammed the phone down. What was this thing that Hawk had with girls? He was fearless. He had nerves of steel. He had a way with the girls that Joe could not understand. Joe picked up the phone and slammed it down again in frustration. There were more important things in life than women! Life was not one big party, dammit!

He began walking home, angry that his brother had ignored him. Or was he angry because Hawk was out having fun and he wasn't? He needed to talk and be with someone tonight. He stopped in his tracks. He would call Mr. Bohr in New Mexico. David Bohr was like a second father to Hawk and him, having raised them during their father's periods of extended absence. He would be able to help with this situation. He turned back to the phone booth.

Using a Bell credit card supplied by his father, Joe called David Bohr in Los Alamos. Bohr's wife Helen answered.

"Joe, honey, it's so late! Is anything the matter?"

"Sorry. I forgot the time. Did I wake you?"

"No, dear. I was watching Johnny Carson."

"Is Mr. Bohr still up?"

"Sorry, Joe. He's not in right now. He got a call this morning and he left to go to the office for a few things to bring to some conference. He told me he's flying somewhere or other tomorrow. Canada, I think. Isn't that where you are? Canada? Give me your number, sweetie—I'll have him call you as soon as he comes in."

"That won't help much. I'm calling from a pay phone near home. Hawk and I don't have a phone of our own. We can't get service to our house."

They chatted for a while. He promised to call more often. It was a good call. Helen was like a mother to the boys since their father never remarried.

He turned and headed home again. Some of his loneliness had disappeared. It was dark outside and the intermittent street lighting cast a weak glow. But, overall, the balmy night was pleasant enough. His sour mood gradually dissolved.

Sleep finally came after a feast of Kraft Dinner and toast.

The next morning, Joe awoke, his body covered in a fine dew of perspiration. He sat bolt upright, struggling to recall his dream. The dream came back in fragments.

He is alone. Walking down a long road. A bus stops and he gets on. The passengers are staring at him. The driver says, "Son, you have to wear clothes to ride this bus." Joe stares down at his naked body and doubles up, covering himself. He tries to back out of the bus, but the door has already closed behind him. The bus hisses as its brakes release and begins to pull away.

There is a smell of diesel fuel and cheap perfume. Joe looks down the aisle. Everyone is staring and laughing.

His eyes jump from face to face. He recognizes no one. "How did I get this way?" he wonders. Then, angry with himself, he thinks: What kind of an idiot would get on a bus without clothes, for Christ's sake? How could I get myself in a fix like this? He tries to sit down, but people push him away. "Freak!" They glare at him. He is trapped on the bus, going who-knows-where, with people who are gawking at him and ridiculing him.

Joe walks down the aisle, gingerly and bent over, looking down at the black rubber floor, searching for a seat. A seat that offers shelter. A safe place away from the leering passengers. He becomes aware of his cold feet and real-izes he is not wearing shoes and the floor is wet. Why is the floor wet? Each time he comes to an empty seat, it is suddenly and mysteriously filled with a belligerent passenger. He is truly dejected. He is unwanted. He wants off the bus! Why can't he figure out a way off?

Joe couldn't hang onto the rest of the dream. He was angry about something he had dreamt, but he could no longer recall what that was.

The alarm clock blinked a bright red digital 5:45. The gray pink shades of dawn were visible through the open window. He groaned a greeting to the new day. Soft billows of crisp fresh cold air rolled over the bedclothes. He hugged the blanket: *Just five more minutes!* It was as if he hadn't slept a wink all night. The bedside alarm clock, which sounded like a submarine alert, went off for a second time and refused to stop beeping until Joe flipped the stop button. He threw back the covers and rolled out of bed with as much grace as an eighteen-year-old could muster.

He went directly to Hawk's room. The door was ajar and the bed had not been slept in. Hawk had not come home last night. Joe hoped that he had enjoyed himself. *Not really. OK, fine, Hawk has a way with girls.* He pushed the thought from his mind.

After a large breakfast and before leaving, Joe paused and left a note for Hawk. It read: "Hawk. Went to the crash site. Got a door open. Going in. Joe."

Then he changed his mind and crunched up the note. He rewrote it to read: "Have gone *there*. Got news. Joe." He absently threw the note onto the kitchen counter and then left for the site.

CHAPTER 6

Los Alamos, 1982

At age fifty-four, David Bohr showed a striking resemblance to his father when he was the same age. His salt-and-pepper brown hair was more salt than pepper. His once lean body was layered with sagging fat after years of neglect. He had a noticeable paunch that even his ever-present loose-fitting cardigan could not hide, and he was beginning to sprout hair in the most unseemly of places.

Bohr's quick smile and friendly demeanor had left permanent crinkles at the sides of his eyes. His wife called them his laugh lines. He was average in height, and stooped slightly when he walked. Sports activity was out of the question because of an arthritic condition from early childhood. This condition caused him to consume buckets of aspirin. All in all, though, considering that he did nothing for exercise besides walking, he was in reasonable shape.

He leaned back in his easy chair, the black leather creaking as if to echo his tired bones. He glanced over at his father's picture on his mahogany office bookshelf. The aging black-and-white photo smiled back agelessly. His father had not only been a brilliant physicist, but a fine man and good father as well. Bohr smiled. He had only fond memories of their days together before leaving home at the age of twenty.

David Bohr was born in Copenhagen in 1928, the youngest of six sons. Their father, the famous physicist Niels Bohr, had won the Nobel Prize for physics six years before David was born. Back in 1913, he had published some crucial papers that made a deep impression on Albert Einstein and other scientists. In his explanation of atomic structure, Niels Bohr had departed from classical mechanics, instead making use of Planck's constant and the quantum theory. The result was a model of the atom in which radiation was emitted only when an electron jumped from one quantum orbit to another. Thus the name *quantum* theory. On the strength of his theory of the atom, Niels Bohr had reached the summit of his career by the age of twenty-eight.

Bohr had inherited his father's intellect and his mother's intuition. He did well in school and graduated with honors in physics and math, after skipping two or three grades along the way. His father, his mentor, would talk at length about the prolific progress of mathematics and physics during the early part of the twentieth century, especially in Germany, between 1905 and 1933. Niels never tired of telling tales about his intellectual colleagues, such as Max Born, and his fellow mathematicians such as Max Planck and Albert Einstein. All were famous in their own lifetimes.

Theoretical mathematics and quantum theory were the hot topics on campuses in the early years of the century. Unlike physical or mechanical physics, which could be proven using physical evidence, theoretical research could only be disproved by other, better theorems based on complex mathematical models. There was no way to physically prove that one theorem was a more accurate model of the universe than another. An example of one such controversial theorem was Heisenberg's principle of uncertainty, which Niels had supported.

Einstein was the most outspoken opponent of the uncertainty principle. Niels told David a favorite story many times. At a conference both Einstein and Bohr attended in 1930, Einstein devised a challenge to the uncertainty principle. Einstein proposed a box filled with radiation with a clock fitted in one side. The clock was designed to open a shutter and allow one photon to escape. When the box was weighed again some time later, the photon's energy and its time of escape could both be measured with arbitrary accuracy. Of course this was not meant to be an actual experiment, only a "thought experiment."

Niels confessed to having spent an unhappy evening, and Einstein a happy one. It was Bohr, however, who had the final triumph, for the next day he had the solution: that the mass could be measured by hanging a compensatory weight under the box. This weight, in turn, imparts a momentum to the box, and there is thus an error in measuring the box's position. Time, according to relativity, a theorem, of course, proposed by Einstein himself, is not absolute, and the error in the position of the box translates into an error in measuring the time. Einstein grudgingly conceded—unwilling to refute his own theory of relativity.

Unfortunately for Einstein, Bohr, and the rest of the physicists, they did not live in a vacuum. The grim reality was that the world outside their isolated university lives was rapidly falling under the jackboot of the Nazis.

In 1943—just four years after he had been made president of the Royal Danish Academy of Sciences and had begun work on a theory of nuclear fission—Niels Bohr learned that the Germans planned to arrest him and make him work in Germany on an atomic project. Niels fled with his family and spent the war years in the U.S., where he participated in the British-American atomic bomb project at Los Alamos. The family moved to New Mexico, and David, at the age of fifteen, had to learn English, and the Mexican and American cultures.

Niels Bohr strongly objected to the tactics and philosophy of the Nazis. He had many friends and colleagues who were Jews and recognized the threat of the Nazis. Many other German and European immigrants would join Bohr in emigrating to the U.S. during the 1930s. Jew and non-Jew alike, they fled to the safety of a country where there was peace and sanity. It was an oasis of decent humanity.

But the Americans could not simply sit back and watch the armies of Nazi Germany destroy their allies. Niels Bohr, the former conscientious objector to war and violence, joined the U.S. team at Los Alamos to work on a weapon that would stop the Germans and stop the war—perhaps all wars.

Bohr would use his intellect to help develop the first A-bomb. He saw the bomb as a Doomsday machine, too powerful to unleash on the world lest there be total annihilation. Bohr could not conceive of the weapon as an actual field weapon because the radius of destruction would be too large. The military, however, saw the Doomsday bomb as the ultimate deterrent to Hitler's march for world domination. Who would have conceived that Bohr's own beloved adopted country would be the one to violate human decency by dropping the A-bomb on the civilian city of Hiroshima?

David was proud of his father for his choice of country and work. David chose as his own career the study and development of quantum physics and subatomic particles—not just theory but a practical application of quantum physics. He was convinced, for example, that space travel would be possible in his lifetime, and that atomic particle energy would someday prove to be crucial.

David's father returned to his native Denmark four years after the end of World War II. David decided to stay in America to continue his studies and be with his girlfriend. Before he left, Niels would introduce David to some of the top-ranking civilian and military minds in the country. Some would become trusted colleagues and friends.

The years from 1948 through 1952, before Niels returned to Denmark, were particularly fascinating for the Bohr family. Their household had become an informal meeting place for local civilian and military minds. They lived a mile or so off base. Their massive dining-room table held fourteen, and it was not unusual for Sunday dinners to be rather large affairs. Over the years, Bohr overheard some interesting developments regarding unexplained phenomena. There had been several incidents of security issues concerning unidentified aircraft, and the military brass was highly sensitive to these reports. They saw them as an affront to the readiness of America's air defense—all the more reason, of course, to perfect the new bomb.

Bohr vividly recalled one such conversation over brandy after a hearty meal filled with stimulating shoptalk. Visiting Commanding General John Mitchell had been quietly discussing a recent incident at Andrews Air Force Base with Roger Baden, an avionics expert who was a colleague of David's father.

Ever the snoop, David had slid up and eavesdropped on the conversation. His best recollection went something as follows:

"Listen, Roger, there was an actual aerial encounter: dogfight maneuvers, rapid acceleration, evasive action. I was sent a copy of the incident report. It has been classified, of course, in the Project Blue Book files."

"Yes, Commander. I have heard rumors. You understand that, as a civilian, I have not seen the actual classified report."

"Consider this as temporarily unclassified, like a few of the other reports we are trying to validate," Mitchell said gruffly. "And I know that you've already seen more than your share of classified material, Roger. It comes with your job."

Roger laughed. "Go on."

David Bohr eased closer still.

"At approximately 2200 hours, Lt. Henry Combs sighted an object flying on a 360-degree pattern from west to east over Andrews Base. The object had one glowing white light. Combs thought it was an aircraft with the wing navigation lights turned off or burned out. He then made a pass to check. The object then took evasive action. First contact was established at about two thousand feet over the base. When the object started taking evasive action, Combs switched both the wing and tail navigation lights off. Since it is perfectly pitch black at ten at night, Combs must have figured that if the object couldn't see him then it couldn't evade him.

"Maneuvering his plane, a T-6," Commander Mitchell went on, looking over at Roger, "so that his exhaust flame would not be noticed in his effort to get the object on his left, he proceeded to close in, but the object quickly flew up and over his aircraft. Then Combs attempted to maneuver the object between his ship and the light of the moon. This was done by making very tight 360-degree turns with flaps down while making a steady climb. This object was able to turn inside of Combs' aircraft even under this condition. Another amazing feature was the quick variation of airspeed from eighty miles per hour to five hundred or six hundred miles per hour."

Roger interrupted him. "Doesn't seem possible. Our best and fastest prototype jet propulsion aircraft couldn't do it, Commander. I've heard rumors of these accelerating speeds before. Those speeds, along with the pressure of the turn, would bust apart any aircraft. The G-force alone would render the pilot unconscious."

The Commander shrugged and continued, "That's the report. Signed by Combs. Combs remained in contact with the object for some ten minutes. He could distinguish the object between the lights of Washington, D.C., and his aircraft. He could only see an oblong ball with one light and no wings and no exhaust flame.

"This boy Combs is quite the pilot," the Commander said. "Sounds like a gutsy one too. Combs pulled back up sharply and came up underneath the object within three hundred to four hundred feet. He then turned his landing lights on the craft. It had a dull gray glow to it and was oblong in shape. Combs ended his report by saying that the object then performed a very tight turn and headed for the east coast at five hundred to six hundred miles per hour."

"Other witnesses?"

"Sure. I know these men personally. They're straight shooters. Lt. Ken Jackson, who described the object as oval. There was also Lt. Glen Stalker, who said the object was a glowing white oval. And Staff Sgt. John J. Kushner, who was on the ground and saw the object make two low passes over the base. I've known J.J. for eight years. He's a no-nonsense career soldier.

"Roger, in his report, Lt. Combs noted that the UFO displayed evasive controlled tactics, the ability to perform tight circles, quick variation of air speed, vertical ascents, and evasive movements. Does this sound like something that any air force can produce?"

"Honestly, no, Commander. I am not privy to the real secret intelligence from the military. I can only speak from where the state of our avionics is today. Our industry, our capability, is nowhere near what you described. Either it's a false claim or a communist prototype, or, I guess, there is a third possibility."

"What's that?"

"It is not terrestrial."

"But why falsify the claim, Roger? Combs and the others had nothing to gain by this report. As a matter of fact, in terms of ridicule, they had more to lose. J.J. was reluctant about filing the report. But he's a military man. His orders were to report any sightings that night. He did his duty."

"Commander, I believe the most likely answer is that the aircraft was a Russian prototype. Possibly unmanned and controlled by remote radio."

"I can't buy that. Our intelligence has told us that the Russians are not technically advanced enough. The war took a lot out of them, as you know."

"I know it did. On the other hand, I also know that the Russians appropriated the best German scientists. Who knows how far along they had advanced before the war ended? Most likely there was research that we will never know about. We lost a big fish when we let the Russians take them."

"I agree. If there is ever a weapons race between the Russians and us, they will probably win. But I don't think they're organized yet. There simply wasn't enough money after the war to fund a project as costly as a supersonic fighter jet like Combs reported."

"Well, Commander, that just leaves option three—an extraterrestrial UFO."

It was shortly after his father had left for Denmark that American Intelligence recruited David Bohr. Back then, U.S. Intelligence was a department within the Department of Defense. Bohr was vetted with a squeaky-clean record. It helped immensely that he was Niels Bohr's son and already known to many inside the agency. His role of assistant physics professor at Columbia was a nice fit.

They didn't expect him to actually spy on anyone. His assignment was to keep the military abreast of new developments in the tight community of physicists. He was to report to his handler any new or significant breakthroughs in the field that he felt would interest the military. Oh yes, and by the way, report any communists—the government was seriously concerned about the leaking of research to the Soviets by sympathetic left-leaning scientists. Bohr advised his handler that there were a few leftists in the group. He never did submit names, and grew increasingly uneasy as the wave of McCarthyism swept the country.

It worried David when Einstein became a vocal advocate of nuclear disarmament. In those days everyone was either "Red" or "Dead." If you criticized American policy, you risked being labeled a commie. David knew that America was going overboard with the McCarthy stuff, but he was fearful of not fitting in the U.S. and so kept his conflicts to himself.

David's field of expertise was quantum mechanics. His father's familiarity with Einstein and his colleagues at Princeton gave him the flexibility to travel and meet informally with many of them. David learned about the latest theories of relativity from the likes of Einstein, Infield, and Hoffman. This was an area of interest for the Department of Defense. The arms race had just been born. David was never clear which specific department branch used his intelligence. Maybe they all shared it. He moved to Chicago in the mid 1950s and joined fellow nuclear scientist Enrico Fermi. Fermi had been a close associate of his father; they had worked together at Los Alamos.

Fermi was the most eminent of all the nuclear physicists in the country. Like David's father, Fermi—in 1938, on the eve of World War II—escaped to the U.S. Fermi's early work on the statistical distribution of elementary particles led him to divide these atomic constituents into two groups known as fermions and bosons, depending on their spin characteristics. This division was thereafter accepted as standard. His subsequent work on radioactivity and atomic structure, which earned him the 1938 Nobel Prize for physics, involved experiments in the production of artificial radioactivity by bombarding matter with neutrons. Fermi experimented with nuclear fission, and this work culminated in the first sustained nuclear reaction, which was produced on December 2, 1942, at the University of Chicago. Further work at the Los Alamos Scientific Laboratory led to the construction of the atomic bomb.

Bohr had begun working on his doctorate in nuclear physics under the tutelage of Fermi. Unlike his father or Fermi, Bohr's field of interest was not atomic applications such as weaponry, but the practical application of nuclear fission, including its effect on accelerated space travel. His understanding of the mathematics of quantum theory was important to the evolving theory of nuclear-propelled flight into deep space.

Now, so many years later, Bohr gazed fondly at the many books and dog-eared binders lined up in his dusty wooden office bookcase, like a mechanic surveying his neatly stacked red tool chests. He was an intellectual and gladly so. He found the logic of these technical theses reassuring.

He vividly recalled when he first read the books. It seemed long ago. He had been young, thirsty for knowledge. He was living happily in Chicago. He was experimenting with the relationship between math and physics. He had earned his Ph.D. and landed a minor teaching job on campus. He had been part of a small but elite group of young physicists, teaching but experimenting and learning at the same time. He had fallen in love with Helen, a grad student in English, and they got married that same year.

Bohr managed to escape becoming either a lab rat or a recluse—partly because Helen was very sociable, and partly because he was naturally affable. People enjoyed his company and he enjoyed theirs. During those years, David and Helen's inner circle of friends was a group of young physicists and their wives.

That situation ended when, without notice, the National Security

Agency sent for him in 1958. A plane whisked him from Chicago to Los Alamos under a veil of secrecy. Helen could be given only a barebones account of the circumstances behind his transfer. Even that censored version of events came as a shock to her, since Bohr had never told her of his affiliation with the NSA.

"You spied on your friends?" she said when he told her.

"Not spied. Reported. You don't understand the consequences of important research falling into Communist hands."

"Oh, David, how could you? You were a snitch!"

"For God's sake, Helen. We are at *war* with the commies, or hasn't anyone told you? It's not an open war, but it's still a war. They spy on us and steal our secrets."

"Secret *weapons*, David, nuclear weapons. Maybe *they* are afraid that we will attack *them*."

"Helen, we would never do that. We need these weapons to defend ourselves against people like that."

"What do you mean we would never do that? We've already done it once. What do you call bombing Hiroshima?'

"Don't start with me about Hiroshima, OK? You know how sensitive I am about that because of my father's involvement."

"David, all I'm saying is watch out for these people, this spy agency."

En route to New Mexico he was told that he was needed on an unusual classified project requiring his exact talents. There were apologies all around for removing him from Chicago, but the circumstances were too important to trust to anyone else, they said. This project would take months, maybe years. While Bohr was upset about being separated from Helen and his friends, it was a comfort to be back in his boyhood home. He visited some old friends and neighborhoods, and he petitioned the DoD to transfer his wife to New Mexico as soon as possible.

His homecoming was not classified, but the project certainly was. The government was convinced that it had found the wreck of an alien spacecraft. The newly formed NSA needed scientists with appropriate intelligence clearance and knowledge of nuclear physics to help in the investigation.

Almost immediately after his final clearance, David Bohr witnessed first-hand the remains of the craft. It had struck a solid canyon wall in the desert and burst into thousands of pieces. There was no mention of alien survivors, not even rumors. The resident scientists were not entirely convinced that the craft was alien. They felt it was likely to be an unmanned Soviet test aircraft.

Bohr managed to convince the government to clear his wife and two other scientists and their spouses to join him in Los Alamos. There were years of work, documentation, and testing ahead—possibly a life's work, when one considered the challenge of reconstructing the badly damaged ship. The couples settled initially in White Rock. Then, after several months, they decided to buy homes in a newer subdivision on Canyon Road that was closer to work in Los Alamos.

It was later rumored that the wreckage of the craft had been found a few miles south of Route 40, about one hundred miles east of Albuquerque, after slamming into a shallow canyon wall. The military had been immediately dispatched to the crash site area. It was secured. It took several months for the appropriate military personnel to be diverted from the war effort to examine the wreckage. The remnants of the mysterious vessel were relocated to Los Alamos Air Force Base because it was the closest secure facility. There was an attempt to reconstruct remnants of the wrecked craft, but it proved fruitless. Initially, the Federal Aviation Agency was called in, but after it became evident that this was not a domestic air crash, the investigators were sworn to secrecy and dismissed.

While it is true that the initial crash site was not too far from Roswell, New Mexico, the urban legends were mostly wrong. There were no live or dead aliens recovered from the wreck. No little green men, no abductions for experimentation, and no secret military cover-up beyond that of protecting the identity of the initial craft. The famous Area 51 and Area 19 were nothing more than high-security testing facilities for Stealth-type aircraft. There were good reasons, of course, for maintaining such fanatically high security around those enterprises. The USAF was afraid of security leaks to the Iron Curtain countries in the wake of the disastrous MI5 defections. Intelligence leaks throughout the Western world were rampant, which meant that the USAF would not begin testing aircraft based on research gathered from the wreck until the 1970s.

The remains of the craft had been transported to the secure USAF base at Los Alamos. The move made sense because of the new and advanced scientific equipment located there. Also, the facility had the protection of high security. There was also tight security in areas adjacent to Los Alamos because of the nuclear development work underway. This kept prying eyes out and prevented intelligence leaks. The team of scientists was able to pursue their research with surprisingly little interference from the press, the military, or politicians. Of course, no one ever made it clear to David Bohr what information, if any, was made available to the government bureaucrats. The American military kept the news of the spacecraft discovery to themselves. Given the arms race, they felt they needed any advantage they could get.

The wreckage itself was peculiar. There was no fire or explosion after impact. The scientists reassembled the fragments as best they could without a schematic or drawing. There was no evidence of electronics, at least not based on our concept of electricity. There were various arrays of green, plastic-like, gelatinous card-sized objects, but their use could not be fathomed. Chairs and part of a control panel were recovered. The panel itself had disintegrated on impact. Several multicolored globs of what appeared to be lights were recovered inside the panel remains.

There were no electrical wires or conduits anywhere. There were, however, hundreds of tube-like segments, made of some kind of plastic-like substance, that wormed their way throughout the craft. There was evidence of a liquid, gel-like substance inside the tubing. The team referred to these tubes as arteries. They postulated that they carried vital energy throughout the craft. Information did not seem to flow through the arteries. It was concluded that information, direction, and control were transmitted through the air, much like our long-wave radio bands: that is, wirelessly.

The craft used an exoskeleton, not unlike the body of a crustacean, as an outer shell for protection and solidity. The outer skin was very strong and resisted extremely high temperatures and tremendous impacts. The scientists were never able to puncture the skin or melt the substance. But, while the skin could not be punctured, it could be fragmented under the right conditions. The conjecture was that the craft, already traveling at tremendously high temperatures and velocity after having entered our atmosphere, blew apart on impact with the solid rock wall of the canyon. Had these circumstances not prevailed, the craft would have survived the crash-landing with little or no harm to the ship.

The team of Los Alamos scientists did manage to gain some insight into the massive gap in technological advancement between the aliens and us. Picture the advances that our civilization has made in electricity, electronics, computing, and science in the last century, Bohr often found himself thinking. Now try to comprehend a civilization that has had another ten thousand centuries to advance its science and inventions. Consider what kinds of gadgets a civilization a million years older and more advanced than ours would be capable of making.

The researchers reached some astounding conclusions about the technology and the possible future direction of our own civilization's technology, as Bohr reported to the DoD in 1960:

Memo
Los Alamos
D. Bohr June 19, 1960
Executive Summary Dept. of Defense
Subject: Extraterrestrial vehicle wreckage

Findings and observations:
1) Electricity did not exist on board the ship. Instead of via electricity, energy was apparently transferred chemically or bio-magnetically.
2) There were no (electronic) computers, as we know them. Computing, as we know it, was performed chemically much as it is in our own biological brains. The ship itself was a brain.
3) A form of radio wave transmitted signals or commands. No wires existed. Computer commands were audio or gesture interpreted.
4) Under the craft's exoskeleton was a thick layer of gelatinous material. This was used to: (a) protect the occupants from blunt force trauma should the craft be impacted by an object in space; b) act as a giant synthetic brain that stored information and provided heat and optical functionality; (c) operate and navigate the craft; (d) transfer energy; and (e) somehow create a field of artificial gravity to cushion against sudden changes in velocity and height.
5) Food was nonexistent. There was no evidence of food storage or processing.
6) The craft appeared to be unmanned. This made little sense because there seemed to be a command center and seating for humanoid-shaped creatures. It is possible that certain sections of the ship are missing from the wreckage, and that those missing

sections could have housed crypts for an alien crew in deep space hibernation. (The team has questioned the military, but were told that any missing sections were unaccounted for.)

7) No weaponry, as we understand it, could be found. It was postulated that it was there, but the team could not locate it.

8) The propulsion system was apparently a matter/antimatter system. There is strong evidence that the damage done to the ship was caused by antimatter annihilation on impact. Most likely the containment apparatus for the anti-matter material failed. The ship also destroyed an immense section of canyon wall when it crashed.

It was Bohr's extensive experience in the theoretical field of quantum mechanics that fueled the discussions and postulations. He was the right person to extrapolate from existing theory and integrate it with the scientific evidence from the wreck.

Good science takes time. Bohr and his team worked for several years to try to uncover any more secrets the craft might offer up. There were important matters of national security to consider. There was the military's insistence that the wreck be examined for clues on how to develop superior military weapons. This would tip the balance of the weapons race in favor of the Americans.

Consequently, the team was audited on a regular basis. Their findings became a national secret. Their research became national security. By the late 1970s, the team, in cooperation with military aeronautics engineers, had begun to develop and experiment with new materials and propulsion systems. They tested several matter/antimatter prototypes, all of which failed. However, since the testing took place near the Los Alamos nuclear facility and testing grounds, no one was any the wiser.

They tested aircraft that incorporated rudimentary biochemical electronics and navigational controls, cold jet propulsion, and a non-metallic superstructure and fuselage skin. Not only were the aircraft incredibly fast, they could not be detected with conventional Doppler radar. There was also a much smaller heat trail because of the improved efficiency of the propulsion system.

The testing was sometimes out of Kirkland AFB, but there was also some flying over the general area of Santa Fe, Albuquerque, and the desert. Although pilots were instructed to limit exposure to the civilian population, there were a few unavoidable instances where pilot error or mechanical failure forced embarassing landings and close encounters with civilians. Leaks of these misadventures became an obsession among the press, especially when the encounters seemed to be close to the famous Area 51 and Roswell. The military continued to dismiss the UFO sightings as urban legend.

Bohr was part of the so-called Smart Team. He was the lead scientist responsible for scientific research. Weapons experts had given up finding anything useful from the wreck, but Bohr also worked with avionics engineers and propulsion specialists from the USAF. His work involved continuing contact with MI7, the RCMP, and the U.S. intelligence agencies because of the technological impact of the research on national security in Britain, Canada, and the U.S.

Bohr never encountered politicians snooping around the lab. Indeed, no politician had that level of security clearance. The White House was aware of the big find, but in non-specific terms. The White House had funded, in its entirety, the research and development of new aircraft based on the research of Bohr's team. They buried the cost under classified research and development expenses.

Over the years, the Americans grew complacent about their technological superiority. The Russians did not. Suddenly, and without notice, the Russians launched the first spaceship, Sputnik. The Arms Race and the Space Race, of course, went hand in hand, and the race was on. Military reasoning was that superiority in space meant superiority below, a philosophy that dated back to when Neanderthals hurled stones at each other.

The spacecraft project, over the course of thirty years, was semi-abandoned or moved to other locations for further development. When scientists were unable to unlock any more of the craft's secrets, the wreckage became redundant. The remains began gathering dust. Bohr had huddled in an adjacent lab for almost thirty years. He was now in his fifties. He had begun with a slide rule and a lot of chalk, and had ended at the beginning of the computer age. He continued to muse on his theories of relativity and space travel. He had in front of him tangible evidence of the reality of space travel, but he had little proof of the validity of his ideas.

Over the years, his computing and general research facilities had improved. In fact, Los Alamos and Bohr's facility were one of the first links to a brand new communications network. The team was able to instantly communicate with various universities and government research agencies using this marvelous invention. It used telephone wires and was called the Internet. But, then, over the years, as the discoveries diminished, the members of the team began retiring or moving on to different jobs.

Finally, he was offered a full professorship at New Mexico State University and retired from the project. Shortly after, the team disbanded for good. The appropriation funds dried up. The wreck was bundled up and sealed away in a nondescript forty-foot cargo container. It was buried in a secret location out in the desert.

CHAPTER 7

London, England

The phone rang and Peter Wright stiffened, upright, almost upsetting his chair. His mind had been drifting throughout the afternoon's rain shower.

"Well, good afternoon, Peter. It's been a few years. Do you know who this is?" The voice had an American twang.

Wright was annoyed to have had his tranquility shattered by this intruder. "Look here," he snapped. "I haven't the faintest idea. Please tell me who you are, or I will jolly well hang up."

The voice chuckled over the line. "It's me, Connelly."

Wright stiffened in his chair. "Not Major Connelly. From the U.S.?"

"The very same. Retired, of course."

"Of course," Wright mumbled, trying to do the math on Connelly's age.

Peter Wright had just recently retired from MI5. He was mildly irritated, yes, but sufficiently intrigued by this phone call from his U.S. colleague of many years before.

"How's the family, Peter?"

Wright's eyes narrowed for a split instant. He grinned as he saw through Connelly's double meaning. "Which family are you referring to, Major?"

Connelly snorted. "Both, I guess."

Wright couldn't help but smile. "Well, my wife is fine and we have retired happily—and quietly, I might add—to the country. As for my dear friends at 'the shop,' I have not kept up many contacts. Once you're out, you're out, so they say. Bit awkward and all that. Generally life has been brilliant. Now, Major, if I know you, and I think I do, you rang me up for a reason."

"Can't fool you, ol' buddy. You remember that project back in the fifties. The one where we were tracking the UFO sightings."

"Yes. That was shelved years ago."

"Right. It was. Died out because the sightings stopped. Before I get into what I have to tell you, can I ask what ever happened to the MI5 files?"

"In the end, we never connected the dots at MI7 or MI5, after the files were transferred to us. The intell never went any place that we could make sense of. We concluded the sightings were Soviets testing secret aircraft. But the file was inconclusive, really. It's been over thirty years, so the file has most likely been declared nonessential and purged. Destroyed."

Connelly's voice crackled over the airwaves. "Do you recall any conversations or meetings with Frank Grayer, based out of Langley?"

"Standard procedure was to record most conversations. Our meeting rooms were always wired. There were a few conversations with Grayer, but nothing that I can recall as significant."

"Has Frank Grayer ever tried to contact you since the Project was retired?"

"I can't recall, Major."

"Project's over. Has been for years. Didn't he just ring you up to say hello?"

"Like an old friend?"

"Exactly."

"We weren't friends, Major."

"Oh, I see. Of course. It was all business. Didn't he try to get you to help him track down a second spaceship?"

"Major, everyone knows that. That happened during the Project. That's not classified."

"For Christ's sake, Peter, has he been in contact *lately*? Surely you can tell me that?"

"No. I haven't heard from Frank in years. Why? Has something happened to him?"

"I've just learned some interesting news that may concern our old project."

Wright's curiosity was piqued. "Learned. Learned how? You are retired. Decommissioned. How is it that you are able to get any news at all? You Yanks handle intelligence matters quite differently from us Brits, you know. Once we are out of the community, we are not supposed to be involved in intelligence matters. Full stop. Out - of - the - game."

"Decommissioned. You make me sound like an old airplane. Maybe we do handle certain types of intelligence in a more relaxed manner than MI5. I *have* always kept my contact list active. Anyway, I was contacted recently by NSA. It seems there is a new lead concerning the project. I am now temporarily unretired. Peter, I want to reassemble the team, briefly.

The major went on to tell Wright that he was contacting those who were involved in the project in the fifties. "I need any intelligence on UFO sightings that we can muster," he said.

"UFOs? Major, what sort of news are you referring to?"

Connelly unconsciously lowered his voice: "NSA thinks they have found another wreck. They think they have a second UFO, possibly the twin to the other one we found. And, if it's intact, I don't have to tell you the importance."

He sketched a few details of the startling story, and then rang off.

Tea in hand, Wright stared out the window as drizzle snaked down the glass. He decided not to tell his wife, Lois, about the call. Not yet. He knew she would have a bloody fit. At her age, that was not something to be taken lightly.

MI5 had become reluctantly involved in the business of UFOs in the early fifties, when the Americans and Europeans had numerous encounters with unknown aircraft. The Americans had for years been focusing on developing nuclear weapons technology. The British had long abandoned that folly and had focused on the young science of intelligence. Why spend money on research when all you had to do was steal it?

The Soviets, meanwhile, had somehow become the spymasters of the planet. Individuals who naively believed that providing both sides with equal information would prevent a nuclear confrontation gleefully supplied them with intellectual property, stolen mainly from Western countries.

World War II had left the world in a state of exhaustion. The thought of more fighting was unpalatable to almost everyone. In the late forties and early fifties, when the Americans were voicing concern about the many fly-bys by potential alien aircraft, British Intelligence reluctantly agreed to help because of a rash of unexplained local sightings on their side of the Atlantic.

Originally, the Americans contacted MI6 the British Foreign Intelligence Service. To be honest, they weren't entirely sure which department to contact because of departmental reorganization at the end of World War II. (MI5 was "our" spies and MI6 was "their" spies.) There were nineteen MI (Military Intelligence) agencies.

NSA was the equivalent to MI6. They had daily interactions with them and felt most comfortable dealing with that department. This matter of alien spacecraft had everyone baffled. It fell between the cracks of authority and responsibility. Someone at the Foreign Office finally made a decision and rang up Peter Wright of MI5 with an unusual assignment.

"Peter, we have a bothersome arrangement going on with the Yanks."

"Yessir."

"Seems they're convinced they have a spaceship on their hands."

"You don't say."

"Blown to bits, I might add."

"Of course."

"You see where I am going."

"Yessir. Russian?"

"Most probably. Peter, I believe you are the best man for the job. You know these Ruskies better than anyone I know."

"Both as MI6 and MI5, sir. But no space research. Just surveillance work."

"You know the spook community better than most, Peter. That's why I want you. The Yanks may have something; they may not. The PM wants to tighten our relationship with them and has offered up our services."

"Yessir. I might point out that I am in the middle of ..."

"Sorry, old boy. Whatever you are on to must be put on hold. I am reassigning you temporarily to MI7."

"Propaganda?"

"Propaganda and censorship is not entirely what the department does, my dear chap."

"What do you mean?"

"MI7 dabbles in extraterrestrial investigation."

"You're joking. You don't believe in that stuff, do you?"

"Me? Oh goodness gracious no. But some do. And I have to admit there have been some curious unexplained occurrences on file."

"Why me? I'm very busy with MI5, sir. We are horribly under-funded. I am undermanned. Frankly, I can't be spared."

"You're better funded than MI7, Wright. The truth be known, my uppers don't want any ridicule or scandal in MI5. They want this assignment outside of MI5. We have had a run of bad luck there, wouldn't you agree?"

"To say the least."

"We can't have a leak about the Secret Intelligence Service chasing flying saucers whilst letting Soviet spies run around loose. Do you understand our dilemma?"

"Certainly, sir."

"Good. Then it's settled. You are temporarily reassigned to MI7 pending further —"

"Sir, if I may interrupt?"

"What is it?"

"We are hot on the heels of a Soviet spy ring here in Britain. This surveillance has been ongoing for two years. My team needs me at this critical juncture."

"What do you propose?"

"I am suggesting that my MI7 assignment be handled clandestinely. I keep leading and working with my MI5 team. In other words, I do both."

"God, Peter. That's a hell of a lot of work for one person."

"I don't see that I have a choice."

"Good show, Wright. We'll make an upperclassman of you yet."

With his strong profile of involvement in Soviet counterespionage, Wright was assigned to the case.

He was one of the few operatives who were unconvinced that the aircraft were test flights by the Soviet Union. As an intelligence officer, he had little budget to speak of, and his intelligence information was pitifully sparse. However, he did familiarize himself with all known sighting reports and read firsthand accounts of these classified occurrences. In the 1960s, his counterpart in America turned out to be Frank Grayer.

They met regularly to exchange intelligence. Unlike Wright, who was a career spook, Grayer worked virtually alone and was not well known in the service. As a matter of fact, he was a virtual unknown in the intelligence community. *Grayer the Ghost.* His file was closed to all but the heads of American and British agencies. Grayer had arrived on the intelligence scene suddenly in the late fifties, working alone on highly classified USAF-related matters. He had the highest-level clearance in the country.

Although the media continued to report false sightings on a regular basis for many years, the genuine military encounters had suddenly stopped in the late fifties, and the intell dried up abruptly. Peter Wright had more pressing internal matters to attend to at MI5. They were experiencing a series of embarrassing defections to the Soviet Union from within their ranks. This meant that the British intelligence had been compromised from within. It meant that the Soviets knew many highly sensitive military and political plans and secrets. There were spies within the agency, and it had been Wright's job for a number of years now to ferret them out.

Wright was a respected member of the world intelligence community. He knew many officers in several countries. Major Connelly happened to be one contact he used to communicate with regularly. However, the UFO project was only one of several he had on the go. While it seemed logical that Connelly would be anxious to get his hands on any intelligence involving the project, it was curious that it was he and not Grayer who was his contact.

Connelly's news was exciting. They may have discovered the crash site of a second UFO. It had long been postulated that the original craft had a twin and that the two ships had traveled the universe as a pair. At first the theory was that one craft had crashed, and the other had tried to contact it. There was, coincidentally, a rash of UFO sightings about that time.

Then, as years went by without any contact, another theory began to take form. This theory held that the second ship had also crashed soon after the first. Either it had crashed as a direct hit on Earth, with a trajectory similar to the first craft, or had crashed doing reconnaissance to find the other craft. In light of this theory, the crash location Connelly had reported made sense—some place in Canada or Russia where the population was sparse and the crash had escaped notice and not been reported.

Wright checked his wristwatch and picked up the telephone. He fished out a weathered business card and dialed the number. "Yes, good afternoon, this is Wright calling. Fine. Thank you for asking. Little bit of a favor. Could you ring up Records for me? No. No. Strictly declassified."

CHAPTER 8

Brandon, Manitoba

Jim Preston knew how to relax and he knew how to fish. Not necessarily in that order. One of Canada's former top spooks, he took pride in having worked for one of the world's top police intelligence agencies. Now in his early semi-retirement, he had been coming to Four Pines Lodge for over twenty-five years. He knew the original owners and had become friendly with the new owners as well. When they raised the rates each year to cash in on the American trade (and the Canadian exchange rate), he was quietly exempted. Consider it a private member rate for retired Canadians, they said.

Preston was truly grateful because he was on a fixed income. He loved this spot and knew the fishing holes by heart. They rarely changed year after year. He swore he had caught the same fish several times. He could tell by small markings and old wounds healed over—

which reminded him a lot of himself. He even talked to the fish as he threw them back in. Gently, of course.

For one week, three times a year, he traveled to this same lodge, to fish, meet old friends, and relax. No drinking anymore—after a close call with a liver ailment, his legendary drinking days were over. But he did like to smoke a good cigar on a regular basis. Seems the only place left on the planet where they let you smoke cigars in peace is the Canadian wilderness, he thought. Bit of an oxymoron, the fresh outdoors and cigar smoking, but the two worked well in tandem. That is, if it wasn't windy. Preston hated the wind because you couldn't taste or smell the cigar properly. Might as well not be smoking at all.

But today was one of those ideal days. A lazy breeze stirred through the trees. Smoke curled from the cigar clenched between Preston's teeth. He threw a cast about fifty feet, admiring the rolling loop of line as it arched over the water's surface and landed with a soft plunk near the far shore. Water rings expanded in wide circles as the bait and hook broke the surface.

Out of the corner of his eye he sensed movement and then a distant splashing sound. He turned toward the sound. He stared in amazement as a figure in the distance jumped from rock to rock, seemingly walking on water, heading directly for him. As the man came closer, Preston recognized him as an RCMP officer dressed in weatherproof clothing.

"Sir, I hate to interrupt, but ..." the officer apologized.

"It's OK ..." Preston was groping for a name.

"Hennings, sir."

"Right. Corporal Hennings. Sorry, remembered the face, but not the name."

"Not a problem. It's a request from Commander Macintosh to join him at your earliest convenience. Would it be convenient, say, tomorrow morning, sir?"

"Choices?" Preston looked inquisitively at the corporal.

"Well, sir, actually, none," the corporal said with an apologetic shrug.

"Thank you, Corporal. I'll be there." Preston dismissed him by turning and reeling his line back in. Half the fun was mastering the cast technique itself, so he didn't mind casting again. Still three good hours of light left.

"Just like the old days, huh?" the desk sergeant said, he glanced toward the coffee urn. The morning sun cast a golden stream through the dusty window as if pointing to the coffee.

"Good morning, Sergeant. It's been a while," Jim Preston said with a half smile.

"He's in. Just go right in. He's expecting you." The sergeant discreetly pressed a hidden button under his standard-issue gray metal desktop, releasing the door lock.

Preston nodded to the sergeant, grabbed his coffee, and opened the door to the commanding officer's office.

"Jim! Good to see you. It's been a long time," Commander Macintosh said, as he looked up from his desk. "Set yourself down, my son."

They shook hands warmly.

Mac, a Newfoundlander, was in his late fifties. His thinning auburn hair was heavily streaked with white. His sideburns and his ear hair had begun to merge. He removed his reading glasses with a dramatic gesture. "Guess you're wondering why you're here?"

Preston took a cautious sip of his steaming coffee. Nothing tasted better than the first cup of the day. "You missed me already?" He peered over the rim of his cup.

Mac laughed. "Yeah, that's it. How did you guess? Listen, sorry to interrupt your fishing, but a matter of national impotence has come up."

"Importance, Mac. Importance."

"Sorry, always get the two confused."

Preston smiled. It was an old joke between them.

"This concerns some of your old buddies in the UFO-chasing business."

Preston's eyebrows lifted but he remained silent.

"Report came in from Elliot Lake a few days ago. Two brothers working near the town found the remains of an aircraft or something. They reported that they had recovered the crash site of some aircraft that had plowed into the side of a hill. They seem to think it's a spacecraft. Maybe UFO."

"Any reported airline or private aircraft crashes in that area?"

"None," Mac replied. "We checked back thirty years. Sure, there had been a few planes that went down, but all have been accounted for."

"Elliot Lake is an old mining town. What about a company aircraft? Or could it be buried mining equipment or a storage container?"

"Not likely. Besides, the young man was clear about the appearance. They said the wreck appeared to be the wing of a large aircraft. Shiny silver. Very shiny. No markings. Not a container."

Jim Preston's eyes narrowed. "Hold on a minute. Would you say it looked like a large wing? Sort of like a boomerang?"

"Why, yes. The report mentions a sort of giant wing. We took that to mean a giant aircraft. Big wing, even bigger airplane. What's your take on it?"

"Never mind, let me see." Preston took the file from Mac. It was sparse. Simply a report of a possible UFO crash site. "Talks about a giant wing being unearthed." It had some personal information on the brothers. Comments by the officer requesting further action. There was a description of the wreck. It was buried in a hillside. Exposed after a landslide. Bright silver metallic wing of some sort. No evidence of fire or damage. Not a scratch. Discovered a few days ago. No photos."

"The file says no visible damage."

"I know. Caught my eye right away. Planes don't crash intact."

"Not where I come from. This thing should have been in pieces."

"Exactly. That's worth looking into."

"The boys' names look familiar," Preston said, looking down at the file folder again.

"They should. You knew their father, Frank Grayer."

"Frank is their father? You sure about that?"

"Some coincidence, huh?" Mac offered. "We ran a check on them. Temporary visas were issued a while back. Frank Grayer DoD is listed as the sponsor. They are his sons."

"Mac, this can't be a coincidence. Think of the odds. Frank has been hunting for UFOs for years. Now his kids stumble onto a crash site?"

"Yeah."

"I'm going to Elliot Lake, Mac. This has to be checked out."

"Thanks for offering," Mac said. "When can you leave?"

"Got some minor housekeeping issues to attend to. Could you arrange for a flight to Sudbury, and a car from there? Mac, I'm assuming that because we are having this conversation, the appropriate clearances are in place."

"Not entirely. The truth is that there is no budget for this type of investigation, and your official status is 'retired.' " Mac half smiled. "I'm dipping into my domestic surveillance budget for your expenses. So live on the cheap. The right people know, so my butt's covered. It's *your* butt that's kind of hanging out there. Can't even issue you a weapon."

Preston's face came close to a smile. "Same old, same old. Hate guns anyway."

"How very Canadian of you!"

Preston was at home relaxing later that day when the phone rang.

"Hello, Preston. It's Connelly."

"Major?" Preston asked. Then he recalled that Connelly was part of the UFO Smart Team in New Mexico.

"The very one. Miss me?"

"Got that right," Preston replied with a laugh. "What are you calling ..."

"I'd like to catch up on old times with my fishing buddies from the fifties. Care to join a few of us?"

A light clicked on in Preston's police-trained head. Too convenient. The coincidences were mounting. The Americans had gotten wind of the crash site at Elliot Lake. But how? That changed the priority somewhat. He quickly said, "Sure would. I know a few good spots in, say, northern Ontario."

Connelly understood right away that Preston already knew about the crash site. "Small world. I was thinking the very same thought. Care to join up with us in, say, Elliot Lake? I hear the smallmouth bass are in season and ready for smoking."

"My mouth is watering. Give me three days."

"No can do, my friend. Two days, max. We'll all meet at the departure lounge, Pearson Airport, Toronto. From there we go to Sudbury. Your tickets are on the way. Bring the right gear. Gotta go." The line went dead.

Preston glanced at his watch. Twenty seconds. Untraceable.

CHAPTER 9

Crash site, Elliot Lake

Joe returned to the crash site the next morning just after sunrise. He brought his bike up to the ship, killed the engine, and sat in the saddle like a cowboy gazing at his herd of cattle. There was this feeling he got when he was close to the craft, a sort of gentle buzzing, a whisper of electric energy.

The first thing Joe had noticed today as he approached the ship was that the door was no longer open. This unnerved him. He slowly slipped off his backpack and took a swig of cold water from his thermos. Staring at the smooth fuselage, he gathered his thoughts.

"Don't be a chicken," he mumbled under his breath.

With his jaw clenched, he reached into his pack and removed his magnetic flashlight and a Swiss Army knife. He pondered the small red knife, weighing it in the palm of his hand. Not much of a defensive weapon. But it might come in handy. You never know. He left the remainder of the pack in a heap beside the bike and proceeded toward the craft.

As before, he tried gingerly placing the magnetic strip of the flashlight on several spots on the smooth fuselage. Lo and behold, the same thing happened. There was a gentle hiss, not as forceful as the first time, and the door opened soundlessly.

Joe closed his eyes and concentrated in a kind of prayer. Mentally steeling himself to ward off the shakes, he craned his neck and peered into the black inner compartment, his feet firmly planted. Wiping his hands against his jeans, he jammed the knife into his rear pocket and his flashlight into a front pocket. His right hand gripped the fuselage by the opening, and he pulled himself upwards and into the craft.

There was very little light inside. Even the morning light coming through the open door seemed to be absorbed into the abyss. Joe could not see any defining walls or compartments. There was only a vague gray-green color throughout that was reminiscent of a hiking trip he and Hawk had taken through underground caves in Arizona. Joe took a tentative step farther inside. Nothing. Silence. He took another. Then another, as he began to inch his way into the craft.

Like a blind man, he instinctively held his hands in front of him to protect himself. Looking furtively from side to side, he could see nothing but darkness. Slowly he got his nerve and started to walk more deliberately away from the doorway. Things were going well. Then, after he had gone several paces into the ship, the door began to close.

Joe sensed the light rapidly disappearing and wheeled around. He launched himself toward the opening, sliding across the floor, hands outstretched. When he was inches from the door, it closed completely. He stared up with his fingers almost touching the door. It had only taken a moment for the door to shut. Daylight disappeared.

"No! No! No! Don't close!" he screamed.

He lay still for a moment, face down on the plastic-like floor. Then he gathered himself up on his haunches and flung his hands toward the door. He ran his fingers over the walls, searching for a crack he could wedge open. He grabbed his knife, ready to pry it open. He found nothing but a smooth surface.

"What have I done?" he moaned out loud, as he pivoted and leaned backwards against the wall. He slowly slid down the wall until he was sitting with his chin on his knees.

After some time his frustration and fear subsided and his mind cleared. All right, if I'm the explorer, I might as well start exploring, he thought. He reached into his pocket, fished out his flashlight, and turned it on. The yellow glow was welcome.

Yellow. Why isn't the light bright white? he thought as he gently tapped the flashlight onto his palm a few times.

Then it came to him. He closed his eyes in frustration.

Damn it! He had forgotten to put in new batteries. An oversight. He broke into a sweat as he mentally calculated how much battery time was left. Not much. Perhaps ten minutes or less.

I've got to find a way out of here fast! he thought. The tune "We Gotta Get Outta This Place" cycled through his head. He sprang to his feet and walked unsteadily down the corridor. The flashlight reflected vague surfaces, but nothing more. He picked up his pace as he walked along a narrow passageway. The light reflected off the walls on both sides of him. He could not discern color or texture. However, he could see markings ahead.

He approached another corridor. He was at a juncture. He had to decide which way to go. Always turn right, he reasoned. Joe pressed on and followed the corridor to the right. He saw what appeared to be two doorways ahead and markings on the floor and wall. His heart leaped. Not so fast, he said to himself, and slowed down. Cautiously, he approached the first entranceway. He ran his right hand along the wall and held the flashlight in his left.

Too bad I don't have both hands free, in case I have to defend myself, he thought.

At that exact moment, his flashlight died. Joe tapped it furiously but to no avail. It was dead. He bit his lip and stood in silence. "I am so screwed," he said out loud.

Total and absolute blackness enveloped him.

He just stood there. Unable to think. Unable to plan. He had no frame of reference or experience that might have guided him to the next move. Was there a next move? He closed his eyes and squished a frustrated thought out of his brain. I need light! his mind screamed.

Incredibly, as he opened his eyes, he was no longer in absolute blackness. At first he thought it might be a trick of the eyes. But it was not. There was a soft, warm, greenish glow coming from the adjacent wall. No, from all the walls. And from the floor. The intensity of the ambient light began to increase, not unlike turning up a dimmer switch.

Joe gazed around. His flimsy flashlight had not revealed the sheer size of the passage and the labyrinth of corridors leading away. He absently pocketed it.

Ironically, he had been so eager to find a way in, but now he was searching for a way out.

As he waited for David Bohr to get on the line, Connelly wondered how well he would remember him after all these years, He knew he was home because Bohr was under ELINT (ELectronic signals INTelligence) surveillance. That meant light, unmanned electronic surveillance by the NSA. Connelly was provided with ELINT on several people for this mission.

"David. Good day. This is —"

"My God. Connelly. It's you," Bohr said. "After so long. Is all well, Major?" His next inclination was to peek outside through the curtains to see if he could spot a Watcher. Get a grip. Who'd watch some old retirement spook anyway?

They chatted for a few moments before the major got to the point.

"Our mutual friends from many years ago have a possible lead on another vessel similar to the one you worked on in Los Alamos. I am assembling the team again for a reconnaissance mission. The political climate of late is not conducive to sharing this opportunity with others. So we may be on our own until a course of action is agreed upon."

Bohr hesitated, his heart beating hard. "Sure. Sure. I understand."

"We are going to Canada. Tickets are on their way to you. See you in Toronto."

Joe stopped momentarily at the doorway. Don't be a baby, he mumbled to himself. This was the third room he had encountered. The others were bare-bones empty. He began to ponder the idea that if he was the one who found this very strange craft, there might be others interested in it as well. He couldn't help feeling he was getting involved in something much bigger than himself.

As soon as he crossed the threshold to the third room, the illumination increased seemingly from everywhere. Joe squinted, and the light intensity diminished somehow to a more comfortable level.

This room was different. It was larger than the others. Joe guessed that the room was about twenty feet in diameter, and perfectly circular. By his best estimates, he figured the room was at the center of the craft, near the nose. The light was such that the room appeared to be a very pale green throughout, with the floor and the walls the exact same color. The showstopper was what appeared to be an instrument panel straight ahead.

The panel was shaped like an upside-down L, with the base angled out at about twenty degrees toward some chairs. The panel's surface was opaque and colorless. In front of it were four white chairs, each shaped like a small, upside-down cross or T bent at a thirty-degree angle, allowing one to either sit up or lean back comfortably. They were a dull, opaque white, and they looked soft yet resilient.

He approached the panel with a mixture of awe and curiosity. His hand reached out and touched the surface. Immediately the blank colorless panel sprang to life with a dazzle of different colors. He jumped back.

Suddenly he heard—or was it sensed?—a sound, like a soft voice. He could not be sure if he actually heard the voice. The garbled sound repeated itself. Then again. Then a different sound, and the panel dimmed to nothing.

Joe walked farther along the ten-foot-long panel, and reached out to touch the surface. Before his hand touched it, the panel ignited and the quizzical voice could be heard again. The same sounds. Then the panel shut down. It was as if the instrument had sensed his intrusion. After having been in contact with Joe just the once, it seemed to have learned and recognized him as someone who did not know what he was doing.

He ran his hands over the nearest chair. It was a soft vinyl-like material. There were no seams or stitching that he could see. The chair appeared to be fabricated from a singular mold. He sat at the base of the T and gently leaned back. The chair seemed to mold itself perfectly around his back and buttocks.

After a while, he decided it was time to move on and discover more about the craft. He was now convinced that this was an extraterrestrial craft. He concluded that he was likely in the main control and navigation room, the bridge. This troubled him because he realized that he had absolutely no business in the control area of a craft that had most likely traveled millions of miles to reach here.

Exiting the room, Joe continued down the right side of the craft. He encountered another entrance farther down the passageway. He peered inside. It was a tiny room, about the size of a shower stall. It was absolutely bare except for a tiny bar of three lights on the far side. He was curious. Leaving the passageway, he stepped inside for a closer view of the light panel. Maybe this was a clue to getting out, he thought. An exit.

As he bent over to investigate the light bar, a hidden door soundlessly closed behind him. He didn't even realize it until he straightened up and looked behind him. Instinctively, his hands flew to where the door had been. He noticed, somehow without surprise, that all evidence of a doorway was gone. The entire room was a circular stall without an exit. Joe threw himself against the spot where the door had been, but his body met with a substance that felt like thick vinyl over steel, and he bounced back, uninjured. Like a trapped rat, he spent the next several minutes running his hands along the walls and exploring every inch in hope of finding an escape.

His hands finally reached the three light bars, and he stopped. The lights were dim and out of focus behind an opaque colorless screen. There were three lights of what appeared to be an identical orange color but different brightness. It occurred to him that there may indeed be three different colors, but his ability to differentiate between them was limited by his lack of optical sophistication. His brain was unable to recognize the different colors and presented them as just one color, orange.

He blinked in concentration, thinking about the consequences of touching any one of the colors. And if so, which color to choose? Were they buttons of some sort? This room could be an alien garbage disposal for all he knew. Maybe the walls would start slowly compacting in on him like in *Star Wars*. Or if he pushed the wrong button, some cosmic incinerating beam might obliterate him.

Enough already, he thought. I can't stay here like this. I'll die for sure before anyone can rescue me from the outside. It comes down to which button I should push.

Wait a minute—the lights have different brightness, he noticed. From dull to brighter. I will choose the dullest. No, hold on, maybe I should choose the brightest. In the end, he chose the least intense light and, reaching out, he touched the panel.

Outside, the air was fresh, and the setting sun filtered through the tight forest greenery like pinpricks of laser.

Joe's head was resting comfortably against his backpack when Hawk found him. His body was outstretched and his legs crossed. His face was expressionless, not unlike a dead person's, which prompted Hawk to reach down to touch him and make sure he was all right.

With surreal speed, Joe's hand flew out and grabbed Hawk's wrist in midair.

"I'm fine," Joe said. He slowly opened his eyes and let go of Hawk's wrist. His voice had a hollow, ghost-like sound to it.

Hawk catapulted back on his haunches and dropped his flashlight. "You scared the crap out of me! What's going on? Why haven't you been home?"

Joe's hands slowly went to his skull. "I have a headache." He tried to stand, but his legs were like rubber, and he collapsed.

Hawk reached out to help him, but drew back at the last second, his hand frozen in midair. Something was not right here. "You OK?"

Joe ran his tongue over his lips. They were parched. "I'm thirsty," he said.

Handing him a water bottle, Hawk asked, "Joe, have you been here all the time?"

Joe took the water and drank greedily. He gazed at Hawk as if coming out of a trance. "What do you mean, 'all the time'? How long have I been here?"

"Well you didn't show last night. And when you still weren't home after I got in after work, I decided to come here to make sure you were all right. Where were you last night?"

"Last night? I ... um ... can't remember. Looks like I lost track of time." Joe was starting to come around. His eyes blinked clarity back into his mind. He took big gulps of the water.

"But Hawk, guess what. I found a way inside. I got inside the ship."

"You're kidding me."

"No kidding." Joe glanced at his watch. "It's eight o'clock! I've lost almost two days."

Hawk reached out his hand. "Come on. Tell me what you can remember when we get back home. I'll drive." He helped him hobble to the ATV.

Once they had rested and eaten, Joe related his adventure to Hawk. As he told the story, his memory began to improve.

Hawk poured Joe another instant decaf coffee and slid in across from him at the chrome kitchen table, the shiny vinyl of the chair squeaking as he sat down.

Cupping his hot coffee mug in his hands, Joe continued. "After I pushed some button, nothing happened at first. All of a sudden I felt a thick slimy kind of goo against my hands. I looked down and the stall was filling up with this green gel. Real fast. Before I could think, it was up to my neck. I took a deep breath. It covered my head. Hawk, I thought I was toast. Then, I started to feel really relaxed. I just forgot about breathing."

"How can you just forget to breathe?"

Joe shrugged. "It was sort of what it must feel like to be in the womb. I didn't feel a need to breathe. It was just there. The oxygen, I mean. Anyway, I began to feel bigger, larger, stronger. Massive. I was more than me. I was beginning to *flow*, sort of. It was definitely an out-of-body experience, I can tell you. As best as I can figure, I was connecting with the ship's brain. It kind of said to me 'get ready to learn!' The first thing I learned was where I was. I was in a Learning Stall. Those are my words because there are no words I know for this place I was in. It can train the occupant about the craft, navigation, weaponry, propulsion—you name it. It is also an infirmary of some kind. The first few seconds were hell. I saw all kinds of images and stuff, but couldn't understand a thing. Nothing made any sense.

"Then, for a moment there was a break, a pause. Next, I saw or heard very simple language and began to understand what it meant. I sensed I was being taught a new language or form of communication. I'm not sure. But it became clear that in order for me to get to the basic training thing, I had to comprehend the language. Hawk, can you imagine? I think I learned a new form of communicating with another …"

"Another what, Joe?"

Joe shrugged. "That's just it. I can't say exactly. Maybe an alien language."

"You think this machine taught you another language?"

"Not really a machine. Something more. I got assimilated," Joe said with a little smile.

"Assimilated? That's a big word, Joe. I didn't know you knew big words like that."

"Hawk, leave me alone, will ya? I'm really tired. I just want to crash now. OK?"

"Sure, Joe." Hawk stared into his brother's bloodshot eyes. "You look like you could use some sleep. There's just one thing."

"What's that?"

"We are going to the RCMP first thing tomorrow. Enough of this mystery stuff. If what you say is true, I think we have to report this, now. This will shake the world. If they aren't prepared to take us seriously and investigate further, I'm going to the press with pictures."

"No. No way, Hawk! I need more time. I don't want strangers poking around the craft. Especially not now that I've begun to learn how this thing works. They will take it away from me! Hell, they might take me away, too. And lock me up for, I don't know, obstruction of something or other."

"God! Relax, Joe." Hawk was concerned about his brother's outburst. "No one's going to take it away from you. But, this thing, especially if it is extraterrestrial, is not yours. This isn't some game like Finders Keepers, you know."

Then he thought, I really have to go to the authorities about this before it gets out of hand.

At that instant, Joe gave him a sharp look. "Hawk, promise me you will come to the site tomorrow and see for yourself. Before you bring in the authorities. Promise."

"I'll sleep on it."

"Hawk, I need you to promise."

Hawk got up and cleared the dishes into the sink. Staring out the night-black window, his face slightly distorted in the reflection, he nodded. "OK. I'll come. If nothing else, to protect you from yourself."

Joe made his way toward his bedroom. Hawk followed him down the hall, turning out the lights along the way. In the darkened passage, Joe slowly turned toward Hawk and said in a soft voice: "I feel different. Smarter, more grown up somehow."

Hawk felt the claws of unease scratch down his back as he caught Joe's eyes. There was a flash of green luminescence behind them, just for an instant, a green ember-like glow visible in the dark hall. Just a trick of the light, he thought.

"You were always a smart kid, Joe," Hawk said. "Good night."

CHAPTER 10

Crash site, Elliot Lake

The dawn of a new day. An important day. Joe sat bolt upright in bed. He was well rested. He had slept the sleep of the dead—no dreams, no tossing or turning, just restful sleep.

Hawk was already up and had breakfast ready when Joe entered the kitchen. "Couldn't sleep," he said abruptly. "Let's eat before we go."

Joe devoured his meal with the manners of a wild dog. He was famished. He had not eaten in two days. After some small talk and his third helping, he said, "Let's rock!" and headed for the door.

Hawk drove the company ATV to the crash site and down the slippery slope to within a few yards of the wreck.

They both stood hesitantly in front of the partially uncovered craft. Some of the bravado had worn off as the danger struck home.

"Joe, you sure you want to do this?"

"All right, I'll admit it … I'm a little scared, but look, I've already been inside once. I got out OK. There is more to do. More to finish. Here, hold my flashlight up against the fuselage and see what happens."

It took several tries but finally the door slid open. Hawk backed away uneasily. "Joe, this is amazing. What a discovery, bro!" Then he looked into the darkness of the craft and said, "We should really get some backup on this."

Joe grabbed him by the elbow and led him inside the craft. "Nothing to be afraid of. Come on, I'll show you what I found."

He nudged Hawk forward down a few passageways. Joe had fresh batteries, but didn't turn the flashlight on because the ship's internal lighting illuminated the passageway.

They stopped in front of a small stall-like room. "After you," Joe said, pointing the way in, but Hawk hesitated. "This is what I call the Learning Stall, Hawk. I have already been here. This is where you learn new things. This room can teach us how to understand the language, and the makeup of the ship. Maybe even fly her."

"I don't want to fly this thing, Joe," Hawk said, frowning as he backed away from the closet-sized room.

Joe laughed as he shoved Hawk into the small space and crammed himself in as well. "What could possibly go wrong? I've already been through this and I survived. Besides, I could use the company."

The door closed almost immediately. Joe reached out confidently and gently touched a dully lit orange button, and the chamber began to fill. The boys waited apprehensively as a clear, light-green gel rose higher and higher up their bodies.

"I don't know about this, Joe," Hawk said, his voice rising in fear. As the gel reached his chin, he was on his tiptoes. "Joe!" He looked like a dog hanging by his neck from a chain. His eyes bulged in terror.

Since Joe was slightly shorter than Hawk, he was already

submerged. Joe's eyes were open and looking back at Hawk. He was perfectly calm.

Suddenly, a peace like he had never felt before came over Hawk. His panic quickly subsided as the gel engulfed his entire body. He too became submerged. The compartment was completely flooded now. Oxygen and breathing did not seem to be an issue, just as Joe had said.

Hawk became tranquil, mesmerized. It was like taking an anesthetic that dulled the pain but kept you more or less awake. His mind became attuned to new and exciting thoughts. He began to hear, understand, and learn the basics of some alien language as it related to our own human culture and language. There was a whirlwind of thought, a kaleidoscope of concepts. It all seemed so fast and so random, like riffling the pages of a book and snatching a word or a sentence here and there.

Many things about human versus alien language and culture and science were revealed to the brothers that day. The ship's brain acted as interpreter. Beginning with what the two species had in common, it managed to link commonalities and then build understanding from there.

Because their entire bodies were tuned directly to the ship's brain, the speed of learning was very fast indeed. The gel acted as a nearly perfect conduit to aid in the transmission of data, learning, and comprehension. It also regulated the temperature of the boys' brains. Because of the molecular agitation during information transfer, a significant degree of heat was generated. The gel dissipated this heat rapidly. Overall, their bodies were maintained at about a hundred degrees Fahrenheit; however, their brains were kept at a temperature of ninety degrees to facilitate an easier transmission without causing a massive headache. They bled slightly from their noses and eyes, but the gel digested the floating red cells.

The craft's intelligence system had already assimilated Joe's human identification system, enabling him to progress at a much quicker pace than his brother. Joe had now advanced to learning about the physical makeup of the craft. How it worked. Where the arteries and circuits were located. Where the propulsion system was located and how it worked. Diagnostics and repair. Once this learning session was over, Joe would have the ability to understand and interpret fluently most of the language and symbols found on board.

Hours passed, but it seemed like the blink of an eye to the twins. Like coming out of a trance, they found themselves seated on the floor outside the chamber. Hawk was slow to move, but Joe was now more accustomed to the effects of the craft, and eased his brother to his feet. He half-carried Hawk to the control room.

"Sit here and lean back until you feel better," he said, easing him into a chair.

Hawk lolled on the chair, but remained upright. His eyes were half open.

Joe had shaken off his grogginess and moved directly to the control panel. He placed the outstretched palm of his right hand about six inches above the surface. The panel flickered to life. Multicolored lights glowed under a translucent surface. A soft voice issued a greeting in English: "Welcome, Joe Grayer."

Joe's eyes flickered wide in surprise, and then he smiled. "Just Joe."

"Thank you for correcting me. Welcome aboard Alpha III, an intergalactic Class Alpha exploratory scout ship, Joe. You have control. Voice activated English and motion."

With the confident assurance of one who knows his craft, Joe touched a sequence of seven lights. "Main," he said, looking up.

The wall directly in front of them disappeared and was replaced by a twenty-foot-wide image in vivid blue and white. "Ship's prints," Joe said. The layout of the craft was displayed. Joe raised his right hand and pointed toward a complex series of symbols. "Damage report." That section of the display enlarged until he held up his hand in a *stop* motion.

Next, he touched a few more buttons, and the image was replaced by a 3-D replica of the craft. "Real-time transparent." It was as if the ship were made of transparent plastic. You could see through walls, levels, arteries, and equipment. Various parts of the image of the craft that were shown in different colors. Joe knew these areas were of concern because they represented possible internal damage. Two spots were blinking. He knew that this was damage that was critical to the survival of the craft. On the positive side, there was no evidence of damage to the external fuselage.

Joe held out his right hand and made a motion similar to screwing in a light bulb. Immediately the image began to rotate.

To get a different view, Joe held up his hand to halt the rotation. "Hawk, look up, look at this."

"My head hurts," Hawk groaned, slouching in his command chair.

"You'll be fine in a minute. Look up at where the wall was. It's like a giant TV screen. Look at the damage report. There's damage to the sections in orange. Do you see?"

"That's a damage report? Looks like a picture of a spaceship."

"Well, you're right. But it's more than a picture. It's a real-time image of what the vessel looks like, and the damage is highlighted in orange so we can see it better. Actually there are other colors, but we don't have the optic range to see them, so those colors look orange or gray to us."

Joe continued by touching more lights. The image changed again, to a view of intricate arteries and biomechanical switching and sensor devices. "Here is where most of the damage is. Look at the diagnostics. These chemicals have breached their containment apparatus and have been contaminated. They have to be replaced."

His hands flew over the control panel. A new image appeared. He continued to explain to Hawk what he saw. "This is the ship's flight data record prior to collision with Earth. The sensing and navigation equipment malfunctioned after heavy contact with meteorites. Hawk, this is amazing! Look here—you can see evidence of a severe loss of momentum. The craft was drawn into the moon's gravitational pull, then into the Earth's pull."

He continued, tapping his teeth with his index finger: "They were lucky. If the craft hadn't been pulled to Earth, our sun would have grabbed it and pulled it into its core. The craft would have been destroyed."

Hawk squinted his eyes in consternation. "You can see all that? I can only see flickering gibberish. The images make no sense to me at all."

Joe shrugged. "I guess your learning has not quite caught up to mine yet. Don't forget I had two days' head start. Take my word for it, though. What's on the screen is the ship's flight record prior to impact. A galactic 'black box.' "

He pointed at the screen and flicked his hand. The image changed instantaneously. It changed so quickly that you had to wonder if the new image hadn't been there all along.

Joe stared intently at the image. "Here is the damage from the impact with Earth. Surprisingly little damage. The ship has the ability to land under extreme circumstances and protect its internal workings. The exterior shell is virtually indestructible."

He turned to Hawk. "It makes sense. This ship had to have traveled for hundreds of years at near light speed. The creators must have calculated that the craft would encounter obstacles in its space travel. The skin had to be super tough to withstand the hits."

Joe reached out his hand, then made a quick closed-fist gesture. The image disappeared. "Time to go. Can you manage?"

"I'm good," Hawk mumbled unconvincingly as he eased himself to his feet.

Joe reached down toward the control panel. A clear blue card, the shape and size of an ordinary playing card, was sticking up through the surface. Joe grabbed it, turned, and walked nonchalantly toward the door. "Our grocery list."

They left the control room and walked down a passageway. Joe stopped abruptly and held his open palm up against the blank wall. The wall disappeared with a soft hiss and they were staring at their ATV twenty feet away.

"How the hell did you do that?" Hawk asked.

"Not exactly sure. Just knew what to do. And voilà! Instant door. Kinda cool, huh?"

"Joe, let's go home. You and I gotta talk," Hawk said wearily. He took a final look around. It was all quite overwhelming.

CHAPTER 11

Elliot Lake

The twins sat at the kitchen table under the early-1970s swag light. Its low-wattage globe cast a glow on both their young faces. Joe handed Hawk the blue card. He decided that the time Hawk spent in the Room would now enable him to recognize the alien symbols.

"Can you make out the symbols on the list?"

"No. It's gibberish," he said peevishly.

"Hawk, you never even looked. Now look."

Hawk was fully recovered from the Learning ordeal on board the spaceship. He took the card from Joe and held it up against the light. It resembled a credit card and was a transparent blue with white symbols etched inside.

Squinting, he said, "Nope, I don't see … Wait a minute. This is starting to make sense. Oh my God, I can understand this. This is, this is amazing. Joe, I can really understand the list." He put the card down, and stared at his brother, his mouth forming a perfect O.

"Hawk, that card contains chemical components that are somehow damaged or missing from the craft. Without these items, the ship will malfunction permanently in a short period of time. These formulations mean nothing to me and we can't show the card to anyone."

"Well, if we can't show anyone the list, how the hell are we going to get the stuff we need to repair the craft?"

"Especially when we don't know what this stuff is."

"You're right," Hawk replied gloomily. "This is an alien grocery list. I doubt if the stuff exists on our planet."

"The list contains chemical symbols. Chemicals are universal, aren't they?"

"I don't know. They could be."

"This is important, Hawk. This spaceship runs on chemistry. It is organic based. There are no metal wires and motors like we're used to. All the devices, all the computers, are organic."

They stared at the table for a few minutes. Hawk got up and poured both of them another coffee. "We're going to have to translate this into English. Then we can go to someone who can make sense of this. If we're in luck, there is some kind of universal Periodic Table, or something close enough for us to use."

"Hawk, you're right. We'll take it to Laurentian University in Sudbury. We can ask the chemistry department for help."

"If someone can tell us what they think these items are, maybe there are brand names and we can buy this stuff. If the chemistry is universal, they could never suspect its origin is extraterrestrial."

"With some luck, we can look up manufacturers in the university reference library."

"Still a long shot."

"Our only shot."

For the next few hours, they translated the alien list into English.

 The next morning the brothers got up, excited.

"Hawk, why don't you call in sick for the next few days?" Joe said. "You go to the university and see what you can find out. I'll go back to the ship. I'm sure there's a lot more to learn. I have a gut feeling there's something that we've overlooked."

"And what's that?"

"Well, for starters, how about the crew, Hawk? Where's the crew?"

"You're right! There were no bodies. No dead smell. Nothing. Joe, we didn't really check out the craft. I'll bet there's a crew somewhere on board. Probably dead, though."

"Right. Exactly why I have to go back in. I know a lot of the ship's layout now. I'm going to try and discover some clue. I'm going to run a different type of scan. There's got to be someone on board, maybe cryogenically preserved. It makes little sense to send an unmanned spaceship millions of miles."

"Unless it was a mistake. Maybe it was designed to go and return, but it couldn't return. Maybe it got damaged. And it just kept going out into deep space. Until it crashed into Earth."

"You mean a drone?"

"Maybe. All right, you check the ship out. I'm going to Laurentian to see if I can get help from the local profs. Maybe I can get some samples. Who knows? See you in a day or so."

Hawk began clearing the table. "And Joe …"

"Yeah?"

"Be careful." Hawk patted him on the shoulder.

Grasping his hand, Joe said, "You, too."

Both brothers had a strong feeling that their lives were about to get complicated.

The flights were delayed in Toronto because of fog in Sudbury.

When he found out, Connelly said, "Screw this." He rented a large Ford station wagon for the group of four. Its plush faux velour luxury seating made up for the length of the five-hour drive ahead. The group was in good spirits.

Just hours before, they had had a reunion in the privacy of the Air Canada lounge in Toronto. David Bohr had flown in from Tempe, Arizona. Connelly from New York. Jim Preston simply drove to the airport. Last to arrive was Peter Wright, coming in from Heathrow. Their arrival flights had come in separately, but all had managed to rendezvous within a three-hour window—only to have the last leg of the journey delayed by fog.

Connelly began talking as they headed north on Highway 400. "Gentlemen, RCMP Officer Hunter will meet us in Sudbury. He has been unable to contact the brothers. One of them has a summer job with Ontario Hydro. Hunter checked with the company. The kid called in sick. They don't expect him in for a few days."

"Do we know where they live?" Bohr asked.

"Sure. Hunter has been to their house but no one was there," Connelly answered.

"Did he not go in and look around?" Preston asked.

"B and E, my friend?" Wright said.

"National security, Peter," Connelly said quickly.

"You need a warrant, guys, we all know this," Wright moaned. "How long can that take?"

"Can't. At least not yet. Besides, the place was empty." Connelly hesitated, and then he half smiled. "All right, we did go in, OK? Hunter was careful."

"We? We who?" Preston said. "Hunter works for the RCMP, remember, not CSIS," he pointed out, referring to the Canadian intelligence counterpart to America's CIA. "The Mounties don't break into private residences!"

"Jimmy boy, Hunter is one of ours," Connelly said. "And yours, too, I guess. He is primarily a CSIS agent, but his cover is as the local RCMP officer. I made a call to Ottawa a few days ago. Hunter is on loan to our, uh, *group* for a while." He glared at Preston.

Wright wrinkled his eyes. "Why would CSIS have an agent in Sudbury, Ontario, of all places? Isn't it kind of quiet up there in the Canadian wilderness?"

"Not as quiet as you would think," Preston said. "We have a problem with organized crime using that region as a national base. Biker gangs seem to like operating out of northern Ontario. It's less obvious, I guess."

"You Canadians never cease to amaze me," Wright said.

"Well, let's go over this one more time," Connelly said to no one in particular as he drove along. "Let's go back in time to 1944. We have always suspected that there were two UFOs, not one, that crashed into Earth back in forty-four. The ships may have received damage en route that forced them down."

"Or Earth was the intended target."

"Yes, David. Or Earth was the target destination. If it was, you would think that they could have done a better job of landing. So, the more reasonable theory is that there was damage incurred either in space or upon entering our atmosphere, and the ships crash-landed. We believe that both spaceships were unmanned."

"Intergalactic drones."

"Yes, drones." Connelly continued the story. "We recover the remains of Ship Number One. It's in bad shape, but we manage to put a lot of Humpty Dumpty back together again. Or, at least the way we think it should go back together. We conclude it is an alien spacecraft because there is no way in hell any military has the gizmos that we found."

"But there was a war on."

"Yes, that's true. The military sat on the discovery once they determined that it wasn't related to the war effort. World War II was in full swing. Because we knew it was not an immediate threat to our nation, it took on a lower priority until after the war. The war ended, and the war on communism began. National security was heightened because the Allies feared the spread of communism throughout the planet. There were enemies everywhere. The military-industrial complex was born. There were a scant few aware of the UFO, and they saw an opportunity to win the arms race with superior weapons and aircraft because of technology discovered from it. The wreck was studied by our friend David here. He had a lab right next door to the craft. He parachuted in his buddies from Chicago U. NSA threw in a few of their own people, and the military assigned me to baby-sit the whole bunch of you."

"Your modesty knows no bounds, Major," David Bohr said from the back seat. "That's a rather condensed version. We learned a lot of good science from our alien wreck. There are projects still underway today that owe their origins to what we were able to glean from the alien technology."

"Major, am I to understand that all that remains of the original team is the four of us?" Wright asked.

"You understand that correctly. It was a small group to begin with. A few have died over the years. One mathematician suffers from dementia. We could not locate two scientists. The military personnel have been reassigned and are no longer relevant. Finally, there is, of course, Frank Grayer. I can't locate him. You two were close, weren't you, David? Have you heard from him?"

"Not for some time now, Major," Bohr said. "I have heard from his boys on a regular basis since they moved away from Los Alamos to Canada, though."

Preston spoke up. "Frank was always a sort of mystery figure. Nice enough, but distant. He and I worked briefly in the Canadian intelligence network. He was convinced that there was more than one spacecraft. He also thought that one had crashed in a remote area of either Canada or the USSR."

"Oh God." Wright said. "I remember the near panic when Frank shared his concerns about the Soviets with the rest of us. We were petrified that the Soviets had secretly recovered the craft. Our fear was that they were developing more advanced weapons and aircraft based on a ship in better condition than the one we had recovered."

"The Soviets were developing aircraft and weapons at a faster pace than us, and with much less capital investment," Preston said. "For a time there we really believed that they had found the second ship. Of course, in the end, the answer had been staring us in the face all along. Our collective paranoia blinded us."

"You're right," Wright said. "It was never the alien technology. It was simply having better spies that allowed the Soviets to advance quicker. They were using our own technology against us. Frank was never totally convinced of this. He spent a lot of time trying to determine if the Soviets had discovered a wrecked spacecraft. But the Russians never did achieve the quality of technology that we had based on the wreckage. Frank was wrong. They never had it. They stole fragments of ours and called it their own. I had a team of Russians working counterespionage. If they'd had a spaceship I would have found out."

"And here we are," Preston said.

Connelly took the hint and concluded, "We're going to check out a solid lead on the second spaceship. Too bad Frank isn't here. This is exactly the kind of lead he was searching for. All those years, and now it pops up."

"And no word on Frank?"

"None. Pity. He would have been over the top about this."

"Well, let me know when we get there," Bohr said, adjusting his seat and stretching back as far as he could. He closed his eyes, listening to the droning of the tires as they drove along. His thoughts drifted back to earlier years when he and Frank first worked together.

In 1958, fourteen years after the wreck had been discovered, Bohr was called in to examine it. Frank Grayer was a bright young test pilot who had volunteered to assist Bohr and the team with various aspects of the reconstruction of the craft. He was also an Air Force Intelligence agent assigned to keep tabs on the project for the brass in Washington. Back then, structure wasn't as centralized as today. Grayer worked directly for the NSA. His reports were then sent to the JCS, the Joint Chiefs of Staff.

President Kennedy had his hands full with the likes of Khrushchev. The President was looking for an edge in the military arms race that would relieve political pressure at home. The JCS had asked NSA to select a young and trustworthy military pilot to work as a team member at Los Alamos to provide additional operations security for Bohr's classified research. Grayer was brought in specifically to control evidence of the activities at Los Alamos and protect it from potential adversaries.

Inside a cavity in the wrecked ship, Bohr had found a silver ball about five inches in diameter. It was stored in a shelf-like mechanism with four other balls. The others appeared damaged somehow and were not silver but a dull gray. Their surfaces had been badly scorched by the heat of the crash. This one, however, was still perfectly round and appeared highly reflective, as if polished.

Bohr spent some time theorizing about the various potential uses of the mystery ball and the mechanism by which it performed its elusive function. It might be a non-nuclear weapon. It had been scanned for radioactivity and was found to be clean. He thought it might have something to do with laser weaponry. Lasers were the latest weapons research going on at the time.

He became convinced that a module he had reconstructed from the wreckage served a purpose related to the silver balls. This device was linked, by a tube, to another, larger object that resembled a portable shower stall. It was barely six feet high and about three feet in diameter. There was an opening on the side where a man could squeeze through and stand upright. Bohr's team had spent years attempting to get these devices to work, which was difficult when you didn't know how they was supposed to work in the first place. They had also managed to fill a two-hundred-gallon reservoir with a green substance saved from the wreck. This green gel was reinserted into the swarm of arteries that surrounded the stall. Then the module was reattached to the stall.

By close examination of the many severed tubes or arteries, the team was able to determine which tubes went where. Energy was supplied by several tubes that were attached to a damaged power core. Bohr had no means of measuring the power because it was not electric. He did have some instruments that detected high levels of magnetic energy fluctuation. He deduced that this meant power was present. He also noticed that, once the power tubes or arteries had been attached, three buttons began to glow on the wall of the stall. He hoped that there was enough power to operate the rest of the device.

All Bohr needed now was a volunteer to insert the shiny silver ball into the module, then enter the stall and activate the three glowing buttons. Grayer, after having received clearance from Washington, was the volunteer.

He asked Grayer to insert the silver ball into the tube that led to the module that was in turn connected to the stall. Firmly grasping the surprisingly heavy ball, Grayer inserted it into the short semi-transparent tube. The ball rolled through the tube and into the device. The module closed with a hiss. Then nothing happened.

Next, with some trepidation, Grayer entered the stall and pressed an orange-colored button that was pulsating intensely. Immediately, the door slid closed, trapping him inside. Already the experiment had gone south. Bohr rushed over and tried to open the door. Then he noticed the module containing the silver ball beginning to vibrate erratically. He raced over and cupped the device in his hands to prevent the tubes from detaching. The module began to get warm, then hot. He let go and dashed to his lab. He returned, wearing insulated gloves, and cupped the thrashing module. The device steamed a little and gave off the odor of burnt hair.

Bohr tried to collect his thoughts. He was deeply troubled about Grayer's fate. He watched in dismay as the stall began to rattle apart. Where the team had made their repairs, the power tubes broke apart one by one, spewing a blinding light. The tubes wriggled and whipped in the air, sending arc after arc of pulsating light around the room. The heat became intense. More arteries popped away from the device. They began to ooze a green gel that temporarily glowed with a bright luminescence. As the substance spread on the floor in pools, the luminescence quickly faded and the gel turned a dark green again.

Without warning, the module stopped vibrating and cooled. Bohr carefully put it down and went to the stall door. He was frantically thinking about how he could get Grayer out, when the door slid open partway. Bohr grabbed at the door with both hands and yanked it open completely. Grayer's body collapsed into his arms. Bohr dragged him away from the stall and wrapped his body in a lab coat. He called for help, but then remembered that they were alone in the complex working late. He made a pillow out of his radiation gloves.

Grayer came to and looked around. His eyes widened. He looked down at his body. He opened and closed his hands. He struggled to get up but was as weak as a baby. There was a faint green glow radiating from behind Grayer's eyes, or so it seemed. Could have been a trick of the light. Grayer's muscles were twitching and his face was distorted.

"Let me help," Bohr said anxiously. "Are you OK, Frank?"

There was a long pause. Grayer stared at the ceiling lights and at the equipment, and then he croaked, "Give me a minute. I think we are."

Bohr felt somewhat relieved to hear this, but Grayer's answer was off-key. "Beg your pardon? I thought you said *we*. Are you sure you're OK?"

After a time, Grayer pulled himself up into a sitting position. He rubbed his temples gently. "You heard me correctly, David. I did say we." He reached out and touched Bohr's shoulder. "Now I want you to prepare yourself for something."

"What are you talking about?"

"There was a transformation of sorts, inside the chamber."

"What kind of change?"

"David, that ball you activated was a hibernation device."

"Can't be. Too small."

"It is what it is. You have to understand that you have activated a crypt-orb, a hibernation device from another planet, another time. You have managed to program my other self, and my other memories, into this now-shared body. This mechanical act of activation has transitioned an alien self to cohabit with my human self."

"By cohabit you mean like a body snatcher?"

"No. I mean that there are two Minds and two Beings sharing one body. Grayer's Being has kindly agreed to share Grayer's human body with Kor from the planet Earth—let's call that Old Earth for clarity."

Bohr drew back. "Frank, have you gone mad? What the hell are you talking about? You're not making any sense." He stumbled backwards. "I'm going for help."

Grayer held up his hand in protest. "Wait, David, let me explain. Please!"

Grayer led Bohr to a small worktable. Together they cleared the clutter and sat down opposite each other. Bohr's eyes never left Grayer's face. It was as if Bohr was looking for the alien within.

"David, I have not been reduced to some kind of zombie. I'm still here. I can talk and think. I know you and everyone else I knew before."

Bohr's eyes narrowed. "You sound fine. Why are you telling me that there is an alien living inside your body? You know that's not possible."

Grayer spoke again, this time with firm authority, his voice taking on a strange resonance:

"David Bohr, my name is Kor. What Frank has told you is absolutely true. Not possible? Of course it's possible, because it has just happened. It is not science fiction. I have not invaded Grayer's body and displaced his soul. I have asked permission to share his human body with his Being. His Being has agreed. His brain took a little convincing."

"Is this a joke?"

"Yes and no, David. We thought it was funny, yes, because we have experienced what's called *transitioning*, a transformation that allows two Minds and two Beings to share the same body. The brain is part of that body. Unfortunately for humans, the brain is convinced it is both body and soul. It isn't. It is a meddlesome organ that needs to be influenced, guided morally, by the Being. Its function is to think, not to Be."

"I think, therefore I am," mused Bohr, half to himself.

Grayer smiled. "That is a human expression that couldn't be more false. It is false because the brain conjured it up. The brain would like to Be, but it cannot Be. It can only think, process information. By default 'I am because I know I am' is technically more accurate."

"You are suggesting that I have transferred an alien soul from the silver ball to your body using that little room? Have I got this right?" Bohr asked.

"I am not sure what you mean by the word 'soul.' That's a religious term. We are not talking about religion. We are discussing cohabitation of beings. David, you are a scientist. You of all people should comprehend the feasibility of what has just happened here."

"And what has just happened, Frank?" Bohr's voice was rising. "Can you explain to me in scientific terms what the hell is going on?"

Grayer (or rather Kor) explained the true function of the ball. It was the means of storing each member of the crew on an interstellar flight without having him or her age unduly. The metallic-looking ball was the encapsulated mind and Being of an alien creature. All his Mind and his Being—his intelligence and his person—were stored in it. This information and his essence, or his Being, was transferred into the human body of Frank Grayer. Grayer was still there, too. He shared his body willingly with the alien once he understood that it was the nature of all Beings to share with others in a collective spirit.

Grayer realized that he had the most to gain—the alien was a highly intelligent soul who wished Grayer no harm, only enlightenment. In exchange for sharing his human body, the alien shared his All with Grayer, and Grayer shared his humanness with him. This happened very quickly. As Grayer explained to Bohr, there is only one Being for each organism. It can never be duplicated. It is important to understand that Beings are the constant and timeless state of eternal joyfulness. The concept of space as defined by time and distance means little to our Beings because, in actuality, space is near-infinite. Because space, like time, is so plentiful, Kor's sharing of Grayer's Being's space—albeit in close proximity to the mortal body of Grayer—was no intrusion.

In the years that followed, only the JCS were advised about Grayer's alien transformation. Bohr never told anyone else. Who would have believed him? The machine itself had self-destructed after the single operation into an irreparable state, so any replication of the event was out of the question. The concept was utterly, well, alien. Grayer was a different person afterwards and everyone who knew him noticed that something had changed. It wasn't a bad change. In fact, most people found Grayer extraordinarily charming. Any changes were not thought of as suspicious and were soon forgotten as people moved on with their daily lives. His unusual behavior became his normal behavior. His alien Being had been assimilated into normal society.

Grayer became most helpful to the team, because it was his ship that they were trying to piece together again. He was a generous guide in their discovery of various new aspects of science. Although he helped them explore new avenues and thoughts, he was careful not to show his hosts too much too soon. Too much technology in the hands of one barbaric nation (or in the midst of a cluster of barbaric nations) could tip the balance of planetary power. His goal was guided discovery.

Grayer in turn found Bohr to be a refreshing student of physics and taught him several axioms regarding space travel. He explained that living creatures, no matter how advanced, were ill adapted to make any substantial space flights because of the time factor. The distances were simply too far between star systems. That is why Kor's civilization had developed a method of distilling an individual's entire Mind and Being into a crypt-orb for storage and subsequent retrieval. His civilization was about a million years more advanced technically than the humans of Earth, and his planet was about five hundred light years farther away than Earth from the beginning of the Big Bang.

Grayer and Bohr developed a deep friendship over the years. The combined Grayer was wise, gentle, and serene, and yet also frisky and adventuresome. The alien's prior identity, Kor, was coded into his aura. Bohr learned to detect a unique alien color encapsulating Grayer's body. Each alien had a uniquely colored aura, called a Signature. Each color combination was unique to each alien being, sort of like a genetic code. One alien could identify another's Signature as easily as a human can read a nametag. Humans were unable to see or decipher these Signatures—or even their own weak auras—because their evolution had not progressed far enough.

Grayer led a normal life—well, if Air Force intelligence was a normal profession, then his was a normal life. Grayer filed his reports with the Joint Chiefs dutifully. He left out certain information, however.

Grayer informed Bohr that the other silver balls constituted the remains of his crew. They had sustained some exterior damage. The digital memories inside were most likely fully intact. Grayer wanted to free the other minds and Beings from the ball, but the damage to the stall ruled that out. There were no technical means of doing it.

As the car droned along the highway, Bohr recalled the awkwardness with which Kor sometimes adapted to the primitive conditions on Earth. It was ironic, really. As a highly evolved human, he had seen all this before or had experienced it through his learning pods. He should have been prepared for the crass nature of the earthly race. Kor was uncomfortable with the brutishness of humans. He could foresee a myriad of human tragedies ahead as this young human race struggled to deal with widespread conflicts due to the flawed and massive egos of individual political and religious leaders. It could all be avoidable, if only sanity would prevail. But, historically, sanity never prevailed—only conflict and the survival of the strongest.

Truth is usually the first victim of history. History is viewed, defined, and recorded by the winners of any conflict. The victorious see themselves as the virtuous. Evil, the defeated opponent, never wins; it is always vanquished. Good, courtesy of the victorious author, always wins over Evil. Of course the victor decides who is Good and who is Evil. That definition is based on outcome.

In 1964, Grayer fell in love and got married, but his relationship ended suddenly and tragically soon after, when his young wife died in a car crash. She was nine months' pregnant with twins.

Miraculously, the twins survived the crash and were born at the scene. Grayer was nonetheless devastated. He changed abruptly into a sullen man. The crash was ruled an accident but, as he confided in Bohr, his only true friend, he was convinced otherwise.

He told Bohr that his vessel had been one of three sent from his planet about five hundred years before. All three vessels sustained damage, most probably by a cluster of asteroids. The ships were programmed to effect repairs at the nearest planet that sustained life and had the necessary chemicals. Earth was chosen. Kor's craft had crashed as it attempted to land. He did not know the fate of the other two ships.

Kor had been commander and chief of the expedition into deep space, and he traveled in the lead ship, Alpha I. A man named Stell was scout ship commander of the second ship, Alpha II. As Grayer told Bohr, back on Old Earth, Kor and Stell had once been brothers and inseparable friends. Unfortunately, a terrible act of treachery had driven them apart years before they left the planet. Now they were sworn enemies, fueled by an ancient family rivalry that dated back hundreds of years before their birth.

It would not be until years later, in 1977, that Kor and Stell would meet again, face to face, in the guises of their New Earth bodies. Stell had transitioned into the body of Corey Wixon, and Grayer believed that it was he who was behind the killing of his wife on that dark night in 1964.

Grayer and his wife, Sara, were returning home from a function in the hills north of the Las Alamos airport. As they rounded a corner, Grayer thought he had spotted Stell's aura in the darkness ahead. Suddenly there were several rifle shots, and both front tires blew. Grayer lost control, and his car careened into the side of a rock face, then flew across the road and flipped over as it rolled down a steep embankment. The car flipped several times, smashing its roof flat and bursting all the windows.

Grayer's body was immediately enveloped in a green hue that protected him from harm. He tried desperately to draw Sara into his envelope. Unfortunately, the severe flipping of the car threw her about like a rag doll. She was killed when her body was thrown from the broken window and crushed beneath the rolling vehicle.

The car came to rest in a cloud of dust. Grayer pulled Sara from under the car, but she was already gone. She had bitten off her tongue. Blood was pouring from her once-beautiful face. Grayer glanced up at the road. A dark figure was outlined against the pale moonlight. Grayer saw the aura and figured that Stell had shot at them and was responsible for Sara's death. In a blink of an eye, the figure disappeared. Grayer held Sara's body close and kept it warm. He thought of the unborn children in her womb. He opened her jacket and placed his hand gently on her maternity dress.

He never saw it, but there was an ever-so-faint glow coming from under the material. The babies inside the womb were still alive! They had somehow known to envelop themselves as protection against the trauma of the crash.

Grayer heard sirens in the distance. The babies' glow was ebbing. The danger of the crash was over, but the children inside the womb sensed that there was the danger of dying because the host was dead. As vital nutrients and oxygen stopped flowing through the umbilical cord, the tiny creatures protected themselves, trying to stay alive within the envelope. They were unaware that time was running out. The envelope could not protect them from this kind of death. The glow faltered as the babies began to weaken.

Grayer held Sara close until the paramedics arrived. They immediately and firmly detached Grayer from her and delivered twin boys—alive—right there beside the wreck. Sara would have been pleased. Grayer was grateful for the children, but his thoughts were full of revenge against Stell.

Frank Grayer raised the twins by himself. Whenever he could, he went off and searched for the missing scout ships and for Stell. Whenever there were sightings of UFOs or abductions, he sensed that he was somehow involved. He flew from country to country but never caught up to him.

The twins bonded well with David Bohr. Grayer entrusted Bohr with the secret of their extraterrestrial genetic inheritance. It was Grayer's intention to raise them as normally as possible, despite their origin. Bohr was sensitive to this and helped out whenever and wherever he could.

When the twins turned thirteen, Grayer suddenly decided to move them away from New Mexico. Only Bohr knew why. Grayer continued to operate from New Mexico and Washington, but traveled more often.

Bohr rarely saw him. The twins were told that they had to go under cover. They were not to try to contact any of their old friends. David Bohr was the only exception. Grayer moved them to Toronto, Canada, to live with Sara's family. That was five years ago now.

Bohr dozed as Preston and Wright talked casually about the various world leaders and their unreported behavior. They talked about affairs of state the way the rest of us might talk about a favorite television program.

CHAPTER 12

Elliot Lake

Hawk walked down the stairs outside by the kitchen, leading into the carport. He noted that the early morning was bright and clear. Ideal convertible weather. The twins shared the 1958 red convertible Corvette. It was Hawk's in name only. It was a gift from their father. Although it was twenty-four years old, it was in pristine shape, thanks to a fiberglass body that never rusted. Its rich red leather seats did show signs of aging—in the wear areas the plastic piping had yellowed and disintegrated.

Hawk folded the top down as gently as he could. It was a tiny black cloth roof with a yellowing plastic back window. It folded neatly into a cavity behind the front two seats.

He took the abandoned expressway out of town and joined Highway 17 heading east toward Sudbury. The trip was uneventful, but Hawk loved to drive. Any excuse to feel the pulsating power of the

Vette was welcomed. He parked in visitors parking by the university's main administration building. He could see the river not far away. The place was fairly quiet because only the co-op students were taking classes. Regular classes began again in September.

He got directions to the Science Building. The chair of chemistry was a Professor Yuichi, originally from Japan. The empty hallway smelled of disinfectant. The building was about thirty years old. He found the professor's office and gently rapped on the door. A voice from within asked him to enter.

Yuichi, a smiling, gentle man who loved his job of teaching young people the joys of scientific discovery, glanced up at the strikingly handsome young man with the piercing black eyes. He stood and shook Hawk's hand with a slight bow of the head. Hawk bowed his head ever so slightly himself, as he shook the professor's hand.

"Sir, my name is Harry Grayer. They call me Hawk."

Professor Yuichi smiled. "Mr. Grayer. Are you a student here?"

"No sir. I plan to complete honors physics at the University of Toronto. I start my fourth and final year this September. If it goes all right, I'll probably go on for my doctorate."

"A wise choice. What brings you to my office this morning? An interest in chemistry, perhaps?"

Hawk reached into his pocket and produced the handwritten list that he and Joe had worked on the previous evening. "Yes. Exactly that. I have a list that I think are chemicals or formulas. I was hoping you could help me identify them."

The professor took the list from Hawk and examined it. "There are some pretty exotic compounds here. What possible reason would you have to search these out? Is this a school project?"

"No sir, no project."

"I don't think I can help," the professor said dismissively. "This list is not something a student should concern himself with. Very advanced. Very technical material. Try the Sciences Resource library and do research on your own."

Hawk leaned toward him with an intensity that made Yuichi pay attention. "Sir, this list is very important to me. I can't tell you why. You'll just have to trust me. I need to get each of these materials right away. Please help me find them."

Professor Yuichi removed his small eyeglasses and polished them slowly. "Perhaps I can be of some assistance. School is not in session, so I am most fortunate to have a few minutes to spare. These compounds are very interesting. Some are organic compounds that are very reactive. So now you say that, not only do you want to know what they are, you need sample materials?"

"Sir, it is the samples that I need. Will you help?"

"Yes, I suppose I will help you, although I am very busy—you are asking a lot of me, young man. Come. We will go to the second floor lab."

The two spent several hours there, finding all the elements and compounds in reference books and research journals. Surprisingly, most of the materials were available commercially and Hawk wrote down their retail names. A few of the materials were being used or developed in new and ongoing research. Two formulations were unknown to science.

Yuichi pointed to the list. "These compounds I can make for you today, my young friend. But see these here? These are two formulations that do not exist. Where did you find such a list?"

"I can't say. Please don't ask. I just need the stuff."

Yuichi put down his pen. "I am intrigued by the two unknowns. I have copied the formulas. You come by tomorrow. Maybe I will have samples by then. Maybe I will give you these samples." He looked away thoughtfully. "Yes, perhaps I can figure this out."

"Sir, I would be so grateful."

"It is I who should thank you. These formulas are fascinating combinations of organic and inorganic materials. Look here, this compound has unstable hydrogen. If it were to come into contact with the right catalyst, it would produce a tremendous amount of energy."

"Energy?"

"Yes. Energy in the form of charged ions transferring from one molecule to the next, its neighbor. This transfer, or traveling, of energy would replicate what we call electrical energy today. Rather than travel along inefficient copper wires, it would travel through a frictionless chemical medium at the speed of light."

"How do you know this?"

"Because it would seem you have given me the formulations for such a chemical medium also. I am hypothesizing that it would act as a conduit for energy."

"How is this important?"

"In and of itself, it is not. But add all of these chemicals in your list together and we have the possibility of a new form of electronic current that could revolutionize the theory of electricity as we know it."

"Electricity based on chemical reactions?"

The professor leaned toward Hawk for emphasis. "Young man, we are talking about the perfect transference of energy without physical contact. No heat loss due to the inefficient carrier. No degradation of energy due to the physical limitations of wires. I believe this opens the possibility of energy transmitted through air."

"You mean wireless electrical transmission? Is that possible?"

"Of course. Think of the power of a lightning strike. Now consider taming such energy through ionic electron transference. The air is a mix of chemicals. This technology you have offered me could free up the radical ions in one chemical compound to react with oxygen and H_2O in the air and be delivered at the other end as a corresponding chemical reaction."

"You mean like a lightning bolt?"

"Yes! And no. Only lower level energy: low amps that could power devices that were themselves attuned to this form of energy."

"So this energy could never power an electrical motor?'

"Not as we define motors today using physical electrical energy. No, this energy would power a whole new class of devices. They would serve similar purposes but be millions of times more efficient."

"So you could have a sort of organic device. Like a living motor?"

"Yes! And more than that, electrified or codified data. Young man, you could create a supercomputer, a super brain. If these formulas prove stable, this may be a breakthrough in certain areas of biochemistry. Perhaps you could be kind enough to permit me to work now. There are chemical suppliers in town that can satisfy your other items on this list."

The professor handed Hawk a list of chemicals by commercial name to ask for.

As Hawk left the campus he was beside himself with joy. He realized how fortunate he was to have found almost everything he needed. He had expected to spend weeks searching for these alien chemicals.

He spent the afternoon driving about the city buying reasonable amounts of various chemical products. By the time the last store closed he had completed his list. He checked into the Radisson Hotel. He would stay overnight and visit the professor again the next day.

While Hawk was pursuing the chemical components, Joe was rapidly learning about the spacecraft. After roaring up to the craft on the Suzuki, he walked about two yards toward the craft. He removed his flashlight from his pocket and gently placed it against the fuselage. This time, he seemed to know exactly where to place the magnetic strip, because the door opened immediately.

After entering, he went directly to the Learning Stall. Instead of a single button, he touched a short series of buttons. Through some code that he had learned, he deliberately instructed the ship to teach him about more detailed workings. How he knew to do this, he could not specifically recall. He just knew.

The chamber flooded but Joe remained lucid, at the edge of consciousness, this time. He began to assimilate knowledge and understanding of so many various elements of the ship. He understood that the craft derived its power, communications, and computing brain both electrochemically and electromagnetically. They interlinked, similar to how a human body's organs work together. There were electrochemical impulses surging through an artery system that ran throughout the ship. Metallic wire electricity became obsolete millennia ago on the aliens' planet.

Over time, the aliens moved beyond electronics to chemically derived impulses that forced matter-less energy through the veins and arteries of artificial-intelligence creations. It worked much like that inertia toy, consisting of five balls, each hanging on a string. The first ball is lifted and then let go, forming an arc as it falls. It strikes ball number two, but that ball remains motionless—it is ball number five that moves instead, instantaneously and in an arc of equivalent length away from the remaining group.

Energy in the craft, in a like manner, traveled through a sophisticated chemical substrate. This was not a chemical reaction. Chemical reactions are slow. In the case of the alien energy transfer, matter did not move. There was no loss from heat transfer because the molecules never had to move. Only the magnetic field surrounding each molecular particle changed polarity enough to influence its next-door neighbor. That ion was charged, which in turn influenced its adjacent molecule. And then the next. All in a nanosecond. Different tasks or commands altered the field accordingly until the energy impulse reached its prescribed receptor. In the case of data transmission, for instance, some energy was coded with a charge and a reciprocal destination.

Electromagnetic forces channeled magnetic energy to perform various mechanical and non-mechanical tasks. Magnetic flux and light were central to the working of the craft. They were the core of the Brain of the ship. Nothing worked without magnetic force. This flux was more efficient than matter. And Joe was taught:

Matter is merely a collection of electrons, protons, neutrons with (relatively) huge spaces between each particle. Light energy allows matter to be visible. Matter is energy coded with certain characteristics to form objects. Electrons and protons (primarily) make up molecules. These particles are charged energy. Clustered Molecules form matter. Light (reflection) allows us to see matter. Relatively, some energy is without substance and cannot be measured by traditional means. Our Being is one such example of undefined energy. It cannot be measured because the measuring tool itself defies traditional definitions of existence. Measurement is one thing relative to another. Our Beings have no relativity

The next thing Joe learned was the theory of intergalactic space travel and propulsion in space. Over the centuries, the alien civilization's technology evolved—from fuel-burning chemical reactions, through nuclear reactions, and finally to matter-antimatter annihilation as the energy source providing the thrust needed to escape the pull of gravity and to propel the mass of the vehicle itself on an interstellar flight.

The ship taught Joe what Earth scientists like David Bohr had just figured out in the last few decades: all material comes in two forms, particles and antiparticles. Any particle has an *antiparticle*, which is identical in every respect except that its electrical charge is opposite. Thus an electron has a negative charge and its antiparticle, called a positron, has a positive charge, but otherwise is identical to an electron. Protons have a positive charge and antiprotons have a negative charge. Just as one electron combines with one proton to result in one atom of hydrogen, a positron and antiproton can combine to produce one antiatom of electrically neutral antihydrogen, an example of antimatter.

This scout ship, Joe learned, ran on an antimatter drive in which liquid hydrogen was mixed with antihydrogen. The hydrogen was heated by adding a tiny amount of antihydrogen. The antihydrogen would be annihilated completely, creating enormous heat and light energy. The resulting exhaust gas propelled the ship at speeds approaching 97 percent of the speed of light. Deceleration was achieved in a similar fashion. The antimatter had to be contained in special magnetic fields surrounding charged-ion traps—a double container, in the event of containment breach.

Once in planetary orbit, or when landing on a planet, the ship would engage an antigravity device. Joe learned that there are three critical stages to planetary landings. First, the craft must slow to entry speed to gain a safe orbit. After orbit has been achieved, the craft applies a decelerating force to break orbit. Second, the craft must again decelerate, countering the effects of gravity using short-duration propulsion spurts. Finally, once the ship's fall has been checked and the ship is in synch with the gravitational pull of the planet, a constant antigravity force is maintained to fly the craft within the planet's atmosphere.

During this phase, unlike the great forces required for initial propulsion, the ship merely has to levitate above the surface of the planet to defeat gravity. It is somewhat like an air bubble in thick syrup; it neither rises nor falls. For sudden acceleration, the ship engages the antimatter drive—for a duration of only microseconds, however. Otherwise, the atmospheric friction could overheat the craft.

The ship was "alive" with various forms of charged energy, which constantly coursed through the arteries or through the air itself. Joe was taught to visualize a small room crammed with the power of thousands of human brains—able to think, communicate, and compute collectively, all instantly. This was the thinking infrastructure of the craft, the intellect of the ship. All parts of the craft were integrated with each other through a liquid gel. The ship, as a result, gave the illusion of being a living organism, yet was totally inorganic.

The ship taught Joe that the universe was created twenty billion years ago. That was the beginning. It was proven that the "Big Bang" was an explosion of incalculable energy. It scattered matter, and some antimatter, in all directions, expanding constantly outwards. Our galaxy and our solar system exist in the middle of the expansion. Ours was not the first system to be created from the cosmic chaos, nor will it be the last. The aliens' solar system was created about a million years sooner than ours. They lived on a planet similar to ours. They had evolved to a more advanced condition than humans on Earth because they had existed longer as a species on an older planet.

Joe discovered that the aliens were a human-based species that was superior to mankind. This was not a surprise—that they were much more technically advanced was obvious. But they were also "spiritually" superior; what you might call mature. From the outset, their civilization had progressed in a manner similar to that of all humans throughout the universe, including those on Earth. The aliens had experienced many distinct and important cultural setbacks in their evolution, such as wars of nationhood, wars of culture, wars of religion, wars of poverty, and wars of family power. For every human civilization, all wars were about power and brutality. The aliens had also experienced the paranoia that still affects humans on Earth.

The aliens' civilization was not different or better than Earth's. It was merely older. It was therefore more sophisticated.

During their regressive war years, the aliens began to comprehend that Mind and Being are not the same. The mind, the brain, was merely an organic computing device. It was subject to rot and disease. It was influenced by early childhood conditioning that impaired rational thought. In other words, the computing device was subjective and not objective, and therefore a faulty organ not to be trusted. It was designed to be the slave of the Being. And, for the aliens, it was becoming so. For humans, the opposite remained true. On Earth, mortal brains, not Beings, ran the planet. "Human beings" were really only half-evolved—they were human, but not yet Beings. They really hadn't got it figured out yet. But it was not entirely the fault of the species—it was the fault of lousy, or at least incomplete, evolution.

For Joe Grayer, this was a humbling learning experience. He gained the perspective that dealing with humans would be the aliens' equivalent of modern humans dealing with prehistoric cavemen. New vistas opened in his mind. He understood the function of the space vehicle. He comprehended the form it had taken. He experienced learning and understanding that would have taken many generations of human evolution to experience and learn. His brain was physically altered by the sheer growth of understanding and learning. Also, he retained an enormous amount of deep physical knowledge about the species and its existence in the universe. In a matter of a few days, Joe had begun his journey from being merely a human, to a human Being.

He emerged from the chamber in a serene mood. He walked slowly down a corridor toward an invisible door and placed his hand on the wall. The door opened silently and Joe stepped from the vessel. He sat down on a rock with his face lifted toward the late afternoon sun. It was still warm outside, slightly muggy. He took a long deep breath. It filled him with a sense of well being. A breeze wafted through his light brown hair, stirring the odd curl that had formed as the Learning Stall's green gel dried. The gel was neither water-based nor oil-based, and left no residue of any kind on his skin, clothes, or hair. He ran his fingers slowly through his hair and gently massaged his scalp. His mind felt somewhat numb from the workout it had just endured. "Brain freeze" was a reasonable description. Joe smiled. He felt like the oldest eighteen-year-old on Earth. In evolutionary terms, he was now about a thousand years more advanced than any other human on the planet.

Suddenly he was hungry. He reached for his backpack, which was still sitting by the bike, and pulled out some sandwiches and bottled water. The water was warm, but it helped wash down the stale sandwiches. After eating, he lay down, resting his head against his black nylon backpack. He still had unfinished business on board the craft. He had not yet discovered the mystery of the missing crew. That is, if they existed at all. If it was true that the aliens could not send living Beings on the long space voyage, then the ship was unmanned, or the crew was in hibernation. The vessel had traveled millions of miles and spent hundreds of years in space. And, as yet, there had been no information on the whereabouts of the crew.

Joe's knowledge of the craft did not provide any additional clues. There seemed to be no facilities for living creatures on board. The ship's layout, as revealed to him, showed no storage for food or waste removal. He decided a further physical inspection of the craft was warranted. He got to his feet a little unsteadily. Fatigue was like a wave washing over him. The inspection would have to wait till tomorrow. Easing himself onto his bike, he went home.

Hawk called about 7:30 that evening. The two had once again prearranged a time for Hawk to call the pay phone near their home.

"Joe! I've got most of the material."

"That's great. When are you coming back?"

"Tomorrow. And guess what? I called home. We got a message from Dad's office saying that he was on his way to Elliot Lake."

CHAPTER 13

Sudbury

The rolling countryside along the route heading north toward Sudbury was a striking contrast to the concrete jungle of Toronto. Connelly and the rest of the travelers noticed a definable tree line as maples, ash, and cherry-wood trees gave way to evergreens. The ground lost its topsoil mile by mile, to be replaced by stark, jutting, white and gray rock. The smooth highway had been blasted out of countless hills, with the gravel created by the blasting helping to pave the road.

Dynamite and road graders forged the road north. Old graffiti were painted, not spray-painted, every few miles on the forty-foot cliffs that lined both sides of the highway. It was a wonder how the people scaled the rock to paint the messages. Magnificent evergreens sprouted from the rocky hillsides that were a constant companion all the way. It seemed incredible that the trees could grow without any apparent soil, but these ones did.

The sky gradually cleared from a pale yellowy blue to a clear deep blue. The air seemed to become increasingly fresh. The clinging layer of smog and pollution slowly disappeared. The trees were a deep bright green and the rocks a dazzling white. What a pleasant drive!

When the team finally arrived in Sudbury, the fog that had shrouded the city had cleared. In the end, ironically, their delayed flight had landed an hour before they got there. Connelly had managed to reach Hunter by car phone, and he was at the airport to meet them. Hunter led them into the terminal restaurant and over lunch they formulated a plan of action.

"Elliot Lake is just a few hours west down the road," Hunter began. "For tonight, I've booked us all in at the Sudbury Radisson Hotel, if that's OK."

Everyone nodded in agreement.

"The brothers that found the wreck have not been seen for a few days, but that area is remote, so it is unlikely they would be seen."

"All right then," Connelly said. "Let's meet early tomorrow morning. Grab some breakfast, and then head out. We'll keep the station wagon for now. Jim and David will drive it to the kids' home in Elliot Lake with Hunter. I've arranged for a helicopter to take Peter and me. We can cover more terrain by air. With any luck we should be able to spot the crash site from the air. We will be in radio contact at all times to direct a ground search. If the boys show up at home, Jim, David, and Hunter will ask them to direct us to the crash. You are to conduct an informal interview to learn what the brothers know. It is to be recorded, of course."

"Anything else?" Preston asked.

"I have managed to acquire some of the documents that you asked for, Major," Wright said.

"Good stuff, anything useful?"

"You will have to judge for yourself. I thought we could all adjourn to a meeting room and review what I have."

Bohr piped up with, "Well, since everyone feels up to some work, I've also brought along some papers, and photos, that may be helpful should the wreck actually be the real thing. These are some of my findings and notes from the first wreck that date back some thirty years."

Connelly stood up. "Why don't you boys start, and Hunter and I will join you as soon as I have made some calls. He and I have to go over some things. I'll make the arrangements for the meeting room. See you in a bit."

The group broke up and each headed toward their own room. Bohr slid the key into his room lock and opened the door. His heart stopped for a second from surprise. Seated there, with his legs comfortably crossed, backlit by the picture window, was Frank Grayer. Two green dots smouldered where his eyes should have been. Grayer rose quickly and embraced his old friend.

"Frank! I'd almost given up on you. Hadn't heard from you for so long."

Grayer smiled warmly. "I know, I know, old friend. But I had little choice. You were, and are, under surveillance. They hoped you would lead them to the boys."

He shut the door quietly and ushered Bohr fully inside. The two men sat across from each other under the window. Grayer drew the inner shade for indirect light.

"I gather you know all about the Elliot Lake find," Bohr said.

"That's why I'm here, David. It seems a strange happenstance that my own sons may have discovered one of the missing ships."

"It is an amazing coincidence. Tell me, Frank, what happened to you? Why did you go deep cover? You know it's been almost four years."

"Well, first things first. I became aware of this recovery operation just yesterday. After I investigated the circumstances, I became convinced that the boys' lives are in danger. Stell either suspects or knows for sure that I have a child or children. He probably suspects that they are my sons from Sara."

"Stell wants to harm the boys? But why? What would he have to gain?"

"I don't know for sure. After I had run into Stell at the NSA meeting in 1977 and had you send the boys to Canada just in case they were in danger, I picked up an unrecognizable Signature aura as I was walking back to the parking lot on the base. I looked up. A pilot was taxiing a small jet on departure, and he had a Signature. But it wasn't Stell's. Probably it was a member of his crew. I ran to the tower and instructed them to terminate the clearance and order the airplane back to the hangar. Unfortunately, I didn't have the required clearance to issue those orders, and the plane took off. I checked the flight plan and it was cleared for Los Angeles. The trail went cold there.

"Then, about a week later, I went back to base. I caught a glimpse of another Signature. I realized that I was being tailed. I did nothing. The next day I was returning to Los Alamos base when I was shot at. I spotted the would-be assassin at the last moment and managed to deflect the bullet."

"I thought you were able to create some kind of force field around your body to protect yourself from harm," Bohr said.

"Normally, that's true. But I don't keep the envelope activated all the time. Only in extreme danger. In this case I only had time to open my hand and deflect the bullet. It was headed straight for my face. I ducked down behind the dash and drove blind for a few seconds until I was clear of the firing zone. When I got home, I contacted Sara's relatives in Toronto and begged them to take in the boys temporarily. I explained that I had some deep-cover work that demanded that I stay away for several months. They agreed to take them in." He paused and looked up. "That was five years ago."

"When was the last time you saw the boys?" Bohr asked, although he suspected he knew the answer already.

"Four years ago. I saw them once in the first year under cover. Although I talk to them frequently by telephone. I'm sure that's not enough for them, though, and that they're angry as hell at me for not being in their lives. They don't understand. There's a lot at stake here on this planet."

"So you and the boys can't be together because you believe that they are in potential danger from Stell's men?"

"That's right. Unlike me, they will have no defense against Stell's powers. It became evident that Stell could find me because of his network of spies. He has the second ship, obviously. It probably isn't damaged. This gives him great mobility. Also, he knows my Signature by sight. It is visible for quite a distance given the right circumstances. Mine is very strong. After years of me chasing him, he reversed the field and has begun to hunt me. I believe he has humanized his entire crew of four. So it's five against one now."

"Why are they trying to eliminate you?"

"David, you and I have covered this ground before. It has to do with power and control. Stell is an embittered megalomaniac. He believes he is the powerful prince of a downtrodden people, when in fact he represents the remnants of an extinct culture. One can guess as to his future plans. I am most likely the person who could mess up his scheme on Earth."

"And the boys?"

"They're related to me by blood. What can I tell you? I had hoped that Stell would never find out about their origins. But he did. He must have. Now they are in danger."

"They are totally innocent."

"Stell doesn't know that, now, does he? He simply sees a potential rival."

"I see."

"Our kind can be killed just as easily as humans if the circumstances are right. All you have to do is catch us unawares and blow our brains out before we can activate the envelope. I guess Stell figured he had a good opportunity to get rid of me with the odds five against one. I realized that he could find the boys by following my Signature. I was putting my sons in danger simply by being near them. I had no choice but to disappear."

"You never told them the reason."

"No, I never did. I stayed with the deep-cover story. The boys changed their last names and disappeared into the Canadian high school system. This spring, Hawk got a job with Ontario Hydro. But he slipped up and reverted back to his name of Grayer on the application. Now everyone knows they are Grayers. He and Joe have no idea of the danger that they're in because they've been so sloppy using their real surname. They used their real name when they reported the crash site."

"I know, Frank. We figured it was Joe and Hawk. But who else knows? What if Stell uses his people on the inside of the Agencies to spy on you and trace the boys?"

"David, we've *all* been under covert surveillance for years."

"I never realized —"

"That's why my contact has been minimal."

"But, Frank, you report to the Secretary of Defense. Surely they can do something."

"They have. They've allowed my people to spy on Stell and other suspected aliens."

"Quid pro quo."

"Exactly. They don't trust either camp and I can't blame them."

"This Elliot Lake discovery is a fluke, then?"

"I must confess I can't explain it."

"What about Connelly?"

"Look at Connelly. How did he get here so quickly? Connelly found out about this discovery too fast. How? He was given a green light from some high authority."

"Connelly doesn't work for Stell. He's one of us. He can be trusted."

"Stell uses people to get intelligence. He's using Connelly to verify the origins of the wreck. If it's genuine, Stell will be here in a flash."

"So Connelly is a dupe?"

"He follows orders, David. You can't get negative about him. These orders come from Stell's direct operatives. I believe he has humanized the remainder of his crew and infiltrated the military for his own purposes."

"He's the puppet master?"

"Exactly. I have to reach the boys. I can't go to them for fear that I'll lead Stell to them."

"I can help."

"Thanks. I was hoping you'd say that. I need you to be my eyes and ears. You're on your way to Elliot Lake, are you not?"

"Yes. The plan is for Jim Preston and me to drive with an RCMP officer called Hunter to Elliot Lake to see if we can find the boys and get them to show us the site. Connelly and Peter Wright are flying there by helicopter to see if they can spot the wreckage by air."

"All right. I need you to let me know if the boys are still safe. If the wreck is one of ours, then we must act swiftly. If it's a false alarm, then I disappear into the night once again."

"Frank, you can't hide out forever. You need to be with Joe and Hawk. You need to explain things to them. They can't go through their whole life not knowing who they really are."

Grayer sounded exhausted and frustrated. "Don't you think I know that? I've been working on a plan to trap Stell and his men, but every time I get close, they get away. They outnumber me. I'm not confident that I could hold off four or five at a time."

"From what you shared with me, you were genetically the most powerful person on your planet."

"That's another story. Still, it would be a fatal mistake to be wrong."

"I understand. What can you do?"

"I can recover the crew of the third craft and use them to help fight Stell."

"That's why this discovery is so important."

"Correct. The wreck fits with my theory of where the ship could have landed. Then there's the fact that my own sons have uncovered a wreck—it's most probably *the* wreck. I must be the one to recover the crew, not Stell."

"And the boys?"

"One way or another I plan to be with my sons. Their cover is blown now that the U.S. military is on the way to Elliot Lake. Everyone knows who they are, right?

"I'm afraid so, Frank."

"Maybe that's a good thing, David, I'm tired of avoiding Stell. I'm going to reunite with the boys and bring them home."

"When?"

"As soon as Elliot Lake plays out. Once I know, then I can act."

"Change of subject, if you don't mind. Helen and I have just talked this morning about that very subject. She received a call from Joe last night. He sounded down. Helen is worried about the boys and how they're living in isolation. She'll be thrilled when she hears about your plans."

"I miss them more than words can describe."

Bohr looked at his watch suddenly. He stood up and picked up his briefcase. "Frank, you'll have to excuse me. I have to attend a briefing with the others. I have some pictures and files from Los Alamos that I thought I could share. It will help refresh everyone's memory."

"Sure. Hey, you're the UFO expert, David. I'm going to step out for a few hours myself."

"You're welcome to use the sofa if you like, if you need a place to sleep."

"I may take you up on that. Have a nice meeting."

Bohr stopped at the door, fumbling for a key. "Almost forgot. Take my key, I'll pick up a spare at the counter."

Grayer gestured about himself. "A key's not going to be necessary, David. How do you think I got in?"

Bohr blushed slightly. "Of course. Silly of me. You got in without one. Secret agent man and all that."

After calling Joe, Hawk had decided to go for a walk and see the sights. He had killed some time just wandering around downtown, checking out the activities.

There were a lot of bars in the city. As a matter of fact, on a per capita basis, Sudbury had more bars than any other city in North America—a dubious distinction explained by the presence of hunters, miners, and lumberjacks, who visited the city from all over.

This was a city full of men. The ratio of men to women was about three to one. No matter how plain-looking a woman you were, if you wanted a man, there was one for you. On the other hand, if you were a man, your choice was drinking, or drinking.

The rest of North America seemed to have exported its population of plain women to Sudbury. It worked out, though—the men were nothing to look at either. The men and women had a system that worked. By about one in the morning, the men had drunk the women pretty enough to be with. The cycle never-ending as the rough men and plain women married each other and had kids who grew up to be just like their parents.

It was no surprise, then, that an extra-good-looking young man like Hawk got many a sideways glance. Everyone knew he was not from around here. He could have had any woman in the city in a moment. But what he wanted was to experience going into a bar alone. So he did. And he wasn't thrown out, even though he was underage, and looked it. Hardly anyone looked up. The bar had a haze so thick you could cut it with a knife, or so the expression goes.

Hawk sat on a bar stool and ordered a Labatt's Lager. (Everyone knew that the local beer tasted like piss and gave you the runs. Even the locals avoided it until they were too drunk to care.) Hawk's young body was not used to the invasion of alcohol into his bloodstream. After one beer, his face was flushed pink. He had another and chatted with a young nickel miner who just got off shift. Pleasant enough conversation. Nickel was the mainstay of the city. There were two mines. This miner was a lifer, as was his father before him. Hawk left the bar feeling more grown up.

Darkness had fallen when he rounded the corner to the front entrance of the hotel. He pushed open one of the Radisson's heavy double wooden front doors. He headed toward his room. Passing by the bar, he thought, "Why not!" He sidled up to the bar and he ordered a beer from the bartender. This bartender was not as easygoing and wanted to card him, but a man at the bar said to give the kid a break and let him have a beer.

"Are you a guest?" the bartender asked. "Let me see your key? OK. One beer, buddy, that's all."

Hawk smiled and took the beer. "Thanks," he said to his new companion, and gave him the international toast.

"*De nada*," came the reply. They chatted about nothing in particular and watched a Montreal Expos baseball game on the smoky overhead TV screen. Hawk didn't notice a figure moving toward him slowly from behind. The figure stopped a few feet behind him.

"What do you think you're doing?" the stranger said in an authoritative voice.

The bartender looked up sharply, certain that the man was an undercover city cop busting Hawk for underage drinking. He instantly regretted giving him the beer. He was going to be nailed for serving a minor.

Hawk whirled around and his eyes widened when he saw who was speaking to him. "Dad! Oh my God. Dad." He threw his arms around him and hugged him. It had been almost four years since they had seen each other. Hawk was breathless with excitement.

Grayer pried himself from his son and held him at arm's length by both shoulders. He was grinning broadly. "You're too young to be in here!" Then he looked over at the bartender with a nod that said everything was all right. "Mind if I join you?"

Hawk practically toppled the stool over as he shifted one position down. Grayer ordered a beer. After it was delivered, he looked around the bar and suggested they move to a booth so that they could have a private conversation.

Once they were alone, Hawk couldn't restrain himself.

"Dad. Joe found a flying saucer! I was there. I was inside. It was too, too cool."

For the next twenty minutes he recounted his adventure aboard the craft and the discoveries he and Joe had made. Grayer couldn't get a word in and he let his son go on and on. More than anything else, he was mostly grateful to be with his son again after so long. He enjoyed every moment. Hawk finished his story by explaining what he was doing in Sudbury.

Grayer asked him for more information on the professor. "He feels that he can replicate these two remaining formulas? Why would he do this? Why would he drop everything and make a strange chemical for a complete stranger?"

"Dad, Professor Yuichi is a scientist."

"That's it? That's your answer?" Grayer's eyebrows rose so high they almost touched each other.

"Yup. For the love of science. To solve a mystery."

"Then you'll have all the material necessary to do repairs?" Grayer asked. Without waiting for an answer he asked, "Did Joe feel that the craft was in good enough shape to fly again?"

"We don't know. I don't even understand how these materials are going to be used to repair the craft."

"Does Joe?"

"Yup. Joe seems to understand a lot more than me about the craft. I think it's because he's spent more time in the Learning Stall."

The conversation lulled a bit. Then Grayer felt compelled to enlighten Hawk. He looked deeply into his son's eyes. "I missed you very much, Hawk. I haven't been entirely truthful about the reason for my absence these past few years."

"You weren't on a secret service mission?"

"Yes. Yes I was. But there was another reason I've stayed away. It's the same reason that I had you stay with your aunt in Toronto and change your name. I'm concerned for your safety."

"Our safety? In Los Alamos?"

"There's a group of people that wish me, and I believe you and Joe also, harm."

"You mean like spies or something."

"Something like that. Look, if I am around you, or even near you, they have a way of tracking me. Don't ask me how, but they do. So our time together is going to have to be short."

The disappointment showed in Hawk's face. "How much time do we have?"

"You're looking at it, kid. For now. After we sort out Elliot Lake, I promise you we won't be separated again."

Hawk's eyes brightened. "Promise?"

"Promise. I didn't realize that you were staying at this hotel. I'll be staying elsewhere tonight—just a precaution to prevent them tracking us here. Tomorrow, you have to go and get the material from the university and then head straight to Joe. I want you and Joe together in Elliot Lake and I want you safe."

"What about you, Dad?"

"You forget what I do for a living. I'm a spy and a spy catcher. I have resources that no one can imagine. I will be safe. It's you boys that I worry about."

"Don't worry about us. We're tough."

Grayer smiled. "I know you are. I count on that for sure." He studied his empty glass and looked across at Hawk. "Hawk, you should also know that David Bohr is here. He's staying here at the Radisson tonight. I would rather you not run into him tonight, so go straight to your room, OK?"

"Mr. Bohr is here? But why?"

"He has been requested by the USAF to help in the investigation and possible identification of the craft you discovered near Elliot Lake. When you and Joe reported a possible UFO find, that triggered a different military-level response than normal. If there's a national security risk, that's one level. The only level that takes priority over that is a legitimate ET sighting or encounter. Our government is somewhat sensitive to this. There have been very few such encounters. This particular discovery, which everyone acknowledges as probably legitimate, is of an extremely sensitive nature. David Bohr has actually had some exposure to similar aircraft in the past. So the government called upon him and a few others to investigate."

Hawk watched the popping beer bubbles in his glass as he put two and two together. "You mean to tell me that David Bohr was involved with UFOs? Dad, Mr. Bohr is a research scientist, a quantum mechanics specialist. His only involvement could have been …"

"Forensic," Grayer said. "He studied the remains of a wrecked alien spacecraft. As a matter of fact, that was practically his life's work. It began in 1958."

"So you do believe me that these things do exist. We really found one."

"If you only knew! Anyway, the government has sent a team familiar with this up here to investigate."

"But Dad, didn't you work closely with Mr. Bohr?"

"We are the best of friends, Harry, and yes, we spent years together at Los Alamos."

"How could you not have known about the UFO?"

"I never said I didn't know."

"You just hid it from Joe and me."

"Hawk, my job is secret. Try to remember that *secret* means just that. I endanger anyone who happens to discover what projects I am working on. I report only to the Secretary of Defense and the U.S. President. He is my commanding officer. I've been through several Presidents and they all treat me the same—total and complete secrecy. It has to be this way. You must trust me on this."

"Yeah, maybe," Hawk said. "But maybe you should try to trust us sometimes, too. How do we know you don't just use all this undercover spy shit so you don't have to bother with us? I mean, we haven't seen you in four years."

The remark stung Grayer like a slap in the face.

"You hardly ever call. For Joe and me it was like you didn't care about us at all."

Grayer looked pained. "Son, that is so off the mark. Someday you'll know the whole story."

Hawk cupped his open palms up in the air in a gesture of resignation. "So you are not going to tell me more than I need to know. See, there you go again, you don't trust anyone, not even me."

"Hawk, I need you to trust me for the next day or so, just a little while longer."

"Yeah, I guess."

"That's not good enough, Hawk. I need you to promise me that you will trust me for the next day or so, whether or not you think I deserve it. Please, Hawk, this is very important to me."

"Yes, OK," Hawk said. "What's a few more days?"

"Good. I want you to go to the university as planned. Get the material you need and then leave town immediately. Get to Joe and tell him about our meeting. I'll join you as soon as I can."

"Gotcha."

"Good. David will contact you in Elliot Lake. Keep an eye out for him. You can trust David. Get him to the site before Connelly's bunch has a chance to move in. I've asked David for his assessment of the situation."

For the next hour father and son caught up on news as best they could. Grayer then left the hotel and Hawk went to his room.

CHAPTER 14

Elliot Lake

Call it a heightened sense of awareness, call it a new instinct, but Joe Grayer was fully energized, with a sense of urgency he had never felt before. Young Joe—who yesterday played practical jokes, sang horribly in the shower, popped adolescent pimples, dreamed of lying in the hot summer sun vegetating and nursing a golden tan, rode his motorbike until his back and legs screamed surrender, and hung out at the A&W—was experiencing a fundamental change of attitude. He now had purpose, drive, and direction. Kid stuff was, well, kid stuff. He was losing his teenage self-deprecation and fortifying his adult self-worth. He mattered. This project mattered.

He felt he must return to his craft as soon as possible. *His* craft? Since when had he thought about this thing as *his*? But it was true— he had assumed a heightened sense of ownership when it came to the spaceship. He knew that every time he entered the stall, he was bonding more and more closely with the vessel. He could almost feel it reach out and talk to him, drawing him in, whispering its secrets to him.

There was a sense of apprehension in the air. A thought kept coming to him: he had to find and free the crew. That's what had percolated in his mind overnight. He knew with certainty, though how he wasn't sure, that there was indeed a crew on board. They were hidden to him. But they were to play an important role in the not-too-distant future.

His brain, like a young muscle, had expanded and been taught how to use more of its massive computing power. He knew new things now. Sleep had provided valuable processing time to catalogue new information. He understood how he was being assimilated into the vessel's aura. The vessel had an aura! That's right. Perhaps it was a collection of the auras of the crew, a sum total of sorts. Who knew? Some beacon that other similar creatures or vessels could find.

The ship's aura was currently very weak. Damaged. It needed vital life-saving materials soon. The ship had been slowly dying for thirty years before its discovery. But that would mean it was alive. No, Joe. It's not alive. It's inorganic. The vessel *holds* Life. It is a space capsule that protects Life artificially in an inorganic environment. The entire vessel was symbiotic to the Life essence of the crew. The crew existed; they were hidden somewhere on board.

Joe absently wolfed down a quick breakfast. He understood that the energy provided by the food would help sustain him. He stuffed his backpack with food and juice and raced out the door.

Seventy miles due east, the team met for breakfast downstairs at the Radisson. The food was always good there. The way Canadians brewed coffee was the best in the world, so Bohr, the Major, and Wright each savored a second cup. Preston, a Canadian, was used to the coffee, but even he enjoyed the hotel's superbly roasted beans.

Like several hotels in town, the Radisson had a helipad in their parking lot. This was one of the few cities in the world that took these helicopter facilities for granted. The pad was necessary because workers and executives needed quick access to the mining industries that Sudbury catered to.

"The chopper picks us up in about an hour, once this morning fog burns off," Connelly said. "David, why don't you and Preston head out now with Hunter here?" He nodded to the RCMP officer. "We'll catch up in no time."

Normally, Bohr might have been a little put out by Connelly's dismissive tone, but he was anxious to find the twins. He gladly jumped at the opportunity to leave for Elliot Lake right away.

Except for Connelly, the group had already checked out. They all walked toward the parking lot, chatting along the way. Once they reached Hunter's car, they shook hands, and Bohr, Preston, and Hunter piled into the station wagon. Hunter rolled down his window to hear Connelly.

"We'll search the area where they say they found the wreckage. When we spot it we can direct you there by radio. I suggest you change shoes, David. Those loafers aren't going to get you very far. We may not be able to land nearby, so we'll just plan as we go along." He patted the car roof in dismissal. "See you when we see you."

Connelly addressed Peter Wright as the car pulled away.

"Peter, thanks for getting that MI5 file. Frank Grayer is a bit of a mystery figure, isn't he?"

"That he is, Major," Wright said, as they walked back to the hotel. "We know that he officially reports to the Secretary of Defense and is listed as an employee of the U.S. DoD as special assistant to the Secretary. We also know he has full access to virtually every secret service department in America."

Connelly whistled. "Holy cow. The only other people with clearance like that are the Joint Chiefs of Staff."

"And your President," Wright added dramatically.

"Are you trying to tell me something?"

"Major, you know how unreliable unsubstantiated intelligence is." He shrugged when he saw the major's cynical expression, and continued, "Anyway, it's difficult to verify some types of intelligence. The unconfirmed report I reviewed concluded that Grayer consulted directly with your President on many important technological issues and intelligence issues. In fact, Grayer has had the ear of several Presidents before this one."

"What sort of technical issues?"

"Well, mostly new aircraft development and defense hardware. Our sources found that peculiar because your Air Force and other consultants are more qualified than Grayer. His educational background wouldn't seem to entitle him to discuss such sensitive and advanced issues with the President. But apparently he does so on a regular basis."

"My sources tell me that they have heard this as well, Peter. Some say he reports regularly to the Joint Chiefs. Not sure about the President, though, anything's possible. The secret service has a muddy budget. The bottom line is, nobody knows who he really works for. He's been in deep cover for about four years."

"Well, we could have used his help here," Wright replied, annoyed. "Everyone knows what's at stake. Between him and Bohr, they're the only really qualified people to head this investigation. And no one knows where he is?"

Connelly shrugged. "I know what I have to do. If Grayer shows, great. If not, we still have Bohr. If this thing is genuine, we lock down the area immediately. Maybe Grayer will show after that."

"I know we covered this last night, but what security arrangements have you made?" Wright understood that they were on Canadian soil, but this was a world security issue. Canada, Britain, and the U.S. had a history of unconditional cooperation, but certain protocols had to be initiated.

"I have our Ottawa people totally in synch with the Canadian Government. They gave us Preston and Hunter immediately. The Canadian Chief of Staff alerted the nearest military base to be on standby for half a platoon. We have permission to bring in our NSA people and military advisors as needed. Just as long as it doesn't look like a Yankee invasion of some sort. We want to attract as little attention as possible. We will have frozen out the media with some training exercise or radiation scare story. It will be a no-fly zone."

Wright chuckled. "I was on the telephone with Whitehall this morning. MI5 and MI7 have had a bit of a squabble going on about jurisdiction. It seems flying saucers fall right in the middle of the two departmental mandates. Of course, that's why I was cleared to come here in the first place. I've had my feet in both camps. Politics and all that. Although I must say, there are only a few people that know about this. Total hush-hush. Section chiefs of MI5 and MI6 only. And the Minister of Defence. Oh yes, and the PM. I asked the Minister to brief the PM because we are fairly certain we have the real thing here."

Connelly raised his eyebrows. "The Prime Minister. Well, you certainly have covered all your bases. If you'll excuse me, I have to make a call. See you in an hour in the lobby."

Connelly placed a call to Washington, D.C., from his room. He attached a device that fit neatly over the mouthpiece of the telephone. There were three small lights on the device. As the call connected, the first light glowed red. When the handshake was complete, the middle light lit yellow. A moment later, the green light went on, indicating that the line was encrypted and safe to use.

"It's Connelly. We're about to leave for the crash sight. Any further instructions?"

There was a pause as the device decoded the encryption. "Good morning, Major. Everything is at the ready here. If the find is genuine, you must immediately quarantine the area and your team. No harm will come to them, but we cannot afford a leak of any kind."

"Sir, we can't keep this a secret for long. Too many people know about the discovery."

"Nonsense. Of course we can. No one knows anything yet. When we do have confirmation, we have the means to lock down the area and stop any information leaks."

"What about the two brothers? God knows who they've told about this."

"Don't worry about them. It is highly unlikely they told anyone besides Hunter. Anyone else would think they're nuts." The voice went silent for a moment, as if the speaker was conferring with another person close by. "Tell me, Major, what news do you have about Frank Grayer? Have you spotted him yet?"

"Uh, no, sir, we haven't seen Frank in years. What makes you think he would just show up here?"

"We expect that he will, Major. Frankly, we have no idea where he is or how to locate him. We believe that the two brothers who discovered the crash site are related to Frank. We believe they're his sons. It's another reason that we believe the find is genuine."

"Hell of a coincidence, considering Frank was so instrumental on the first wreck."

"Too much of a coincidence, don't you think? I want you to detain his sons. They're not to escape your custody, Major. Use any methods you deem appropriate, but don't let them slip away. If you have his children in custody, Grayer will not be far behind."

"You make him sound almost like a criminal. I've known Frank for many years. He's as trustworthy as you or I."

The voice was curt. "I'm not going to argue the point. I never said he was a criminal. But he *is* a person of extreme interest to this government. I mean, to this project. We will use his offspring as bait if we have to. Do I make myself perfectly clear?"

"Yes, sir."

"Good. Fine. You are to detain the brothers as soon as you make contact. Take them into protective custody. Hunter will cooperate. For their personal protection, I suggest you use a mild tranquilizer. Hunter will accommodate you on this issue also."

"Then what?"

"Then wait for dear old dad to show. Without question he must be tranquilized. Either use some trickery, or shoot him with a tranquilizer dart."

Connelly was shocked. "Shoot Frank? Are you mad? I thought we needed him for this project. How can tranquilizing him possibly be necessary? He would never be a problem—we know each other too well."

"Don't count on that, Major. Your relationship was a long time ago. Frank has to be brought in. If you are able to, you bring him in. Understood?"

Connelly's mood had changed from sweet to sour. The gray foggy day was beginning to depress him. The sense of adventure had just gone out of the mission. There were elements to this whole affair that seemed to be getting further and further out of his control. Someone was pulling strings and keeping everyone else in the dark. He didn't like it one bit. He slammed the door shut as he left the room.

Hawk was closing his door when a gruff man, mumbling to himself, stormed by him, brushing him slightly as he passed. Rude bastard, Hawk thought. Some people really need their coffee in the morning.

Hawk went straight to the university. He went to the professor's office and the lab. But Yuichi was nowhere to be found. Hawk raced to the student office.

"I'm looking for Professor Yuichi. We were supposed to meet this morning."

"The professor left a message that he might not be in today," the secretary said.

Hawk looked at her, perplexed. "Is he ill?"

She shrugged indifferently. "Don't know. He called in. That's all I know."

"Where does he live?"

"Confidential. Please leave me alone," she said, in a voice that threatened *harassment*.

"Surely you can tell me. He's expecting me today."

"Look, his home phone number is public knowledge," she said, handing Hawk a slip of paper with a phone number on it. "Have a nice day. You can use the pay phone over there."

Joe had a plan and a goal. He walked briskly up to the fuselage of the craft. He held his hand outward like a cop directing traffic and strode forward without pausing. To an observer it would have appeared that he was intent on walking into the side of the craft, probably breaking his nose in the process. All of a sudden, though, the door flew open with a click and a whoosh of air. Joe kept on walking straight through as if it were perfectly normal for this to happen. The door slid closed silently behind him.

He headed immediately to the control room. He sat in the command chair and touched a series of controls on the panel. A soft voice welcomed him aboard and he grunted an acknowledgement. He put the damage report on the screen and studied it for several minutes, acquiring close-ups and other information that appeared on the screen instantly. His hands flew all over the panel. He attempted a few voice commands, but was gently rebuffed. He stuck to touching a series of lights on the control panel. Then, he absently rubbed his hands against his pants and bit his lip. He was going to try to power up the vessel.

His hands gave succinct orders to the computer. On screen came a view of the matter/antimatter drive module. It seemed intact. Joe then went to a damage-report view of the same module. All was intact; there was no breach. He sent a command to the ship's energy drive. He was attempting to activate the power.

His command, in reality, fed a few grains of matter into the matter/antimatter drive module. Onto the screen came a pop-up monitor providing a large visual of the actual device itself. It was a heat indicator. Strange symbols changed rapidly. Joe understood the symbols clearly. There was heat energy, lots of it. The matter/antimatter reactor was functioning.

Next, he transferred some of the energy to the thrusters. A rumble like a rolling thunderstorm broke the silence. Then the craft started to vibrate. Then it began to undulate, and then to shake violently. The rumble became louder and louder. Joe braced himself to the deck like a sailor in a storm. Suddenly, there was a loud wail like a warning horn. The soft voice warned Joe that the vessel was under trauma. Her hull temperature was high and some of the internals were getting hot. The vessel's monitoring system recommended aborting the attempted maneuver before any damage occurred.

Joe's heart was racing so fast that he thought he was having some kind of attack. He checked the ship's monitors and decided to stop what he was doing. He touched a few controls and the vessel imme-

diately fell silent. A little shaken, he got up from the chair, held his
arm up and out, and closed his fist. Everything shut down. He had
failed. He felt slightly nauseous from the adrenalin rush. He went
outside and sat down heavily on the ground. His right leg was shaking, tapping up and down on its own.

He calmed down, eventually. He sat and stared at the partially
exposed vessel. He tried to review what had gone wrong. The ship
should have had enough power to break free. The more he stared, the
more something seemed out of place. Suddenly it came to him. The
craft was buried *deeper* in the ground than before. There's only one
thing that could have happened, he realized: he had directed the craft in
the wrong direction. He had driven the vessel deeper into the hillside.

He jumped up. "I have to go in the exact opposite direction," he
said out loud, shaking his head in disbelief at his error.

Joe re-entered the control room with buoyant optimism. The
panel and screen came to life and he repeated the same procedure,
but with different directional coordinates. The same thing happened
again. There was loud rumbling and stomach-churning vibration. He
remembered a trick he had just learned in the Learning Stall. He gave
a new command.

The walls of the room dissolved into a 360-degree visual of the
vessel's surroundings. Where the ship was buried in the hillside, the
wall was dark, and where they had dug away and freed the ship, Joe
could see daylight. He could see the forest. It seemed as if he was staring right through the ship's hull at his Suzuki. It appeared to be right in
front of him. "Should have done this in the first place," he mumbled.

The view was as clear as if Joe was merely a few yards away from his
motorcycle. The image was also in perfect 3-D. He felt that he could
reach out and touch his dirt bike. He held his hand up and slowly opened
his closed fist, spreading his fingers. The view of his bike enlarged, then
enlarged again. Now his bike seemed just inches away.

Reality came back with a rumble and a sudden jerking force that threw him forward from the chair onto the control panel. A second later, and just as unexpected, there was a force in the opposite direction. Joe crashed back into his chair. It had all happened in the wink of an eye. He looked to where his bike had been. It was gone.

Joe's hands flew to the control panel. Sensors indicated that the vessel was no longer on the planet's surface. He touched a few more buttons. The deck dissolved before his eyes. The floor disappeared and was replaced by a perfect 3-D image of the ground directly below the vessel. Instantly, he jumped up and clawed for the chair. He instinctively feared he would fall to the ground below. His eyes saw the ground before his brain remembered that there was a firm deck at his feet.

He giggled nervously, still clinging to his chair. He slid down and placed one foot, then the other, carefully onto the transparent deck. It was as if he were levitating above the ground. His face became one big fat grin as the significance of his achievement began to dawn on him. He looked up and then down, then all around him. He began to circle the chair, keeping one hand on it as he walked slowly around. His Suzuki was directly below him, maybe thirty feet down. The treetops were at eye level. The giant crater where the vessel had crash-landed was now empty. Empty because Joe was in the vessel and the vessel had broken free of its Earthbound grave.

The ship was programmed to break the gravitational pull and hover. Having learned how to perform various flight commands during his time in the Learning Stall, Joe had practiced a crude version of this program prior to takeoff. He had given the ship an instruction to avoid being flung into the atmosphere as the ship broke the gravity: break free, and then stop and hover at some reasonable distance above the planet. Joe was never clear what the distance should be, because he still had difficulty calibrating from English to the alien language.

He gave the ship the discretion to choose a hover height above the ground. It chose about thirty feet.

Although he and Hawk had been certified private pilots since the age of sixteen, their training and instruction hardly covered anything like this.

Joe was enthralled with the barrage of visual stimuli. The craft was completely still. There was no sense of flight or motion. Yet Joe was aware that he was flying—or whatever you call sitting perfectly still in midair thirty feet above the ground. He left the dubious safety of his chair and walked, seemingly through the air, toward one of the walls. All the view panels were functioning, so the view was as if Joe himself were hovering above the ground. There were no walls, floor, or ceiling to look at. He held his hand out in anticipation of reaching the boundary of the wall. He touched the wall. It was as if he was touching a windowpane, and yet there was no distortion. He had the sense of walking on air across the forest canopy. A God-like experience. His senses were overwhelmed.

He may have lost track of time. A soft voice issued a caution. The craft was not operating at an efficiency level that would support remaining aloft for much longer. It was recommended that the vessel descend to save energy. Repairs had to be made in order to achieve flight. Hovering at this height was possible, but flying any higher was very unlikely without repairing the damage from the crash.

Joe knew what to do. He returned to the control panel and touched a series of lights. Without warning, the craft lost altitude and nosed toward the ground. In slow motion, it would have looked like a leaf falling to the ground. In normal time, the craft crashed, with a bone-jarring thud, back more or less into the crater it had left. The internal artificial gravity protected Joe from harm, but the crash still hurt. He realized that he had failed to land the craft neatly.

When he had been learning to fly a plane, he'd always had problems with the landings. His plane would always lose altitude quickly and the wheels would thump on the ground, jarring his body. Landings were definitely not Joe's strong suit.

CHAPTER 15

Sudbury

As he rounded a corner on his way to the entrance to the Student Union building, Hawk saw Yuichi motioning to him.

"I was looking for you," Hawk said.

Yuichi guided Hawk roughly to a stand of trees. "You were looking for me! I was looking for you! I have been up all night working on these formulations." He seemed stressed. "My young friend, you must tell me where you attained this information. Surely it is highly classified. Are you involved in some kind of spy ring? Perhaps I should call the authorities?"

"Sir, I assure you ..."

"Don't lie to me, my young friend. Where did you get these formulas?" Yuichi's eyes looked all about in a gesture of paranoia.

"Please professor, let me explain."

Hawk couldn't explain anything. He knew that, so he stalled, hoping to find some inspired answer. "Uh, what in particular is the source of your concern?"

"That is not an explanation!" Yuichi squawked. "The two formulations you gave to me to reproduce are a giant leap forward in biochemistry! Nothing even close to this technology exists on Earth. "

"And ...?"

"And, my young friend, you are not a Nobel Prize scientist. Where the hell did you come up with these?"

Hawk didn't even attempt to answer. "With all due respect, Sir. were you able to make the material?"

"Yes," Yuichi said grudgingly, yet proudly, eyeing Hawk carefully.

Hawk took a deep breath. "Can I have the samples?"

Yuichi began to rub his upper lip with his hand. "Young man. You seem not to understand. What you gave me to replicate does not exist as a scientific formula, not yet. These represent a significant breakthrough. I would rank it up there with the discovery of penicillin. No, what am I thinking? Way beyond penicillin."

Hawk was in a fix. "Mr. Yuichi, no doubt this is true. But I have a desperate need for these chemicals to ... to ... fix ... my ..."

"Go on!"

"My ... I'm sorry. I can't say. I'm sorry." Hawk was somewhat prepared for this eventuality. "I have money," he continued. "I will pay you for the chemicals."

Yuichi was intrigued. "Oh, really. How much would you pay for them?"

"I have two thousand dollars in an envelope."

"That's a lot of money for so young a student."

"I work."

"I will consider your offer."

"Please, Professor ..."

Yuichi ignored Hawk as his mind drifted to his chemical creations. He scratched his chin in thought like he did so often in the lecture hall in front of his students. He couldn't stop thinking about the compound that had unstable hydrogen held together with an amazingly clever complex binder.

Yuichi gave in. He sighed. He had been up most of the night concocting the chemicals. "You have broken no laws, as far as I know. These chemicals you seek are yours for the taking. They are ready at the lab."

Hawk was relieved. "Thank you."

When they got back to the lab, the professor slowly turned to Hawk. "I know I do not deserve the privilege, but whatever you are working on, would you consider allowing me to join you?"

Hawk was speechless. Talk about an attitude swing.

Yuichi continued cautiously, "You have discovered something important. Or—do not take offense—more likely someone you work with has discovered or developed new technology. If I can be of use, please allow me the honor of accompanying you."

"Sir, as much as I would be honored to have you, I'm afraid that is not possible. You would be wise to forget me and these chemicals."

"We would win a Nobel Prize," Yuichi countered. There was no smile. He wasn't kidding.

"We might. Then again, you might be interfering in matters you don't understand."

Yuichi handed him a cardboard box. "You will find everything I promised in this box. Good luck to you. You are very young to be carrying such a burden."

Hawk bowed his head slightly and took the box. "Professor. I owe you more than you can imagine. Here's the money I promised you."

Yuichi took the envelope with the cash. "You would be quite surprised how far-reaching my imagination is, my young friend."

Yuichi watched as Hawk left the building. Normally a sedate man, he was in a state of disbelief. This complex formulary was astounding. In and of itself it was straightforward—if you merely had the brilliance to conceive of it. It was so obvious. Why hadn't anyone thought of it before? He was going to be famous! These chemical compounds would revolutionize the field of electrochemical engineering. He had kept his notes. It was now a matter of keeping the formulas under wraps until a trademark lawyer could protect them for him. Yuichi's mind buzzed with images of receiving, modestly, of course, his Nobel Prize in chemistry. Wait, there's more! Another prize for his related impact on physics.

He was actually rubbing his hands in glee as a man came up behind him until he was practically touching his shoulder. He jumped in fright.

"Oh, pardon me, Professor. I did not mean to startle you," the man said.

Yuichi whirled around and gawked at him. The man started talking but the professor couldn't quite make out the words. They were droning in his head. He looked deeper and deeper into the dark, almost black, eyes of the stranger, eyes that were like swirling pools of blue-black water. The water had no beginning. It had no end.

"You are no longer interested in the chemical discovery," the stranger intoned. "You cannot recall specifically what you were working on."

Yuichi stated blankly, "I have no recollection."

"You were visited by a young man, but you cannot recall what he wanted. You cannot recall what he looked like."

"I can't seem to remember this young man. A student, perhaps, I cannot recall."

"There is an envelope in your hand. Please give that to me. It doesn't belong to you."

"It is not mine."

"No doubt you have a record or notes of an experiment you did yesterday. Give them to me."

Yuichi handed him his sheaf of papers.

"Is there more?"

"No."

"These are of no use to you. Would you mind if I took them?" the man asked.

"These are useless to me. Please take them."

"Should anyone ask you about the young man and the events of yesterday, you seem to have forgotten."

"I seem to have forgotten."

"I will leave you now. Once I am gone, you will feel like a little nap. Rest. I was never here. You have silly dreams sometimes. But you are a good man. A happy man. You feel good about yourself."

Yuichi dreamt of a leaf bobbing down a black gurgling stream. Pulled along by the water, it gently bumped against small rocks and fallen logs. The leaf snagged and then freed itself, coursing along the babbling brook. The leaf began a lazy turn that became a spinning eddy. It paused then flew over the side of a waterfall. Falling and falling and falling.

He came to with a start. He felt surprisingly energetic and well rested after his nap. He smiled as he thought how much he enjoyed the restful, uneventful days of the summer holidays.

About the time Yuichi was waking up, the station wagon was almost at Elliot Lake. The radio crackled.

"This is Connelly. Come in, David."

Bohr fumbled for the radio handset. He pressed the TALK button. "David here."

"We've had a delay. The chopper we ordered had a minor mechanical problem."

"Is it fixed?"

"It's fixed, but the guy who fixes it can't be the same guy that certifies it. Some damn civil aviation law. Now we have to wait for it to be certified. It turns out that the only qualified inspector is out of the area. We're grounded until they can get us a replacement chopper or the inspector shows up."

"We'll be there well before you, by the sounds of it. We'll try to locate the brothers."

A frustrated Connelly mumbled as he replaced the handset: "This crap doesn't happen in the military, I tell ya."

Unbeknownst to him, Hawk was traveling behind the three team members on Highway 17 toward his house. His Corvette was cruising at sixty-five miles per hour. He had a nagging sense of urgency. He just wanted to get the craft all fixed up. He thought about what it would be like to have his father rejoin Joe and him. They would be like a family. He pushed the sports car a little faster, and the speedometer needle tickled seventy-five.

It took an hour or so to reach his house. His father had warned him about the three men in the vehicle and about the helicopter on its way. Hawk approached his house slowly, with the Corvette's 427 engine barely above idle. The throaty gurgle of the engine still sounded loud above the crunching of the gravel.

Catching sight of the wagon parked in front of their house, he stopped abruptly, then eased the Vette into a driveway down the block in front of an abandoned, boarded-up house out of sight of his own house. He carefully pushed the car door shut with both hands. Then he picked up the box of material, walked to the side of the abandoned house, and peeked around the corner.

Hawk jerked his head back again. Two men were sitting in the station wagon. David Bohr was sitting on the front step. He wanted to run and greet his dear friend, but he knew better. There would be time for that later.

He was tempted to try reaching the crash site by foot but knew he couldn't manage the trip because the box was too awkward and heavy. He had little doubt that Joe was at the site. He doubted he could get to the ATV without the men noticing. He paced for about ten minutes, and then snuck another look. All three men were leaning against the station wagon, talking. One lit a cigar.

Hawk figured that they were waiting to rendezvous with the helicopter. Once they were on the copter, they were sure to spot the crash site. What about Joe?

He came up with Plan A. He would sneak by the group and get his ATV, and hope he could get to the crash site before the chopper. He knew the plan was deficient because his move would alert the men and make him look like a fugitive.

Plan B would be to drive up to them as if it were a perfectly normal day. He would ask them what the problem was. Would they let him take his carton, jump on the ATV, and take off? Not bloody likely. They would insist that he take them to the crash site.

So Plan A it was. In his mind's eye he saw the ATV roar to life. He saw himself drive past the astonished men and get to Joe before the helicopter arrived.

He needed to hide the package before running toward his house. He could swing back with the ATV and retrieve it before going to meet Joe. He looked around. Off to one side of the driveway was a metal garden shed with two narrow sliding doors. He pried them apart and placed the awkward carton inside the shed. The doors squealed in protest as he shut them.

Lithe as a deer, he bounded across the street toward his carport. He made his way behind a row of houses until he was directly behind his own house. As he crept up to the carport he snuck a look at the men, who were facing away from him. He eased his way into the carport and up to the ATV.

The keys! He knew they were on the kitchen counter in a saucer. He was caught out in the open. If he didn't move immediately, the men would surely spot him. If he went inside, he risked being caught. If he didn't, he couldn't start the ATV. He went inside.

Bounding up the short flight of three stairs, he entered the kitchen and went straight to the counter. The keys weren't there. The saucer had spare car keys in it, but no ATV keys. He went through the drawers, checked the counter, and the table. No keys. Resting his hand against the kitchen counter, he took a moment to think. Was it possible that he'd left them on the seat of the ATV, or that they'd fallen to the floor? Who drove last?

He eased himself out through the side door that led to the carport and crept toward the ATV. The seat was just out of sight. He had to walk around in full view of the men in order to see if the keys were inside. If they were, he would jump in and race out of there. He leaned over and looked. No keys.

A booming voice shattered his nerves like a pistol shot. "Looking for these?"

Hawk jumped backwards and spun around with a cry. A large man in his early sixties was dangling a set of keys from his fingers. He was grinning like he had just swallowed the canary.

"Yes," was all Hawk could say. He reached for the keys instinctively.

The man snatched them back into his palm. "Not so fast, young man." He eyed him up and down. "Are you one of the Grayer brothers?"

"Yes, I'm Hawk."

"Come with me, please." Preston gently guided Hawk's elbow toward the street. Gesturing toward his vehicle he said, "I believe you know these two gentlemen."

Bohr launched himself from his leaning position against the side of the wagon toward Hawk. "My God, Harry! Is that you?"

"Mr. Bohr!" Hawk forgot about his dilemma, broke into a smile, and ran and hugged the man. "But please don't call me Harry. I like to be called Hawk."

"Well … Hawk … you're all grown up. And now you can call me David." Bohr pushed him away for a better perspective. "Look at you! Strong and handsome as ever."

"Caught him trying to leave, sudden-like," Preston said, imitating a southern drawl as he dangled the ATV keys from his hand.

"Never mind the theatrics, Jim," Bohr said, looking at the former officer. "Hawk, that gentleman is Agent Jim Preston and this is Officer Hunter. Both are RCMP."

"Officer Hunter and I have met. I think that's why you're here, isn't it?"

Bohr laughed. "Of course. Of course. Almost forgot."

There was an awkward silence. Then Preston said, "Hawk, we would like to talk to you. Is it possible for all of us to go inside? I need to use the facilities, too."

"I guess. The door isn't locked, as you know."

"I know," Hunter said. Then he quickly added, "We didn't want to barge right in. Thought we'd wait till you got home." He quickly changed the subject. "How come you're not at work?"

Hawk studied Hunter coolly. "I took a few days off." Then he reached out his hand to Bohr and his smile returned. "Come on in."

The group split up when they entered. Hunter stayed in the kitchen. Preston went toward the bathroom. Hawk and Bohr walked into the small living room. They sat and looked out the twelve-pane bay window that faced onto the deserted street. Empty except for the station wagon out front.

"Hawk," Bohr began in a whisper, "I've seen your father. He's in Sudbury."

"I know, he told me."

"He did? When did you see him?"

"Last night. He told me as much as he knew about why you're here."

"Hawk, he asked me not to let you out of my sight."

"Mr. Bohr—I mean, David—my father and I trust you. It's the others who worry him. He told me I could trust you, and I do, of course. I have known you most of my life. It's just that Dad has concerns for all our safety—me, Joe, and probably you, too."

"Your father was supposed to meet me in my room last night. We've only had a brief conversation, yesterday afternoon. He never came back. You're going to have to trust the whole team, Harry. Nothing will happen to any of us."

"Can you show me the crash site?"

"Do you want me to take you there?"

"Yes. Where's Joe?"

"He's probably there now. He spends all his time there. David, it's a real alien ship of some kind. I have been inside. I've seen things you wouldn't believe."

"Oh, wouldn't I? You'd be surprised about what I know about spaceships, Hawk."

"Sorry, of course you would. I forgot. Dad told me a little about the Project at Los Alamos."

"That vessel was a wreck. Are you saying this one is intact?"

"Entirely. Inside and out. I saw some detailed schematic on a monitor of some kind. There is damage, but almost everything works, or so I was told."

"Told by whom?"

"By Joe. I told you that he's spent a lot of time on board. He's learned a lot about the ship. He tells me a lot about what goes on. He says I'll catch up in time."

Bohr stood up. "Hawk, we must get to the site as soon as we can. A discovery like this is monumental. We must get on with it."

The two other men entered the room.

"Hawk, we'd like you to lead us to the crash site so that we can evaluate the security situation and such things," Preston said.

Hunter nodded. "Son, if this is a real spaceship, think about what kind of security nightmare we've got on our hands."

"Please, Hawk, your father would have wanted it this way," Bohr said gently. "He never specified not to take us there, did he?"

"You're right."

"Well, let's get on with it then. We can still be there before the others," Bohr said.

"Others?" Hawk asked innocently for the benefit of the cops.

"There's a helicopter on its way from Sudbury. They should be here within the hour," Bohr said. "They'll find it with or without us if they have to. Let's get there first, Hawk."

"All right. I'll take you. Let me change clothes. You might want to change into other clothes and shoes, too."

Hawk walked down the hall. His mind was racing. How would he be able to give these cops the slip? What about David? He was here to help, but right now he was no real help at all. As he entered his bedroom a hand grabbed him from behind. The other hand covered his mouth. Hawk jerked and kicked out.

"Stop it, Hawk. It's me. Quiet!"

"Joe?"

Joe grinned and put a finger to his lip. "Quiet! We have to escape." He pointed to the open window.

Hawk didn't wait for an explanation. He flew out the window right after Joe. They raced across the back lawn to the shelter of the abandoned house behind. Hawk kept looking over his shoulder to see if they were being pursued. He thought he caught a glimpse of someone in the kitchen window as he rounded the corner of the neighbor's house. Hawk disappeared behind the house just steps behind Joe.

"I saw their car, and then I saw the Vette parked where it shouldn't be," Joe said on the run. "Thought I'd take a little look-see. I snuck into the house. Didn't like what I heard. I parked the bike over here."

"Joe, David Bohr's here. He's our friend! You know we can trust him. He's like a father to us."

"Right now it's only you and me," Joe said with determination. "Hawk, you've got to see what I've been able to do. Besides, I'm not giving my ship up. At least not yet."

Joe rolled the bike out and Hawk jumped on behind him. "Joe. The chemicals we need. I hid them in the shed beside the Vette. It's going to be tough to ride and carry the carton at the same time."

"We have no choice. We can't use the Vette on the trail," Joe yelled over the roar of the engine. "We must get back to the ship and we can only get there by bike. We have to repair the damage before we're discovered."

The bike leaped ahead, front wheel high in the air.

The brothers managed to double back around the subdivision. Joe let the bike idle and coasted quietly to the location of the hidden material. He helped load the fifty-pound carton onto Hawk's lap.

It was a delicate balancing act for Hawk, holding onto the carton and balancing on the back of the bike. The pair drove through the subdivision as fast as Hawk's discomfort would allow. His knees and thighs dug into the side of the bike until they hurt like mad. It was tough going. The box split open after Joe struck a deep pothole, making it all the harder to hold.

No one followed them. There was an old hiking path at the end of a block of homes in their tiny subdivision. This path led to the hill above the crash site. It was identifiable by two dark-brown painted posts on either side of the path. There was a faded yellow inscription carved into a sign on one post. It read: The Canterbury Trail. The first part of the word was more faded and, at first glance, it looked like "bury Trail."

The motorbike passed easily between the two posts, and they followed the trail toward the woods. Hawk again found it difficult holding onto the carton as the motorbike snaked precariously down the steep slope of the hill. They had to stop twice after the box dumped its contents. Finally they made it to the bottom. Hawk slid off the rear of the bike, clutching the box. Joe leaned the bike against a small pile of stones and dirt.

"Come on, Hawk," Joe said, walking through the door of the ship.

Hawk struggled through the narrow door. He was walking as if he had been riding a horse. He followed Joe around the craft. He was amazed at how much knowledge his brother had gleaned from his time on board and, presumably, in the Learning Stall. He observed that his brother's outward physical appearance seemed to correspond to a newfound inner maturity. His boyish physique seemed to have bulked or toned somehow into a man's more solid body. His jaw seemed more set. Those large penetrating eyes that he had in common with Hawk were even more unnerving. Their brown-black color seemed to over-power the whites of his eyes. A pointed stare from Joe could stop an attacking tiger in mid-launch, or so it would seem.

Hawk handed over his precious cargo of chemicals from the university lab. Over the next two hours, Joe managed to replenish and repair the electrochemical devices throughout the craft.

As they worked, Hawk dropped the bombshell about his meeting with their father. Unlike Hawk, Joe didn't seem at all perturbed about why his father had reappeared after a four-year absence. Both of them, though, questioned his role in this mystery. In the middle of all this strange activity, it was hard to know what to believe. Had their father really meant it when he told Hawk he was coming back to be with them?

Joe strode confidently up and down passageways as if it was his very own ship. He pulled out vein-like liquid circuits. He replaced complex bio-grids. His focus was complete. The time passed quickly. When they were finished, Joe asked Hawk to follow him to the control room.

"Watch the screen, Hawk."

Hawk watched as the ship's huge main monitor screen came to life. The image had pure 100 percent definition. Various images and characters spun and scrolled as the craft evaluated its own health. The evaluation was completed in three seconds flat. The damage report indicated that one more material was needed to return the ship to normal.

"Look there on the chart," Joe said, as he checked the screen. "We're missing one of the ingredients."

Hawk handed Joe the blue card. Joe compared the list on the card to the screen.

"Here it is. We missed one of the chemicals."

"That's not possible," Hawk moaned. "I got all the chemicals. I must have dropped a bottle along the way. I'll go back and retrace our steps. It can't be far. I bet it was when we were bouncing down the hill."

"You're probably right. Hang on, I'll go with you." Joe turned his back to the screen and began walking toward the door. He raised his hand and made a fist. The screen went blank and was a plain wall again. Hawk looked back and did a theatrical double take. He followed

Joe down the corridor. Joe gently touched the wall and a door winked open, so fast you could swear it was open all along.

Just like that, the boys were back outside again. As they backtracked up the hill, Hawk continued to fill Joe in on some of the interesting details of his trip to Sudbury, Yuichi, and more of his conversation with their father. The bars and the girls he saw in Sudbury. They laughed, pushing each other and horsing around.

They never heard the chopper land, because it did so while Joe was performing the maintenance on the craft. Nor would it have been visible from their vantage point. They didn't hear the trained agents coming up on them until it was too late.

There was the crackle of a twig breaking and Connelly strode in. "Well, I'll be damned! If it ain't the Hardy boys!" he said.

The brothers turned and faced the two men coming toward them. Their instinct was to flee, but each held the other in check with a hand gesture.

"Good God Almighty. Major, will you look at that." Peter Wright was gazing past the brothers, down at the silver craft lodged awkwardly half in and half out of a huge crater, its majestic wing tipped precariously downward. Everyone in the group turned and stared. It was impossible not to. The sight was magnificent. Dug into the hillside, the glistening silver wing looked like a silver plate thrown into the dirt by an angry child.

Connelly broke the silence. "Which one of you is Harry?"

"The name is Hawk," Hawk said.

Connelly seemed annoyed by Hawk's suspicious demeanor. "Son, you filed a report about a possible UFO crash site. That's why we're here. *You* called the authorities, remember?"

"I remember. It was an airplane, not a UFO, that I reported. Well, both, I guess. More an airplane than a UFO. At the time."

"You call *that* an airplane?"

"No, sir. I call that a UFO."

"Well ...?"

"Times change, sir."

"Never mind. We're here because you called us here. Why are you looking annoyed?"

Wright spoke up. "I'm no aeronautical engineer, Major, but that looks a lot like the New Mexico wreck."

"Well, boys, show us what you found." Connelly gestured toward the craft and nudged the two of them along.

The awkward pitch of the vessel caught Connelly's eye. "I thought you said the thing was buried in a hillside." He pointed to the gaping crater. "Doesn't look much buried to me."

The boys kept their mouths shut.

The group stopped beside Joe's motocross bike and stared upwards at the leaning craft. It appeared flawless. There were no scratches, dents, or visible damage. It looked ready to fly. It was clearly resting mostly outside the crater.

The twins remained silent, unable to figure out what to say or do next.

"Are you telling me that the two of you dug this thing out?" Connelly said. "Just how the hell did you ever manage that? Peter, look at the size of the crater."

"It's a very big hole, Major. I can't imagine how these young men were able to dig this much soil away.

Connelly looked at the boys warily. "Almost looks like it has been flown."

"Major, if they flew it, why land it right back into the same hole?" Wright asked. "Doesn't make any sense."

It was time to redirect this conversation. Joe spoke up. "It took a long time to dig it out." He nodded toward Hawk for support.

Hawk nodded vigorously in agreement.

"Then we towed it out some of the way. This is as far as we got."

"Towed it! With what, a Sherman tank?" Connelly asked.

"An ATV?" Hawk said.

"Bullshit!" Connelly said, with a laugh.

"The ATV is stronger than it looks. We worked really hard digging most of it out," Hawk said. It wasn't much of an explanation, but it was all they had.

Joe kept the story going. "Really hard. Day and night."

Wright looked in a circle around the dig site. "I would have to say that it would be impossible to dislodge a thing this size without professional equipment. I don't see any around."

"We used our ATV to tip it and rock it out," Hawk said.

"Our ATV is strong, and the ship is lighter than it looks," Joe said.

"Don't be silly, son," Connelly replied. "Who helped you dig it out and how did you do it?"

Both brothers shrugged.

Connelly lost his patience. "It's not important. We've both seen a craft just like this one before. Or pieces of it, anyway. I know this is the real thing. Peter, do you concur?"

"I do indeed. We have much to do."

Connelly ushered the group away from the ship toward the woods where the helicopter was waiting. "The pilot's waiting for us. We'll take the chopper back." He pointed into the woods.

Joe held back. "Hold on, what about my bike?" He nodded toward his motorcycle. Wright was standing beside it, absently admiring and inspecting the machine.

"Leave it," Connelly said.

"No way. I'm not leaving my bike."

Connelly paused. "OK, then. Your brother comes with us. Just a little insurance that you'll show up."

"We don't have to come with you," Hawk said.

"Oh yes you do. National security. You boys are now Persons of Interest."

Wright nodded, walking toward the group. "National security, my boy. He has the authority." He led Hawk toward the woods and the waiting helicopter.

Joe saw the trio disappear through the thick July foliage. A few minutes later, he could hear the whining of the turbines as the helicopter engines warmed up. The revs increased and Joe could hear the thudding of the blades cut through the humid air. Moments later the helicopter roared overhead, splashing the area with its downdraft. Connelly gave Joe a "hurry up" signal from the open door.

Joe walked to his bike and sat while the chopper hovered. He turned the ignition and kicked down on the starter. The helicopter was kicking up a lot of dust. It disappeared in a cloud, then banked sharply and flew out of sight.

This wasn't the ending to their adventure that Joe had envisioned. The authorities had taken over. He and Hawk would be taken into temporary custody, no doubt. They would be sworn to secrecy. The world would never know about their discovery.

He dismounted, shut off the motor, and walked his bike up the hill. His mind was playing through various scenarios. They had Hawk in custody. He was a hostage, in fact. They would send a team of scientists down here and figure out how to open the door. They would probably take the craft away for study, and then learn how to work it. They would find the crew and capture them. He and Joe would be studied and held captive for the rest of their days.

"Can't let that happen," he mumbled under his breath.

They were in a jam. They needed their father. Where was he?

Joe reached the crest of the hill. He passed by a blue-and-yellow object half lying on the ground. He almost ignored it, he was so deep in thought. Then his mind kicked in and he looked back. It was the missing canister. Joe reached down and snatched it up.

I'm not going back, he thought. Hawk is not in any real danger. At least not yet.

He raced back down the hill, practically tripping over himself and the motorbike. What was he to do with the bike? With a grin, he opened the door to the craft and shoved it inside. The handlebars jammed in the entranceway, but he twisted them sideways and they popped through. He looked around, found a storage room, and deposited the bike inside.

Then he went to the bridge and figured out where the missing chemical compound was supposed to be put. He took the canister and emptied its contents into a molded container inside a wall panel. Then he walked back to the control panel and pulled up a damage report. Everything was now operational. He fired up the matter/antimatter reactor and checked the heat readout. All was normal. Next he transferred heat to the thrusters. Finally, he gently applied antigravity and slow forward thrust.

The vessel responded smoothly and quietly. There was some jerkiness as Joe familiarized himself with the controls. He put up a total-surround 360° visual monitor. For a few moments he felt vertigo. It was as if he was walking on air through the treetops. The vessel began to yaw and was starting to turn clockwise. As a beginner pilot, Joe had little idea had to correct this condition. The situation worsened. The craft began to spin erratically, faster and faster like a top. Amazingly, Joe had no sensation of the ship's rotation itself. The craft was somehow cushioning him against the effects of the violent motion. However, the huge monitor was showing a spinning forest outside, and that was beginning to sicken him. He shut off the view screen temporarily to stop the effect.

A pictorial representation of the spinning vessel jumped onto the screen. A soft voice offered Joe a suggestion as to how to stabilize the craft. He did so immediately. The spinning abated. He resumed the outside visual, but kept a few pop-up boxes running, showing him the stability, temperature, magnetic heading, ground speed, pitch, and yaw.

The crater disappeared from sight as Joe flew slowly over the forest. He was gaining too much altitude, so he trimmed the ship and decreased thrust. It leveled out nicely. The burning questions were what to do next and where to go—what kind of place could he find suitable for hiding the craft? And what about Hawk? He had to find a place close by so he could rescue him.

Meanwhile, he couldn't let himself be spotted. They would be sending the copter back to find out what became of him. He couldn't hide in the forest because it wasn't dense enough to offer the coverage he needed. There were no caves large enough to fly into.

Then, off to the west, he spotted a building. It was a deserted auction arena. He knew of this place. Years ago, there had been a centralized pork and beef auction facility here. The business was abandoned, like everything else, when the mine shut down. There, in the middle of the grounds, stood a large arena where the cattle and hogs had been bought and sold. Joe swooped down for a closer look. The empty building looked rough from lack of upkeep, but the structure itself appeared solid. He flew to the spot and circled slowly at about ten feet above the ground. The area was deserted and overgrown with vegetation.

Joe stopped in front of the massive entrance doors. They were not quite wide enough for the craft to enter. He nosed the vessel up against the doors until they were touching. He then applied a hit of thrust. Immediately, the doors blew apart, sending shards of wood and metal inward. The ship stopped about ten feet in, and he killed the thrusters and shut down the reactor. Finally, he released the antigravity. The ship crashed straight down like a rock. The drop jolted him.

I'm going to have to work on that landing of mine, he thought.

He searched the screen and saw that the arena was deserted. He shut down the controls. Then he retrieved his bike and rolled it out onto the concrete floor of the building. Pigeons flew about, beating their wings in protest against the intrusion. Swallows buzzed him, sending him the same message. This empty building was their territory. The pungent odor of cattle droppings still lingered in the humid air. The cloud of dust kicked up by the landing lingered, suspended in the windless afternoon.

His plan was to rescue Hawk and try to contact his father without being caught. With any luck, no one would find the ship. He was sure his father would guide Hawk and him on what course of action to take next.

Joe's plan had to include getting away from the arena without being spotted by the helicopter. The search was probably already on for him. He could follow the road from the arena back into town. From there, he would play it by ear. At the very least, the ship would be safe from detection. He rolled the bike outside and squinted into the afternoon sun. He debated about waiting until nightfall.

That question was answered immediately when he heard the helicopter in the distance. He had just enough time to push the bike back in through the broken doorway before the helicopter swooped in from the east. It flew directly overhead. Joe inched toward the doors and craned his neck to look outside. The roar of the engines suddenly increased again as the helicopter began to circle the arena. Joe couldn't see the aircraft, but he knew it was hovering nearby.

Then, as quickly as it had come, the helicopter left and flew toward the west. Joe sat for a while on his haunches before finding a more comfortable spot to sit and wait out the search. Around dusk, the helicopter roared back over the arena without pausing. Its huge searchlight panned the ground for clues to the whereabouts of the vanished spacecraft.

Joe waited till darkness before easing the motorbike out again. Some stars were visible and a half moon was rising in the east. There was a surprising amount of light at this time of year, illuminating the road clearly enough for him to navigate without concern. He headed back to Elliot Lake.

CHAPTER 16

Near Elliott Lake

When the road was fully exposed to the night sky and young moon, Joe could see well enough to leave the bike's light off. However, every so often, a thick overgrowth of trees with areas of dark shadow made the drive dangerous and required him to turn it on.

The night air was moist and pungent with the northern fragrance of evergreens. There was an undercurrent of dankness in the air. When he drove through fog clouds, he could smell the raw odor of fermenting vegetation mixed with the fragrance of pine needles. Pure Canadian wilderness.

The trip back to his house in Elliot Lake took over an hour. Joe wasn't in a hurry. He was formulating a plan as he drove along. First, he hoped Hawk was at the house and hadn't been taken elsewhere. Second, he would get as close as possible to the house, ditch the bike, and rescue Hawk.

Every time he pictured the rescue, his brain came up with disastrous results.

Before he knew it, he was just a few blocks away. He slowed the bike, headlight off. He stored the bike at an abandoned house a block away and went the rest of the way on foot.

His house was in darkness. There were no cars around. The station wagon that had been parked in front was gone. What if Hawk wasn't here? His heart raced anxiously at the possibility. The house appeared empty. A trick, he thought. He didn't like it. It was too obvious. Surely they expected him to come back for Hawk. Didn't they? He didn't know what to think.

He crawled toward the house through the back yard. At one time it had been a fine, green, well-managed lawn. Over time, nature had reclaimed the area, adorning the area with a multitude of dandelions and wildflowers. Joe used the overgrown foliage as a cover and crawled up to a basement window on the west side of the house. He knew this window would open for him.

He slid inside and froze, waiting for any sound of activity. His heart was beating fast. He willed himself to relax. Slowly, ever so slowly, he took one step after another toward the basement stairway. He had to stifle a cry when his shin struck something. Finally, he made it to the staircase and cautiously raised his foot. He walked on the outside edges of the stairs but there was still some creaking. He turned the doorknob gently. He knew it didn't lock. The door opened a crack. He peeked around the corner. Nothing but the shadows of the moon playing across the hallway and kitchen. He slid through the door and crept down the hall toward the living room.

As he rounded the corner, he smelled the scent of human plus something else. His nose twitched as he continued toward the living room. He caught the faint odor of cigar. Cigar! Joe froze in mid-step. That RCMP fellow, Jim Preston—he smoked cigars. He turned to leave.

"Too late, Joe. I have you covered," a voice called out. A figure rose from the shadows and moved toward him, pistol in hand.

Joe raised his arms.

"Put your hands down. This isn't some western movie." Preston laughed, waving the gun. "Reach for the sky!" He shook his head. "Not likely," he mumbled. The truth was that he was uncomfortable with guns. The one he held now was a loaner from Connelly.

"We figured you'd come back," Preston said. "Come to rescue your brother, have you?"

Joe kept his mouth shut as long as he could, then blurted out, "Where's Hawk?"

"Safe." Preston reached for a walkie-talkie and squeezed the button. "This is Preston. The Eagle has landed! Right into my arms."

A voice crackled back. "Good work. Give us a minute or so."

"Come on, where's Hawk?" Joe repeated, straining to see Preston in the shadows.

There was a sudden movement into the room. A voice from behind spoke. "He's safe, son. Don't worry, he's OK."

Both Joe and Preston spun toward the voice. Preston immediately raised his weapon. "Freeze!" he screamed—more out of fright than authority.

"You do not need that weapon, officer. We're all friends here," Frank Grayer said. His voice had a soothing, steady tone reminiscent of a gently flowing stream. He continued with what sounded like a chant, which Joe remotely recognized but could not understand.

Preston's eyes glazed over. "We're friends here."

"This weapon isn't necessary."

"What the hell am I doing with a weapon?"

"Your weapon is safest in the toilet where it cannot hurt anyone."

"My weapon belongs in the toilet. That's for sure."

"You know where the toilet is."

"I know where the toilet is." With that Preston left the room. Joe could hear the toilet flush. Preston returned. "All done."

"You are feeling good about yourself. As you should, because you are a fine officer. You feel the need to rest."

"I've got to sit down and rest for a while," Preston said, slumping down with a thump into the living room easy chair.

Joe raced over to his father. He hugged him hard, then began laughing. "Where have you been?"

"I know. I *know* I've been away too long. I missed you, both of you, very much."

Joe looked toward Preston. "What have you done to this guy? How did you do that? It's hilarious."

Grayer smiled and tousled Joe's hair. Then he gently grabbed his shoulders. "Joe, it's not meant to be funny. We have to free Hawk, and quickly. Connelly is holding him captive, on orders from Washington. Connelly still thinks he works for the U.S. Defense Intelligence Agency. He doesn't know that the operation has been compromised. Connelly is really working for someone else."

Just then headlights became visible through the living room window. "They're here," Joe said.

Grayer spoke quietly to the seated man. "Officer Preston, you are tired. You need rest. Now is a good time to close your eyes and to rest. You will not remember the past few minutes. Joe and I were not here. You fell asleep waiting in the darkness for Joe. He never came."

"Oh yeah, and don't go Number Two in the john. It'll back up," Joe added.

"Quick, Joe, follow me," Grayer said. "We'll go out the bedroom window, then circle round."

Joe slid through the window effortlessly. Grayer followed, landing on all fours like a cat.

"I hear them. They just entered," Joe said.

"Yup. There's going to be a little confusion for a minute or so. They'll probably do a ground search for you. Let's go around front and see if Hawk's with them."

The two ran stealthily around the side of the house, stopping at the corner. They could see the station wagon and an unmarked police car haphazardly parked out front. Slumped in the rear of the unmarked car was the body of Hawk.

The pair dashed toward the street, anxious to get to Hawk. "They must have sedated him," Grayer hissed as he ran.

Hawk was alone. His mouth was slightly open, with dribble snaking down his chin. His eyes were shut peacefully. His head was resting against the windowpane.

Joe looked at the dash. "No keys in the ignition. Looks like the doors are locked, too."

Grayer fished what looked like a key chain out of his pocket. It was actually a skeleton key chain with a dozen small and intricate tools dangling from the chain. He selected one and inserted the tool into the car door lock. It failed to open. Slightly annoyed, Grayer flipped the chain and selected another tool. This time the door clicked open.

Grayer instinctively swung his closed fist upwards and whacked the plastic dome light as it came on. The plastic shattered, and the bulb extinguished as it broke. The car interior went black. He reached over and opened the rear passenger door for Joe. Then he slid behind the wheel and bent down, examining the ignition.

Joe got in beside his brother and held his head away from the glass window. Taking Hawk's head between his hands, he began talking to him to see if he could bring him around.

Meanwhile, Grayer was studying his B-and-E tool chain. He made a selection, inserted the tool, and fiddled with the ignition. The engine turned over a few times, and then it started. "It pays to be a secret agent, son," he said with a laugh.

He pulled away with the headlights off. Joe looked back at the house and shouted in alarm. There was a commotion as the house disgorged its occupants onto the front lawn. They were charging toward the car. Grayer floored it, spraying a shower of stones behind the vehicle as they pulled away from the house. Then he flicked the lights on and asked Joe for directions to the spacecraft.

"Dad, my bike is up ahead. I can't leave it."

"Forget about the bike!"

"I can't. Why don't I drive it and you follow in the car?"

"Joe, we don't have much of a lead on them. There may not be time to stop."

"Dad, we may need the bike!"

Grayer thought for a moment. "You may be right. I have an idea. Which way to the bike?"

As Joe was directing his father, Hawk was starting to come around. His eyes flickered open, and he squinted as he looked about the car. He tried to moisten his lips with his tongue.

"Joe, what are you doing here?" he croaked.

Joe held him by his shoulders, but Hawk's head lolled around lazily. He couldn't keep his chin up. His eyes started to close again.

"Hawk! *Hawk!* Don't fall asleep on me," Joe said. "Wake up!"

Hawk responded after Joe's not-so-gentle shaking. He groaned and opened his eyes groggily. "The Major gave me a needle. It happened so quickly. I feel so tired." Then he lost track of what he was saying. He sat quietly, his head nodding along with the bouncing motion of the car as it struck pothole after pothole.

As they approached the abandoned house where Joe had left the bike, Grayer said, "Joe, listen. We're never going to lose them. You take Hawk and get back to the ship."

"What about you?"

"I'm going to divert the posse away from you boys. I'll head in the opposite direction down 17 back toward Sudbury."

A car was fishtailing down the road behind them, its headlights blazing in their rear-view mirror. "No time to talk. Joe, help Hawk. Then run for cover. Don't start the bike right away. They may spot you."

Joe dragged Hawk awkwardly from the vehicle. He kicked the door shut and his father sped off.

Joe pulled Hawk into some brush a few feet from his bike.

Seconds later the station wagon sped by. It appeared as if it was Connelly, Preston, and Hunter who were in pursuit. As the wagon rounded the corner, Joe saw a second vehicle appear from nowhere and join the pursuit. It must have come in from the highway. Joe wondered who it was.

Time passed slowly as Joe cradled his brother, waiting for him to come to. About a half hour later, he contemplated starting the bike and going back to the arena. But Hawk didn't seem quite up to the trip yet. "How do you feel, Hawk? Ready to travel?"

"The spirit's willing but the body sucks."

"We'll wait a while longer."

A car without lights rounded the corner and drove slowly by. There was an occasional burst of a powerful searchlight from its passenger window. The light traveled over the derelict homes and overgrown lawns.

The boys lay flat on the ground as the light swept over their hiding place. The light momentarily blinded Joe. He thought for sure they had been discovered. He was ready to make a run for it. Then he thought about the bike and wondered if it was hidden from view. He strained his neck as he watched the light wash over the bike. The car drove away.

Something must have gone wrong with their father, or why else would their pursuers backtrack and begin to look for them? Joe decided to leave before they came back again. "Hawk, we have to leave now before these people find us."

Hawk nodded, "I think I can do it. Just help me a bit, Joe."

Joe helped Hawk over to the bike and mounted the machine. With a swing of his arm, he pulled Hawk up behind him on the bike. "Whatever you do, hold on!" he said.

Hawk's head was resting on Joe's shoulder. His arms were wrapped around Joe's midriff. He was as weak as a kitten.

Joe started the machine, held the clutch, and engaged first gear. They edged out of the driveway and began to cruise cautiously down the deserted suburban road. Joe turned onto the road that led toward the arena. He could see the arena in the distance.

"How ya doing, Hawk?"

"Better. I guess. Just don't make any sudden moves."

"You just hold on so I don't have to pick your sorry ass off the road."

The words were no sooner out of his mouth than a pair of headlights snapped on thirty feet away. A vehicle screeched its tires and raced toward them from behind.

"It's a trap! Hawk, hold tight!" Joe screamed and goosed the throttle. The motorbike leapt up, the front wheel flying two feet off the ground. Hawk was practically standing up in back because of the severe angle. His hands slid away from Joe's body. He tried to hold tight and managed to ride the rear pegs. Adrenalin pumped through his body, countering the drug. He grabbed Joe around the waist with renewed strength.

They roared down the road, accelerating just faster than the car that was following them. After a few minutes, it looked as if they might lose their pursuers. Joe leaned his head down, burying his chin in the handlebar. Hawk followed suit, the back of Joe's shirt whipping at his ears.

"Let's rock, Joe!"

"Someone's feeling better."

Just then, a second pair of headlights jumped into view. Another car was headed straight for them. It slid sideways, blocking the road. Joe hit the brakes and geared down simultaneously. Forgetting about Hawk, he leaned the bike down hard into a left turn. Joe's knee scraped the pavement as he buried the bike. Hawk flew over the bike, unable to hold onto Joe's shirt. He tumbled down onto the black pavement, remnants of the shirt still in his hands.

"You OK?" Joe screamed.

Hawk howled in pain but somehow staggered to his feet and limped over to the fallen bike. Joe picked it up, and the two jumped aboard. Joe headed away from the car that blocked their path, popping a wheelie as he took off. Suddenly the first car came careering around the corner from the opposite direction, just one block away. It was heading straight for them.

Joe slammed on the brakes again and slid sideways to a stop. "They have us boxed in!"

"Joe, get us off the road to where the cars can't follow," Hawk said, pointing at a space between two houses. There was a flimsy homemade fence joining the two properties. It was made of hand-crafted branches nailed together. The fence touched the walls of the adjoining homes.

Joe looked in every direction. There was no choice. He gave the bike full throttle and aimed toward the wooden fence. They bounced up the curb and skidded across the lawn toward the fence. It disinte-grated on impact.

Directly behind them, one of the cars screeched to a halt. Two men jumped out and began to pursue them. As fast as the men were, the boys were a fraction faster, bouncing across the back lawn toward the neighboring property behind. Then their luck ran out. There was another fence. This time it was a chain link fence. A quick glance told Joe that the fence was in good shape.

Joe began to circle the back yard, looking for a way out. The bike was kicking up waves of grass and dirt with each turn. One of the men, his gun drawn, was blocking any escape back through the broken fence. The other man pulled out his pistol and yelled at them to stop the bike and get off.

Joe began to slow the bike, then, without warning, he gunned the engine and the bike leaped away. There was a kid's swing set in the corner of the property. It had a small stainless steel slide about five feet high. Joe aimed for the slide. Just before they hit it, he jerked the front wheel up off the ground as if attempting a wheelie. The front forks caved as they slammed into the slide, then recovered. The bike raced up the slide and flew over the fence. Behind them the slide collapsed.

As luck would have it, their landing was softened by a sizable compost pile in the corner of the lot directly behind the house. Both boys went flying head over heels.

Without missing a beat, they jumped back on the bike and raced through the back yard. Joe gave his pursuers a backward glance.

"Hawk. Duck! These silly asses are going to shoot at us." As if on cue, two shots rang out. In the next moment the boys were safely out of range.

Not trusting the roads anymore, they cut a zigzag pattern cross-country, through various abandoned yards. Joe managed to navigate back to the road that led to the arena. No sign of pursuit. They drove slowly back to the arena and the spaceship.

It could be that the ship was their new home, Joe thought. All else was lost.

CHAPTER 17

East of Elliot Lake

Grayer, still behind the wheel of the diversionary car, prayed that his boys would make it to the ship.

As he drove along Highway 17, the memories came surging back. Although Grayer had been aware for many years of Stell's presence moving in many of the same circles as he—and although he had strong suspicions about the night of that terrible car crash in 1964—it was not until 1977 that the two alien infiltrates met face to face.

Both Grayer and Wixon were present for a meeting of the National Military Joint Intelligence Center. The point of the meeting, ironically, was to discuss the disposal of the remnants of the spacecraft found in New Mexico.

Once the two Beings were in the same building, each immediately sensed the other's Signature. Their Signatures got closer and closer until they converged on the same floor. Grayer got off the elevator, and there, not twenty feet away, was his nemesis from another time and another planet. Instinctively, both protected themselves with their green aura.

"Kor!" Wixon blurted out.

"Stell! It is you. You're alive," Grayer said.

"You survived. I was misled by the DoD. I understood that all those on board perished in the crash."

Grayer's eyebrows rose in sarcasm. "Evidently not."

The two stood feet apart in the lobby of a government building with surveillance cameras and audio monitoring everywhere. In a silent truce, the two disengaged their aura defenses. Grayer nodded toward a back stairwell, and the two disappeared from camera view.

"Kor, we must discuss the Directive," Stell said.

"You mean our pre-launch planning?"

"Yes. I think it's obvious that the plans must change due to our marooned status."

"It would seem that we are *not* marooned here. I assume your ship survived the landing, or you wouldn't be here."

"Our ship is in excellent shape."

"Then how do you feel 'marooned'?"

"Marooned may be a poor choice of words. Let's put it another way. Is it not opportunistic that we arrived on this planet? This planet is suitable for colonization, I am sure we both agree."

"Listen to me, Stell. My primary concern is with the inhabitants. They are not primitives. Our species cannot assimilate into a thriving semi-evolved society such as these humans have here. It would destroy them. We would be relegated to nothing more than the body snatchers you and I already are."

"I disagree. These humans are primitive by all civilized standards. It is not a crime to assimilate them. It is for their own good."

"Stell, I know them. I have spent time studying them. Their minds are too advanced for assimilation. You would be condemning them to slavery for the rest of their lives."

"I've studied them too, don't forget."

"This planet was not chosen as our primary target destination. It is a fluke that we are here, not a planned directive. We should move on."

"Kor, think of it!" Stell said with a grand flourish. "What would they do? How would they stop us?"

"Rebel, for one thing. They are wild, often violent, and unpredictable."

Neither side was making any headway. Grayer could see Stell's explosive personality coming out.

"You are not royalty here, Kor," Stell said. "You are an explorer just like the rest of us. What you say is not law. In this time and place, all our history has changed. We have moved on through space and time, but all those others are long gone. Your family no longer rules the planet. There is no planet. Everyone has been dead for centuries."

"Stell, what are you saying?"

"As the first to land on Earth, Kor, I claim the right of this planet as the land of the Family Abishot. My family, my land, my planet."

"No, Stell, I cannot allow that. This place is claimed under our ancient laws as belonging to the Family of Narok, the ruling family of our ancestral home. My family. The family who sponsored this journey to begin with."

"Ruling family! Family of tyrants and thieves, you mean. Our home no longer exists, or have you forgotten?"

"I have not forgotten," Grayer said softly. "Our home and many of our friends are gone."

"It was your family's pride that cost the lives of so many, was it not, my Prince?" Stell practically spat out the words. "Oh yes, the mighty Prince Kor. He who would rescue all the souls of our planet. Safe here on Earth. But what of the poor souls back home? What of them?"

Just then, a voice crackled at Grayer's belt. "Commander, the Joint Chiefs are waiting for you."

"On my way," Grayer said into his handset. Looking back at Stell, he said, "We are not finished yet, you and I."

"Oh, yes we are, my Prince. Only one of us can rule this place. It is my family, the Abishot, that claims that right. You have no power to stop me. You are alone. I have the others from our ship. They all survived. They are committed to my family and me. Here, on this planet, your family power does not exist. You are redundant. You are expendable."

"You can't harm me, Stell. You know that."

"Not alone. No. But I have my crew. Five against one. Together we can dispatch you to the Heavens, my Prince." Stell turned and walked back into the foyer.

Grayer spoke into the handset. "Nora, please have David Bohr at Los Alamos call me ASAP. Interrupt the meeting, but don't say who's calling."

Grayer excused himself and left the meeting room when the call came in. "David, old chum," he said, taking the call in an empty office nearby. "Disaster. Stell, from Old Earth, is alive. His name is Corey Wixon. He's here, in the next room. He holds an old grudge against me."

"Grudge?"

"I guess grudge is not the right word. It goes way back in time. Our two houses, our families, are enemies."

"And he sees himself as your enemy still, even here on Earth?"

"He means to harm me in any way possible now that I don't have the protection of my palace guards."

"Stell's ship survived intact?"

"Yes. It would seem so."

"Has he revealed himself to the others?"

"No. I don't think so. Perhaps H knows. Wixon reports directly to H."

"Too bad. I'd give anything to get inside a working spaceship."

"I have a plan, and I need to ask your help. The boys' safety, and possibly yours, is at stake. Please help me move them right away to a safe place in Canada. I have already made arrangements. The boys know you; they trust you. Just take them to the departure area at Los Alamos. Someone will meet all of you there and put them on a plane. I don't want you to know where, just in case you're compromised."

"Frank, I'll do as you ask, of course. Do you think Stell would go after the boys?"

"I'm not taking any chances. He could threaten them to get to me."

"When will I hear from you?"

"In due course. Thank you for being such a good friend."

"You can always count on me, Frank."

Grayer was a bit of an enigma. He was AIA (Air Force Intelligence) when he worked at Los Alamos, but quickly moved up the ranks until he was based in Washington with the Defense Department. He landed a job working closely for the Secretary of Defense. Inexplicably, his profile became inaccessible to anyone other than the Secretary or the President himself.

For the next five years, between 1977 and 1982, it was a cat-and-mouse game. After the encounter with Stell, Grayer had gone undercover. Both sides had the intelligence resources to track the other. Stell had many agents reporting to him. Grayer, on the other hand, had access to the Joint Chiefs of Staff and the President.

Both sides knew that finding the third spaceship would tip the balance of power. Stell's crew had followed him loyally. With the right incentive, the crew of Alpha III would follow whoever activated them. They had no close family ties to either House, although Kor felt confident that they would be loyal to him.

Because of his position, Grayer had been able to intercept the intradepartmental chatter at DIA when the call came in about the spaceship. He did not immediately guess the identity of the other crew members loyal to Stell, but he was able to uncover messages concerning his sons and a UFO site in Canada. By backtracking the messages, he deduced that Stell's men were Cringen and O'Sullivan.

Grayer had flown immediately to Sudbury and established a covert position there. He had followed the activities of the team from Toronto through to Elliot Lake. Then, through a communications intercept, he learned that Cringen, O'Sullivan, and Stell were on their way to Canada.

It was then that he decided to make his presence known to his sons and do everything in his power to protect them from harm.

Grayer was jarred out of his reverie when his car struck a gaping pothole in the road. He skillfully corrected the car back onto the center of the road. It felt sluggish to him as he accelerated down the poorly lit road. He had broken a tie rod and bent the wheel rim. It was going to be impossible to outdistance his pursuers. Time was what he needed to allow his sons to gain more distance from Stell's men.

CHAPTER 18

Near Elliott Lake

Joe skidded the bike to a stop about three hundred yards from the arena and switched it off. "Hawk, what if someone has found the ship? What if this is a trap?"

"Seems quiet enough. Where's the ship? I can't believe you actually flew the thing all the way here by yourself!"

Joe grinned proudly. "It's hidden inside the arena. I landed right in the middle of the floor. Let's walk the rest of the way so we don't get spotted if there is anyone hanging around."

All was quiet, except for the steady ticking of the bike's aluminum engine block as it cooled down. The dark outline of the deserted arena looked ominous as it reflected the bluish-white moonlight. The twins' sneakers ground the fine gravel with a steady crunch. There was a distinctly musky early-night odor that began to join with light wisps of fog creeping through the lower marshy forest.

Hawk shivered despite the warm temperature. He looked from side to side. "Doesn't it feel too quiet?"

"Yeah, it does," Joe said, with a shiver of his own.

In the darkness, Hawk saw that unnerving glint of green hue in his brother's eyes. He wondered how much he had changed in his brief time alone on the spacecraft.

They edged up to a small clump of bramble bushes about five yards from the arena's entrance.

"I was going to suggest splitting up," Hawk whispered. "You go around back and I'll go to the front."

"We don't know if there even *is* a back way in. If there is, we don't know if it's locked or not."

"So why bother?"

"Exactly," Joe said, confused by Hawk's roundabout logic. "OK. We go in together."

Hawk rolled his eyes. "It's your party, bro. Lead the way."

As they got closer to the gaping doors, Hawk saw the damage that the ship had done earlier to the arena's entrance. He whistled softly as he inspected the broken wood splintered all over the ground and the jagged hole halfway up the wall where the doors met. The remains of the giant doors hung lazily from one hinge on each side. They were fixed at impossible angles, as if they were bowing toward the boys, bidding them to enter.

"What the hell happened here?" Hawk asked.

"Doors weren't big enough."

They passed through the doorway, careful not to disturb the wooden doors or make a noise.

"God. Joe, will ya look at that!"

Even in the weak moonlight that penetrated the many cracks in the ceiling and walls, the magnificence of the silver vessel, regally seated in the middle of the floor, was unmistakable. It was practically luminescent on its own. The ship's perfectly curved lines looked like richly polished sterling silver against the darkness.

Joe nodded and walked straight to the hull. With Hawk at his side, he raised his hand, as if taking an oath in court, and continued his pace. At the last second a door winked silently open. The entranceway was pitch black against the silvery hull.

Joe led the way to the bridge. "Hawk, we have to get you back into the Learning Stall as soon as possible. I don't think I can fly and navigate by myself, especially at low altitude. I'm going to need some assistance." He motioned to the control panel with a sweep of his hand.

"You have control, Joe," the soft female voice said.

Hawk cocked his head to one side. "Did you program the computer to talk like this?"

"No. It just learned to respond to me in a manner that pleased me."

"Hmm, quick learner. I could have told it what pleased you, too," Hawk said.

Joe ignored the taunt and studied the screen. "Everything seems in order. Except ..."

"Except what?"

"A funny reading from inside the ship. A life form has been detected. Its color tells me it's under some kind of duress or stress."

Hawk rushed to the panel. "What the hell are you talking about? This is creeping me out, bro."

"How could he or she get in?" Joe said, mostly to himself.

"Maybe he was here all the time. Maybe he is trying to get out."

"You could be right. Could be one of our missing crew."

"What do you mean, *our* crew? Where is it?"

"Right where we want to go. Just outside the Learning Stall. Sprawled by the door in the corridor."

"Not exactly hiding."

"Not conscious either, from what I can see on the monitor."

"Unconscious? Oh great! That's all we need. An unconscious alien. Are you sure?"

"Yup, pretty sure," Joe said, examining the monitor.

"Let's go investigate!" Hawk said, with more bravado than he actually felt.

"Your bravery knows no bounds, Hawk. OK. Let's go!"

The twins proceeded cautiously down the passageway toward the Learning Stall. The vessel was utterly silent. The passageway was adequately lit by an indirect luminescence. They were both used to the light green glow by now. They rounded the corner before the Learning Stall and gasped at what they saw. There was a body of a man, lying crumpled on the floor. His head was face down, resting on his right arm. He appeared to be dead.

Hawk approached the body and peered down. "He's human! Thank God. I don't think I could deal with some alien right now, thank you very much."

The two of them gently rolled the body over.

"David! Mr. Bohr!" they said at the same time.

"Joe, help me with him," Hawk said, as he cradled Bohr's head in his arms. Instinct took over. Both brothers held their hands to his skull and gently rubbed in one-inch circles. They looked at each other, then back at the prone figure.

Both brothers nodded simultaneously. "He will be fine," Joe said.

Almost at that very instant, Bohr's eyes flickered open and he looked around, dazed. He frowned, and then he recognized the boys. Saying their names, he struggled to get up. He sat on his haunches to rest for a moment.

"Dizzy a bit. Sorry," Bohr managed to say.

As Bohr came to, Hawk glanced down at his own hands. How had they known to do those circular movements? He couldn't hold back: "What the hell did we just do? What ... I just don't get it." Then, looking at Bohr, he said, "David, how did you ever find us? How did you get aboard?"

Joe mouthed the word "David" quizzically at Hawk.

Hawk explained out loud. "He told me he wants us to call him *David*, not Mr. Bohr any longer. We're all grown up now, see."

"Whatever."

"Help me get to the control room, will you boys?" Bohr said weakly.

"There's much I have to explain."

When they were seated facing the panel, Bohr looked around with a grin of grim satisfaction. "It's just as I had imagined. Magnificent, isn't it? I couldn't get the monitors to work for me. Had to wait for you boys to work this damned thing."

The twins were both surprised and relieved that Bohr was here to share in their discovery.

"The third ship," Bohr said. "I often dreamed of finding an identical working model of the vessel that was found in the desert. Now here I am sitting in its control room! This machine actually works!"

"David," Joe said, trying the new name on for size, "will you tell us what you know about this ship?"

"I suspect we don't have enough time for that before the rest get here."

The twins looked at each other in alarm.

"Let me explain. If you will recall, Peter Wright was aboard the helicopter that landed close to the crash site. He, Connelly, and the pilot. The pilot stayed with the helicopter while Wright and Connelly investigated the crash site. When they got to the site, they came upon the two of you, climbing up the hill away from the craft.

"While you two and the Major were talking to each other, Peter had maneuvered himself around to your motorbike. Coincidentally, he had just visited MI5 before leaving England. They lent him a prototype of a new homing device. Very powerful. New chips and tiny battery. He pulled it from his pocket and slipped it under the seat of the motorbike when no one was looking.

"He had the frequency programmed on his satellite telephone, also brand new technology, so he was able to track your bike wherever you went. When you landed here, he and I followed your signal. You must have had the bike on board. We didn't tell the others because we weren't sure the bike and the ship would be together."

"Fine. But how did you get inside?" Joe asked. "I thought I was the only one that could do that."

"I theorized how to gain access to the craft from my studies of the Los Alamos wreck. It operates in two ways. First, mechanically, using electromagnetism to trigger the opening device. Or it—and by *it* I mean the ship's huge brain—is somehow able to recognize the person and opens the hatch for them when there is some recognizable gesture. I figure it's some higher form of voice recognition. Wright happened to bring along a few items, one of which was a magnetic strip, and I was able to open the hatch door with that. It took some time, but I was able to trigger the door to open magnetically. I went in, but Wright refused to. He said someone had to keep watch."

"And ...?" Joe said.

"And nothing really. I explored the ship. I was able to fit some clues of the Los Alamos crash investigation together. It was fascinating to see how close we'd been when we were guessing how it all came together. We were mostly correct. Your father was instrumental near the end of the research. He had a very good feel for where things went. He saw other things that were missing so we could simulate that portion of the craft to make it all fit together logically.

"This ship has recognition capabilities. It didn't recognize me. I guess it saw me merely as an intruder. I found the control room. I sat where we are now. There must be some biological activation code because when I attempted to touch the panel, there was an audio sound like a warning. I pulled back my hand. The lights on the panel dimmed as if in some kind of sleep mode. Since I knew nothing about how to operate the machinery, I decided to vacate this room and explore elsewhere.

"I had spent twenty years examining one of these starships. I wasn't about to give up easily. I wandered down various aisles and passageways. Portions of what I had learned from Los Alamos came back to me. I found the Learning Stall by sheer accident. I had no idea where it was located on board, because all we had found were fragments of the ship. But I knew what the Stall could do."

The twins looked at each another in concern.

"Don't worry! I couldn't get to square one. I don't have what it takes, I guess. My human metabolism wouldn't support the device. It failed dismally and I was rejected. That's why you found me in the hall in an inappropriate position."

"It showed you *nothing*?" Joe asked.

"After I entered the room, the door closed quickly behind me. There were three round lights on the wall directly at eye level. I waited and waited but nothing happened. Then I got concerned. I couldn't just stand there until I was discovered—or worse, until I died. So I pressed the buttons at random. All of a sudden, there was this green goop flooding the room. The level rose so fast I didn't have a chance to think. Next thing I remember is seeing you boys."

"It seems strange that you weren't able to access the system," Joe said. "You may have accidentally hit the wrong buttons. Hawk and I both have been able to use the Learning Stall in order to understand how to run this aircraft."

"You and Hawk must have a certain metabolism that's symbiotic to the makeup of this ship. I'm convinced I don't. I lost consciousness, though."

"Do you recall being submerged in the gel?" Hawk asked.

"No."

"So nothing has changed with you. You feel no different? No smarter or generally more aware of, well, things?"

"Nothing that I can figure."

"David, you said that you left Peter Wright waiting outside. We didn't see anyone."

"No doubt. That must have been hours ago. He must have gone for help. If that's the case, you boys have a time-constraint problem."

"He's right, Hawk," Joe said. "I'm sure Wright will lead the others here. What do you think we should do?"

"Good question," Hawk said. "I don't think we would get into much trouble if we just gave up the ship. On the other hand, who are we giving the ship up to? These guys tried to shoot us a few hours ago."

"Shoot you?" Bohr sounded shocked. "You must be mistaken."

"Hey, they shot at us. Probably to scare us into stopping, but it was a shooting nevertheless. My guess is that there is way more to this story than we've been told."

"I agree with Hawk," Joe said. "They claimed to be government agents, but they came after us with a vengeance. They fired at us. We barely escaped. What happens if they figure we're better off dead than alive?"

Bohr had been thinking deeply. He slapped his knee gently. "Boys, we have to get this spaceship out of here before Peter and the others return. We need time to figure out a sensible course of action. I agree with you, this shooting business sounds wrong. We have to find a secure hiding place for the ship, now that this one is blown."

"David, are you planning to come with us?"

"If I'm welcome."

"Of course you are," Hawk said. "We can use all your experience."

"We should leave now."

"Not without my bike, we don't!" Joe said.

"Joe's right," Hawk said. "We should take the bike with us. It saved my neck once already."

"I'm going outside. I'll bring it in after I remove the homing device," Joe said.

"Are you sure you want to take that chance?" Bohr asked. "What if the others arrive or have already arrived and are waiting for you? There could be an ambush waiting for you."

Joe commanded a sensor monitor to activate. He studied the monitor. "Looks quiet to me." As he left the control room and exited the ship, he said, "I won't be long!"

Moonlight filtered through the damaged parts of the building. Joe's eyes traveled around the perimeter of the inside of the structure. Everything seemed OK. He proceeded to the front doors, his hands resting on the swaying broken door. Cautiously he peered through the opening, sensitive to any unusual activity or movement. All was dead quiet. *Too quiet* was what Hawk had said earlier.

Joe couldn't see his bike from this distance. He knew it was about three hundred yards back down the road. He decided to jog because he was out in the open. The less time he was exposed, the better. He ran through the parking area down to the road. He watched both sides of the road for an ambush, and ahead down the road for any car's lights or movement. All was quiet except for the crunching of the gravel under his sneakers.

He caught a glimpse of his yellow bike ahead, partially hidden in the bushes. Just then he stepped in a pothole and went over on his ankle. He cursed as he fell. He broke his fall with his hand, and he yelped as the gravel particles dug into his palm, ripping the skin. He got up on one foot, then limped and hopped toward his bike.

Just then a car appeared down the road and began screaming toward him. Joe could see a cloud of dust scatter in the moonlight. With renewed vigor, he hopped and hobbled toward his bike. He frantically fished for his keys in his pants pocket as he bounced down the road. The key chain caught on the inside of his pant lining and he gave it a sharp tug. The lining tore and the keys flew out of his hand onto the gravel. Joe immediately fell to his knees, groping for the keys. The car was almost on him. They surely would have seen him by now.

He spotted a glint of a metal key reflected in the moonlight. He grabbed at the key chain, wrapped the keys safely in his palm, and jumped to his feet. He stood up in plain view of the car's headlights.

Joe ignored the pain in his left ankle and ran for his bike. He jumped aboard. The engine caught, second try.

The car braked and turned into a lazy half-spin in the loose gravel. The driver attempted to point the nose of the vehicle directly at Joe, but it was too late—the car had already traveled past the bike. The car was swallowed up in a huge cloud of dust. Joe used the opportunity to jerk the Suzuki out of the bushes and around the back of the car. The passengers were half in and half out of the vehicle as he screamed past them on the bike. Back into the car they jumped. Huge plumes of dust erupted from the rear wheels as the car skidded to accelerate. The car lunged forward, following Joe toward the arena.

Joe traveled the three hundred yards quickly. He laid down a full throttle. The bike approached eighty miles per hour, close to its top speed. As he neared the arena, he glanced back at the car right on his tail. He charged at the arena's busted doors and drove straight through. He didn't dare slow down too much or they would be on him. He had a problem, though—how to open the door to the spaceship without losing valuable seconds.

He raced up to the side of the parked spaceship and then abruptly hit both brakes at once. The bike skidded and screeched. As he approached the fuselage, he held out his hand in the Open Door command, which looked like a high five. The door opened as he passed. At that exact instant, the chase car exploded through the remainder of the arena doors and bore down on Joe.

Joe laid the bike down in a curve so tight that one peg lit up sparks as it scorched the concrete floor. That helped slow the bike down. He finished the circle neatly and sped toward the open hatch door.

Inches from the door, he hit the rear brake hard and lifted the front forks in a circus-like wheelie. The bike slammed against the fuselage as the handlebars refused to squeeze through the opening. The maneuver had not gone as he had imagined. Joe was thrown over the handlebars straight through the opening and flung tumbling down the passageway.

Injured but still mobile, Joe scrambled to his feet and charged back to get his bike. He grabbed the bent handlebars and twisted them sideways to help ease them through the opening. The handlebars cleared. He grabbed the bike frame and began to wrestle the bike inside.

Just then there was a flash of light. He glanced up and saw a car's headlamp. He couldn't believe his eyes—the car was going to ram the ship! He dove backwards out of the way. The car plowed into the rear wheel of the Suzuki, propelling the bike forward. The bouncing bike flew past Joe, barely missing him. There was a grinding explosion as the car's grille burst through the portal of the ship. A cloud of wet antifreeze and particles of plastic and metal blew over and past Joe.

The crushed metal car hood, complete with dangling chrome hood ornament, stopped inches from his nose.

In shock, Joe tried to close the door. It began to close, crushing pieces of metal and plastic in its path, but then it stopped suddenly. There was an audio warning alarm. The door began to reverse itself and open. Joe quickly stopped it; he did not want to leave an opening for the attackers. He stared at the wreck and pondered for a moment. He thought he heard voices coming from inside the car interior. That gave him the motivation to move. Quickly. He limped toward the control room, pulling himself along the walls.

Hawk and Bohr practically fell out of their seats when they saw him come in. They rushed to his side. He was covered in blood from the many tiny cuts courtesy of the exploding car grille. His kneecap was scraped and his jeans were tattered.

"God, Joe. You're a sight!" Bohr said. "What happened? We felt the whole ship shake."

Joe looked down at himself. "It's not as bad as it looks. We don't have much time, I'm afraid."

He limped over to the panel and performed a few functions. The green-gray walls disintegrated and were replaced by a 360-degree total-surround visual of the inside of the arena.

Bohr gasped, absolutely stunned by the magnificence of the sight. Hawk and Joe had seen this trick before, so they focused on the task at hand.

"Joe, there seems to be a Chevy up our ass," Hawk observed caustically, pointing to a monitor showing the partially destroyed sedan sticking out from the side of the craft.

The images were difficult to distinguish in the poor light. "We need more light," Joe said matter-of-factly. "Watch this, Hawk." Ignoring the blood dripping from his many wounds onto the pristine control panel and the floor, he made a strange gesture in the air.

At that moment an observer standing outside the ship would have seen the entire fuselage, ever so slowly, begin to glow—dim at first, then brighter and brighter. The light enabled the trio to see into the shadows for the first time. The darkness melted away quickly until the arena's outer walls were visible. That was when the three spotted their pursuers. Four men were standing in a group, staring at the spacecraft. The men, aware that they had been seen, remained perfectly still.

Bohr pointed toward the destroyed doors at the far end of the building. "Look, there's Peter. It looks like another car is behind him in the parking lot."

Hawk nodded toward the group of men watching the craft. "Joe, I'm thinking these were the guys that chased you in here and almost killed you."

"I'm thinking the same thing, Hawk."

"This picture is very wrong. They don't have a scratch on them. Their car is totaled and they walk away without a scratch. I swear their hair isn't even messed."

"Great seatbelts," Joe said softly. He was trying to recall a memory that was relevant to this situation, but it wouldn't come.

"The men are yelling something to Peter," Bohr said. "Any audio to go with this great picture?"

"I don't know how everything works yet, David. No audio."

Hawk grabbed Joe's arm. "Look, it's a tow rope!"

"Peter has brought them a rope to pull the wreckage from the ship," Bohr guessed. "They're going to use one car to pull the other out of the ship."

"I think you're right." Joe shook his head in dismay. "We have to get out of here."

"And fast!" Hawk's voice went up half an octave.

"Hold on," Bohr said, grabbing Joe's arm before he could program the liftoff. "Let them hook up the rope to both vehicles. "They don't know how well, or poorly, you can fly. Hell, they don't even know if we can take off. Let them hook up, and then blast off."

"I don't know about blasting off, but I think I see your plan," Hawk said. "It's a smart way to dislodge the wrecked car."

"It's risky, David," Joe said. "If we don't take off fast enough, they could gain access to the ship. Then we'd be done for."

"Joe, if we do nothing, we're done for," Hawk said. "Let's try it."

There was no time to quibble. The men had attached the towrope from the frame of the one car to the twisted frame of the wrecked car. Joe checked to see that the antigravity generator was powered up. It was. Just as the car by the door engaged in reverse, Joe programmed a takeoff.

The ship began to rise sluggishly. Joe's heart hammered against his chest. Having never maneuvered like this before, he didn't know what to expect. The drag from both cars was more than he had anticipated. The vessel crashed back down onto the concrete floor. The three men were sent sprawling. Joe jumped back up to his feet and ran to the panel.

He upped the power and repeated the takeoff sequence. The craft lurched upwards and the thick nylon towline snapped taut. The craft was about five feet off the ground. One of the men ran toward the ship, jumped, and caught the line. It was Cringen. He began to work his way toward the hull of the craft. The spaceship began to climb but the movement was jerky. There was a good chance it would fall again. Joe applied more power. The ship rose twenty feet into the air. It dragged the tow car skidding across the concrete floor, its tires screaming in protest and gushing out black smoke.

Cringen was scurrying up the rope like a rat trying to gain access to a ship by climbing the anchor cable. He was balancing somehow on top of the rope, not hanging upside down by his feet and hands. The trio looked on in alarm.

"If he makes it to the door, he might be able to enter once the wrecked car is wrenched free," Bohr said.

"My thought exactly," Joe said, applying more antigravity lift.

The ship rose until it bumped up against the roof of the arena. They were up about forty feet. The second car was now dangling about two feet off the ground, swinging from side to side like a body from a hangman's noose.

"Give it more juice!" Hawk said.

Joe complied and the ship began to tremble in protest. Suddenly a pair of overhead steel girders failed simultaneously. The spaceship exploded through the roof in a shower of wood, steel, and aluminum debris. There was a tremendous cloud of dust, then a sudden lurch upwards. As the tow car got caught in the superstructure of the arena's roof, there was a tug backwards, but that was only momentary. The lower car ripped the jammed auto from the side of the fuselage, and both cars came tumbling down like a kite with a broken strut.

The tow car was first to land. It blew all its tires on impact. The force of the fall broke the spine of the vehicle. The other car was already damaged, but it managed to compress itself like an accordion as it slammed into the thick concrete floor. The dust and grime of twenty years exploded over the floor like an atomic bomb.

"Shut the door, Joe!" Hawk yelled.

Joe closed the door remotely from the control panel, and the ship catapulted skywards.

CHAPTER 19

East of Elliot Lake

Hours earlier, Grayer had watched as his two sons exited his car and ran, crouched down, into a clump of thick bushes, hidden from the road. He accelerated as fast as the automobile allowed. He noted grimly how painfully slow and antiquated these combustion vehicles were. He felt like Fred Flintstone using his bare feet to propel his auto. Fortunately, his pursuers were dealing with the same conditions.

He was pleased to see that the station wagon had passed by his sons' hiding spot without slowing down. They were safe for now. He focused on redirecting the pursuit away from Elliot Lake. He buried the accelerator into the floorboards. Grayer was not concerned about the danger of crashing, because of his ability to deflect injury. The car behind him was more cautious. Even with the stakes so high, there was a limit to the amount of risk the humans were willing to take. He was gradually pulling away, but his car was shuddering violently.

Just as he was leaving the subdivision, he sensed a tremendous psychic push. He felt a Signature close by. No, more than one. Several Signatures were heading his way at a very fast clip. They roared right past his car. The occupants of both cars stared as they passed each other. Grayer had seen him clearly—it was Stell, in Corey Wixon's body.

Stell's car took five hundred feet to stop and turn around. It joined in the chase. Grayer knew that Stell had him in his sights, and that this time he had backup. With him were James Cringen and Steve O'Sullivan, both high-ranking DIA. Between the three of them, they possibly had the collective power to terminate Frank Grayer. Within minutes, Stell and his men overtook the first chase vehicle driven by Connelly, Preston, and Hunter.

The conclusion was inevitable. Stell had selected a supercharged Chrysler, while Grayer was driving a standard-issue Chevy sedan. The Chrysler would overtake the Chevrolet. It was just a matter of time.

Grayer raced down the abandoned highway that led away from the town. He could see the lights of his adversaries in his rear-view mirror. He was a scant few minutes ahead. He turned onto Highway 17 and headed east toward Sudbury. Traffic was light this evening. He easily passed the few cars that he encountered. He watched the two cars behind him weave in and out of traffic. He worked the Chevy hard, never letting up on the throttle.

A warning light on the dash began to flicker red, then came on bright and steady. The coolant-temperature warning light was indicating an overheated engine, due to either lack of coolant or a leak. No sooner had the light come on than Grayer could smell the sickly sweet aroma of antifreeze coolant.

Wisps of steam uncurled from under the hood. Suddenly the hose blew off the radiator and blew coolant all over the inside of the hood. The engine block became soaked and the coolant vaporized in a huge cloud of steam. The steam cloud gushed from under the hood and covered the windshield, obscuring his vision of the road ahead. The wet spark plug harness began to short against the hot engine block. The motor misfired and the vehicle began to lose velocity.

Grayer knew that the pistons would seize up inside the hot engine cylinders at any time. When that happened, the car would stop, and he would be in mortal danger.

The Chrysler was bearing down on him. As a preemptive strike, he doused the lights, wrenched the steering wheel around and aimed the disabled car straight at the grille of the oncoming vehicle.

For Stell, who was driving the big Chrysler, it all happened so fast. He saw the brake lights up ahead, but didn't comprehend what that meant soon enough. Then the red lights disappeared and the road ahead went black. Stell was perplexed. What had happened to the car? The Chrysler burst through the remnants of a cloud of steam, and directly ahead was the Chevy. Coming fast. No lights. No time to react. Just brace!

"Use *it*! Use *it* now!" Stell screamed to his passengers.

The words were barely out of his mouth when his entire body was enveloped in a transparent green globe. The orb would protect him from injury. At the same instant, the two vehicles collided head-on. The two front ends rose in a fatal last dance and exploded in a ball of flame and engine liquids. The impact fused parts of the two engine blocks together. The grilles of both cars disintegrated into shards of plastic, glass, and metal that blew fifty feet into the air and rained down on the wrecks and the road. The rear seats joined the front seats and collapsed under the dash together. The roof of the Chrysler opened like the top of a convertible. Both of the cars' rear axles folded and their differentials went flying.

The impact was so severe that it drove the Chevy back thirty feet. There was a rending, screeching sound as the metal of the cars tore along the pavement. Both cars were joined at the nose, forming a flattened A. The fused wreck came to a grinding halt in the middle of the highway.

Then silence—the silence of expectation.

Stell, Cringen, and O'Sullivan were thrown clear of the crash upon impact. Grayer, meanwhile, had activated his protective orb and rolled out of the Chevy just prior to impact.

Grayer watched from a safe distance, as three green orbs erupted from the car like popcorn popping off a pan. The orbs fell to the ground and rolled a short distance. The green shield dissolved around each of them. They each got up and brushed themselves off. It was hardly necessary; their bodies never came into contact with the crash or the ground. They gathered and looked in his direction. They had spotted his Signature.

He began to jog east in order to continue to draw them away from Elliot Lake. He went about thirty yards before turning around to look at his pursuers. They were not taking the bait. They must have guessed his trick. The trio headed back down the highway toward Elliot Lake. Grayer hesitated, then reluctantly followed.

Twenty minutes later, a Bell telephone repair truck whizzed past him. He watched from a distance as one of the three stepped out in front of the truck with his arm in the air. He was holding a badge of some kind in his outstretched hand. The truck screeched to a halt, and the three went to the driver's door.

The driver exclaimed, "Lord tunderin Jesus, Officer! I seen a big smashup back there a ways. You guys OK?"

Cringen's eyes locked onto the driver's eyes. He *pushed* the human with a slight nod of his head. Smiling, he mesmerized the poor soul. "All is well," he said. "You feel the need to help us. You kindly offer your truck for us to use."

The driver's eyes immediately dulled over. "Take my truck."

"You are very kind," Cringen replied as he opened the door and helped the man from the vehicle. He signaled to the others, and they climbed into the truck.

"There is a man behind us. He is chasing us." Cringen nodded down the highway. "You passed him. Tall, dark hair, dressed in a dark jacket and slacks. He is a dangerous man. He caused the crash."

"He caused the crash," the driver intoned flatly.

"That's correct. You must disable him to prevent him from running away. Then you must turn him over to the police. Do you understand?"

"I understand. Stop him. This is a police matter."

"A very bad man. That's right, my friend."

Cringen laughed as he drove off.

"Grayer is going to handle him easily. Why play with the poor man?" O'Sullivan asked.

"It will further delay him. It might buy us some time."

Several minutes later, Grayer jogged up to the Bell truck driver.

"How's it goin, eh?" the driver said. He recognized Grayer as the one to fear, the bad man, the one he must hold for the police. He must stop him.

"Fine," Grayer replied, studying the man's face.

"See the crash back there?" the Bell driver asked.

Something was out of kilter. Grayer could sense it. His eyes locked onto the man's eyes. "Yes ... yes, I did," he said. He could sense that the man was in a state of hypnotic suggestion. "Did you talk to my friends?"

"Some friends!" the driver snorted before he could help himself.

He cursed his big mouth. His hand flew to his mouth as if to stop the words. Too late.

Grayer smiled. "What do you mean?" He decided to *push* him a little to see if he could unravel the implanted suggestion. "Tell me, friend, what did the men say to you?"

The Bell driver immediately fell under Grayer's power. "They told me that it was a good idea if I gave them my truck. They also told me you had caused the crash."

"I see. What's your name, friend?"

"Alex Shaw."

"Well, Alex, I want you to forget what these men said to you." Grayer *pushed* a little harder, watching the man's eyes. Alex began to feel very much at ease. It was as if he were resting at home in his Lazy Boy chair. He was going to snooze before dinner. That's it—a little snooze before dinner.

"You feel more like yourself, Alex. You are no longer confused. Forget what those men told you. They were mistaken. It is as it was before you stopped to talk to those men. You are not in a dream. You can wake up. Now!"

The man blinked and then started as he looked at Grayer. "Where the hell did you come from?"

"It seems there was an accident. You lent someone your truck to go for help."

"Not bloody likely. Company policy. Nobody drives the truck except me." Then he looked a little confused. "Why would I give someone my truck? I remember that I radioed in the crash."

"Is there someone coming to help?" Grayer asked. He could tell the poor man was sick about losing his truck.

"Yup. Second Bell truck should be here soon."

True to his word, a second, larger truck pulled up to the pair as they walked back toward town. The truck stopped, and the passenger rolled down his window. "Shaw! Where the hell's your truck?"

Shaw looked over at Grayer as if could somehow verify his story. "Lent it to some fellers so they could bring back help."

Two men climbed down from the cab. The driver of the second truck looked at Shaw in disbelief. "I can't believe you did that! Have you lost your mind? We've already called the accident in to the OPP." He shook his head. The man knew that Shaw wasn't the sharpest tool in the shed, but he had never seen him do something so stupid before.

Grayer could hear a faint wail of a distant siren. He sighed. Then he nodded his head abruptly toward the ground and looked back at the trio. His voice took on a strange and powerful timbre. Some might say it resembled the siren call of the mermaid or the hiss of a snake. It was deep; it was sharp; it was otherworldly. It was also impossible not to obey.

Grayer ushered the three Bell guys off to the side of the road so a passing car wouldn't hit them. "The police are coming. You will be fine. You will remember nothing."

He jumped up into the cab and started the engine. He saw red flashing lights in the rear-view mirror, reflected in the night fog. He slammed the door shut as he pulled away and headed for Elliot Lake, hoping he wouldn't arrive too late.

CHAPTER 20

Near Elliot Lake

High above the arena, the trio gazed down through the transparent floor of the ship at the commotion below, happy to have escaped their attackers moments before. The sleek spaceship hovered soundlessly at three hundred feet like a hawk hunting mice. Its speed was zero knots. The sensation on board was not unlike the buoyancy one feels in a hot-air balloon. There was no sense of motion or height—just a quiet, peaceful sense of well being.

A yellow-white ball of flame erupted from the wreck of twisted metal tangled on the arena floor. A bright cascade of sparks from a battery short ignited gasoline fumes that had formed above spilled fuel from the cars. The runny fuel caught fire with a whoosh as the gas sucked in as much oxygen as possible. The concrete floor became a sea of flame as the fire traveled from one pool of spilled gasoline to the next like hungry bright-orange koi snapping at pond food. Human figures could be seen scurrying from the building out to the safety of the parking lot.

Hawk pointed down at several figures fleeing the building, dashing away from the flames. They threw open the doors of a truck and piled inside.

At that moment, one of the gas tanks below blew apart and spewed a cloud of yellow-orange flame toward the wall of the building. The flames seared the arena wall and ignited the chemical vapors from a large pile of fertilizer and farm feed that had been decomposing for two decades. There was a violent intake of air and a hideous display of raw force as the entire building, sharing the pressure equally on all its walls, lifted from the ground.

With an earsplitting boom, the system disgorged its awesome shockwave of energy. The building disintegrated outwards in all directions. There was an enormous plume of yellow flame. The roof shattered in shards of wood and steel. The walls lost definition and became a rolling wave of fragmented debris that radiated out for four hundred feet in a circle around the epicenter of the arena.

The punching shock of the explosion lifted the rear end of the Bell truck on a wave of screeching dust and debris. The momentum pushed it down the road like a child's toy. The nose of the vehicle scraped the dirt, threatening to overturn the whole truck. Luckily for the occupants, that did not happen. The rear end slapped down on the road and bounced a few times. The truck was wrapped in clouds of choking debris as it fled down the road.

The spaceship was buffeted violently but briefly by the shock wave as it leapt upwards from the center of the explosion. The air warped with the intensity of the heat. Outside the ship, the smell was one of burnt gas and rotted fertilizer. A putrid mushroom cloud enveloped the craft. The ground below disappeared in billowing black smoke and dust.

"Time to leave!" Joe said. He was amazed at the intensity of the blast. His hands gently grazed the panel and the vessel accelerated with a flash of speed. An outside observer would have thought it simply vanished.

Inside the ship, its own artificial gravity defied the laws of Earth physics. The occupants felt practically no G-forces as the vessel shot toward space. The bioelectrics sensed the change in pressure within nanoseconds and adjusted the internal pressure and artificial gravity accordingly.

The vessel rocketed to twenty thousand feet, then steadied as Joe trimmed it. The heading was 090.

"Not sure how Canada's radar or NORAD's system works," Joe said. "Don't want them to pick us up on their radar. I think we're still outside Toronto's Air Traffic Control Zone. I've leveled out at about twenty thousand feet above ground level."

"Joe, did you see that wicked explosion down there?" Hawk burst out. He had been glued to the screen along with the other two.

"I thought we would never lose that car from our door. It was jammed solid. Lucky thing for us they tried to tow it out."

"Lucky indeed!" Bohr offered. "That reminds me. We'd better search the craft for unwanted visitors."

"I hope we shut the door before that guy had a chance to come on board," Joe said. "Did you guys see if he fell or not?"

"Couldn't see," Bohr said. "Too much dust."

"No one could have survived that fall," Hawk said.

"I didn't see anyone fall," Bohr said. "He may be on board."

Joe ran a quick scan. "I'm getting a life sign reading near the portal door. We have an intruder. It must be monkey man."

Hawk rushed over. "Where?"

"There. Right there …" Joe couldn't believe his eyes. "It's gone. The reading disappeared."

Bohr and Hawk scoured the craft on foot, systematically checking every corner of the ship. They found nothing. It must have been
a false reading.

After they had completed the search, Bohr said, "What now? Do
we turn ourselves in to the authorities?"

Joe had a devilish grin on his blood-splattered face. "Anybody up
for some fun?" His eyebrows were raised in a Jack Nicholson grin.

"Fun?" Bohr was genuinely perplexed.

Hawk laughed and nodded eagerly like a dog waiting to go outside.
He knew that Joe was planning to take it to the max.

Bohr studied the injured boy in front of him with measured calm-
ness and parental concern. "Joe, you look a mess. Let's get you some
medical attention and dressings."

Joe grinned as he walked over and put his hand on Bohr's shoulder. "It's not all that bad. Really, it isn't. More little cuts than anything.
Look, Hawk and I want to do this. Right, Hawk? Want to see what
this baby will do?"

"You bet, bro! Buckle up, David!"

Bohr looked at his command seat, foolishly hoping to find a seatbelt there. Of course there was none.

Both brothers had the biggest dumb-ass grins on their faces. Their
youth overrode any caution. Their pent-up adrenalin needed release.

"Ready for some special effects, David?" Joe said coyly.

He caressed the control panel, and the floor disappeared. Bohr
screamed, clawing for his white command chair. The twins howled
with laughter. Bohr scrambled into the safety of the chair and leaned
back, shaking his head back and forth.

"Not funny. No, really, *not funny.*"

The boys took their chairs, tears of laughter rimming their eyes.

"I could have had a heart attack!" Bohr said.

"David, this ship can and will do amazing things. And *I* know how to fly her!" At Joe's command, the ship began to accelerate rapidly.

The three crew members had a total view of the ship's surroundings. It was like being in a hot-air balloon without the basket. The visual effect was somewhat disquieting. Joe flew the craft like an F14. It hung for a moment and then arched gracefully downwards, accelerating to Mach 1. The vessel's heading was due east. From their height, they saw the early morning dawn. A flawless orange-gold sun winked at them from the horizon to the east. It was so glorious that they had to squint to protect their eyes.

To be honest, Joe had no real plan. He had no set course. He was flying for the thrill of it. He saw little difference between this joyride and bombing around on his bike—except that this was closer to flying like Superman. No floor, no walls, no ceiling, and no restrictions. It was the ultimate ride. Indeed, Superman would have been jealous.

Joe dove toward the ground at a sickening speed. Both Hawk and Bohr were holding their breath, eyes like saucers. Joe let out a tribal howl as the visual thrill traveled through his body. There was a sensation of falling down an elevator shaft thousands of feet deep. Lacking the sensation of extreme G-forces, the visual rush was perplexingly overwhelming. He pulled up vertically at four hundred feet above ground and continued, parallel to the ground, at Mach 2.

The ship was capable of determining the contours of the land. She rose and fell automatically to avoid obstacles. The effect was like watching footage of the countryside played at very high speed.

For the next hour, the three flew like they were strapped to the belly of a cruise missile. They weaved in and out of valleys and above fields. They soared up the sheer sides of cliffs and crested mountain tops, blowing billows of snow-dust in their wake. They skirted urban areas to avoid arousing attention. The ship was silent and flew gracefully—it left no footprint on the environment except for a small circular shockwave as the craft passed overhead. Other than that, there was no evidence that they had passed by.

As the craft reached the Atlantic shoreline, the trio reached a consensus. They would go toward South America and avoid the radars of Atlantic Canada, NORAD, and Europe. Joe knew that most civil aviation craft flew no higher than about thirty-five thousand feet. He accelerated and rose nimbly to sixty thousand feet. To see the ground fall away so rapidly was brain-numbing. They felt that at that level, they would be beyond the reach of civilian radar.

As the ship gained height, the shoreline lost definition and the snaking urban and rural roads disappeared until the planet itself began to form below. The gray Atlantic waves crashing into the New Brunswick shore resembled a thin ribbon.

"Will ya just look at that!"

"It's amazing."

"Amazing."

"It's a planet. Not a place. Look, you can see an actual curve in the horizon."

"Amazing."

"All right, crew. Where do we go?" Joe asked.

"Good question, Joe, where *do* we go?" Hawk said.

"Hawk's right," Bohr said. "We have a problem. We are most assuredly wanted by some government, or by all the military in the western hemisphere, by now. Where is a safe place for us to go?"

"OK, David, how do we get out of this jam?" Joe asked.

"We go somewhere away from the U.S," Bohr said.

"I agree. How about somewhere unfriendly to America?"

"There's so many to choose from," Hawk said.

"Very funny," Bohr said. "Look, we just need time to work out this situation. Then we contact your father in Washington for help."

"OK," Hawk said, "so the plan ends up being that we look for a phone booth in a nasty country—someplace far away from home, where the crazies can't get us."

Joe had an idea. "How about Cuba? At least to start."

Bohr thought hard. "I like it! Even if their radar picked up the spaceship, who would care? It's not as if they would contact the U.S. or alert the world. Cuba is isolated."

"Cuba it is, then," Joe said.

CHAPTER 21

Elliot Lake

For a ghost town, Elliot Lake was home to a lot of activity lately. Grayer drove the big diesel Bell truck down the main highway into town and headed for the boys' house. He would be able to pick up any clues from there. He wheeled the heavy truck through the wide subdivision streets until it reached its destination.

Grayer turned off the engine. Leaving the keys in the ignition, he walked across the street toward the house. He went inside through the carport door by the kitchen. He wasn't expecting to find anyone at home.

Peter Wright was humming to himself while waiting for the coffee machine to finish. He spun around and looked at Grayer as the door opened.

"Frank?"

Grayer extended his hand. "The very same. It's been many years." He was curious about what role Wright had in this whole affair.

"Indeed. Indeed it has." Wright let go of the handshake. "You don't look a day older than when I last saw you." This man truly hadn't aged a year since they'd last met many years ago in New Mexico, he thought.

"Thanks. Nothing like deep-cover work to keep you fit," Grayer replied.

Wright laughed. "Deep cover. My favorite. Always sounds so mysterious, doesn't it?"

"Just lonely work." Grayer said with a sigh. "Nothing lonelier. You can't contact your friends, the few that are left. You can't see your family near often enough. And the Agency can't or won't recognize your sacrifice, because it would compromise your intell."

Grayer took a fresh-brewed coffee from Wright and sat at the kitchen table. "Covert action means that there is no publicity," he said. "It's for the good of the nation, but it's not the kind of work you do if you crave attention."

Wright sat down across from him, coffee in hand. "You are preaching to the choir. After thirty years, all I got was a meager pension and a stiff handshake. Oh yes, and they changed the locks on my way out the door. They actually did change the locks the day I left!"

Grayer smiled. He knew that Wright had been instrumental in uncovering a senior Soviet mole inside MI5. There was a significant political price to pay for this, however, because in the UK, senior bureaucrats tend to be appointed to positions of power by their friends. When Wright exposed evidence of not just one but *several* improprieties within MI5 and MI6, the British Peerage closed ranks. Wright was not within those ranks.

The Establishment was not prepared for the embarrassment of having one of its own caught spying for the Soviet Union. It was preposterous. Why would a member of their ranks stoop to working for the classless Russians? The British upper crust were a privileged class. They attended the best schools and dated each other's sisters or brothers. That's what privilege meant. They were better than the masses and expected to be treated accordingly. And, for the most part, they were. The cheeky nickname for these types was "Range Rovers," after the expensive jeeps they drove. When he had proven that there was a leak at the highest level inside the Agency, Wright had crossed a very dangerous line.

"Let's move on to other topics, shall we?" Grayer said. "Have you seen my sons?"

Wright let out a low whistle. "Have I? What a family! Your sons have stolen a bloody spaceship, Frank!"

Grayer coughed up part of his coffee, and not all of it was acting. He never would never have guessed that the boys could get the craft airborne. "Peter, do you know how silly that sounds?" he said with a hearty laugh.

"Laugh all you want. I was there. The Americans want this machine badly, Frank. I mean, even more badly than you would imagine. This has not been treated like some archeological find. If we look beyond the obvious significance of the find, the treatment of the situation by the U.S. government has been highly irregular. There's a desperation in their efforts to recover this vessel that I cannot comprehend."

Grayer listened patiently as Wright came to the end of the story: "As I watched the two cars dangling from the ship, there was this most bizarre spectacle of a person scrambling almost vertically up the tow rope toward the ship's door. It was supernatural. I had never seen this man before. Then the ship smashed up through the roof. What a mess! Both cars fall. There's a hell of a racket. Can't see much because of the dust and debris. Next thing I know the building's gone. Blown up."

"What happened to the spaceship?"

"Dunno. It disappeared in the mess and confusion."

"So it didn't blow up with the building?"

"Not as far as I know. Anyway, we all piled into this truck just as the building exploded. Blew the truck down the road. Thought we were finished, but we came out of it all right. No injuries, and only minor damage. Incredible, really. We turned and looked back. The building was gone, just a big fire. The spaceship was gone too. We headed back here. Connelly radioed in for a helicopter, but I guess there was some problem getting one. Then this other fellow, I forget his name, took the mike and made another radio call. This time they got a different answer. He said things had been taken care of. When we arrived here, Preston and Hunter took off in the telephone truck. A helicopter came and picked up the others just before you arrived."

"What happens next?" Grayer asked.

"Well, I would think our role as a 'recovery' team is over. We identified the ship as a UFO. Our purpose wasn't supposed to be to capture a runaway spaceship; it was to identify the remains of a crashed one." Wright had had enough of this little adventure. Time to fly home.

"What about David? What's happened to him?"

"He's still missing. So is that crazy monkey guy who went up the rope."

"That's why you're still here, isn't it? Can't just leave David behind, right?"

Wright smiled. "Just like the U.S. Marines, I guess. Preston promised to send a government car for me as soon as possible. I'm going back to the arena to look for clues."

Grayer stood up and went to the kitchen window. It faced west toward the arena—the last known position of the spacecraft and his sons. He was thinking about how the story of the recovery was probably just a front for Stell to acquire the craft for himself. He realized that this was never a sanctioned government operation.

"Peter, you mentioned the DIA before, that the DIA wants to recover this craft."

"Yes."

Grayer turned around to face him. "Why did you say DIA? What makes you think the DIA is involved?"

"Oh, they're involved all right. Connelly was covert DIA back in the fifties. I would bet that this fellow Hunter, or whatever his real name is, is a part of operations, and works for the DIA. Too many coincidences in operational timing. These new people that showed up today, they must be DIA, or Department of Defense."

"They aren't," Grayer said. "If Department of Defense were involved I'd know about it. That's who I work for, Peter. I work under the Secretary of Defense."

"Hold on, Frank." Wright was shaking his head in denial. "Connelly contacted me in England. He also contacted Bohr and others. I got clearance personally at the highest MI5 level. The Prime Minister's office approved my involvement. Preston got RCMP clearance from Ottawa. The U.S. government is very involved here."

Wright was beginning to realize that both the Canadian and British governments had been unofficially contacted by someone high up within the U.S. intelligence community. High enough to bypass the American protocols. It seemed everyone was in the know except the American government. That's a first, he thought.

Grayer turned back and talked to the window. "I handle the most delicate of defense issues for our government, Peter. It never reached my department. I never knew about the op until yesterday, and I had to dig for the information. I guarantee that the DoD was not aware of any action to recover a crashed UFO in Canada."

"Frank, no one took this seriously until twelve hours ago! Why would they bump this upstairs to the top DoD? These must be field agents like Connelly. Just here to gather Human Intelligence."

Grayer answered him without turning. "Certain intell from agencies like the DIA, NSA, and CIA are channeled through to the Department of Defense on a request or need-to-know basis. I know that there is an open request that any UFO activity, no matter what size, be forwarded to the Defense Department. It is the standing order from the Joint Chiefs of Staff that this intell be sent to my personal file. For My Eyes Only. *My* discretion on course of action. That never happened in this case, did it? Perhaps someone figured that I did not 'need to know.' "

"Who would have that kind of clout?"

"I have a very good idea who."

"Frank, I don't know exactly what's going on in Washington, but I can tell you that this place was crawling with U.S. federal agents. DIA, NSA, who knows? I can also tell you that they outranked Connelly— who was the one who originally recruited us for this operation. Once the new group came in, Connelly faded into the background."

"Did the name Wixon come up in any conversation?" Grayer asked. "Did the men address each other by name?"

"Yes, I picked up two names. There was Jim Cringen. Hunter seemed to know him. Connelly called the other chap Steve. I'm sure that Connelly reported to this Steve person. No mention of Wixon, sorry."

"Wixon's involved. I'm sure that he has recruited some ranking DIA or other intelligence agency personnel. There is a possible covert operation going on here. I am going to have to get back to Washington to see if I can sort this out."

Grayer handed Wright his Department of Defense business card. "Let me know if you find anything on David Bohr. You know that he's a friend of mine."

Wright nodded and slipped his hand into his jacket pocket. He took out a slightly tattered business card. It was a plain white card with Wright's real name and a tiny replica of the queen's crest in the top right-hand corner. It had the old Whitehall MI5 address and phone number. The phone number was scratched out and another number, presumably his home phone, had been scrawled overtop.

Wright laughed. "I told you they changed the locks—well, they also cancelled my phone privileges as well, fancy that."

Wright was interested in how Grayer's career had progressed from AIA in Los Alamos to Assistant to the Secretary of Defense. Grayer was candid with Wright, and they chatted until they heard honking from the driveway.

Two nondescript cars were parked in front. Daylight was dawning gray and orange in the east, casting ghostly early-morning shadows across the fog-soaked subdivision. Grayer and Wright left the house and went to the parked cars. They were both pros. There were no goodbyes or awkward moments. Both men gave the other a smile and a nod. Wright signed for the one car, and Grayer managed to get a lift back into Sudbury in the other.

As they pulled away, Grayer looked backwards at Wright, whose sedan turned down the road heading west. He looked at the bungalow his two sons had called home for the last few months. He knew he would never see Elliot Lake again. He knew they wouldn't either.

He reached forward from the rear seat and tapped one of the Canadian agents on the shoulder. "You boys mind if I use your car phone?"

CHAPTER 22

East coast of North America

The Caribbean and South America would be ideal to fly over without causing much of a stir. Their collective military equipment was meager. The boys could frolic without causing trouble at home.

Joe was easing into his newfound role as commander of the spacecraft. Because of his time in the Learning Stall, he learned tasks faster and more easily than he could have before. His training as a private pilot must have helped, but he grasped piloting the spacecraft with uncanny ease. He wanted more flight experience, though. He headed east over the Atlantic Ocean. At about five hundred miles due east of Moncton, New Brunswick, he changed his heading from ninety to about a hundred and ninety, heading south-southwest. That is, he turned right.

Within minutes, they all noted Long Island off the starboard side in the far distance. The vessel traveled effortlessly down the Atlantic coast, maintaining an altitude of sixty thousand feet. A half-hour later, the coast of Florida was clearly evident off the starboard. Joe knew Cuba lay just south of Key West. He waited until he estimated he was almost abeam Cuba, then banked the ship into a sharp right-hand dive. At an astounding speed, the vessel scorched from the east toward the sandy island.

"Hawk, David, feel like some Cuban sand?"

"Joe, this thing is amazing," Hawk said. "I know we're falling fast, but I don't feel the G's."

"Hawk's right, Bohr said. "I had no idea that the craft was this capable. It's surreal." He saw the island of Cuba race toward them. He felt no sensation of speed.

Joe smiled the smile of a teenager taking his buddies on a joyride in Dad's new Porsche.

Joe thought idly that Cuba's radar operators might think the incoming spaceship was a missile, except missiles don't travel that fast. It would certainly confuse the technicians studying the equipment. He had to smile. He relished the thought of messing with them.

He had another thought pop into his head. No reason, it just did. Joe was curious how close to the ocean itself he could maneuver the craft. This was still a trial run, for heaven's sake! He swooped down several miles east off the Cuban coast and ran, parallel to the water, at Mach 2. He descended lower and lower, until he was five feet above the rolling blue-green waves.

"Um, Joe, aren't we flying a little low?"

"Relax, David. This is a test flight. A trial run. We're test pilots today."

"Swell."

There was a rooster tail ninety feet high behind the ship as it sucked in the water in passing and then blew it high in the air. A huge circle of cloudy seawater formed a perfect white O around the center of the ship. It was a sight to see. The odd rogue wave slapped the spacecraft's nose and was vaporized instantly, the force of the impact tugging at the ship like invisible hands trying to pull the craft into the water. From above the craft it would have looked like a white line being drawn across the Atlantic Ocean, heading straight toward Cuba like a speeding arrow.

"Joe, look ahead, coming on fast," Bohr said.

"I see it."

Up ahead there was sea traffic. At their tremendous speed, the waves were practically a blur. They were on top of the traffic in seconds. Joe flicked the controls to avoid hitting an oceangoing trawler. He regained his original course, not on purpose, exactly, but because of some newly learned habit. Within another second or two, they came upon a small fleet of fishing boats. The ship zigged and zagged to avoid hitting them. They flipped the craft at a ninety-degree angle to force the tight turn, its wing tip slicing the water. Joe was careful not to fly directly over the boats, to avoid damaging the tiny vessels with the wake and wash of the shockwave.

He decided it was time to increase altitude and went to three hundred feet. He slowed down to Mach 0.7 when the sandbars off Cuba's eastern shore came into view. The full, open, 360-degree view in the control room gave the crew of three a magnificent view of the island.

"Cuba," he said.

"You're telling me," Hawk said.

"What a sight. It's beautiful," Bohr said.

"Look at the beaches. Let's stop and go for a quick swim," Hawk said.

"Tourist," Joe said with a sneer.

They continued their approach toward the pristine white sandy beaches that made the island a paradise. Tall royal palms swayed in the gentle Caribbean breeze.

Joe slowed to 250 miles per hour. It felt downright sluggish.

"I can almost smell the flowers."

"Me, too."

"Me, three."

The foliage thickened as the trio flew over land. Neat yet terribly shabby shanty houses appeared beneath them as they left the ocean behind. These were replaced by worker farms, and then by a scattering of larger haciendas left over from the American era.

Finally, they flew over the colorful suburban buildings that dotted the outskirts of Havana. They chose to avoid flying directly over the city itself, and flew over its northern suburbs at three hundred feet. People gawked in surprise, but it happened so fast they weren't sure what it was they had seen. Was it a U.S. missile attack? What made it even weirder for them, of course, was that the ship flew without sound.

As the ship left the island, the reverse happened. Buildings were replaced by homes, then resort developments, then the beaches, and then the ocean.

The west side of Cuba held most of the large resorts. It tended to be the haven for foreign investors. Cuba was building a thriving tourism trade with partners from abroad. It was mostly the Spanish hoteliers who were brave and savvy enough to foot the bill to build world-class resorts. They took a huge risk, because the Cuban government was thought by many to be unreliable and untrustworthy as a partner. Of course, that wasn't true. In fact, quite the opposite was the case—the Cubans understood the importance of the tourist trade. But that trade was with Europeans and Canadians, not their U.S. neighbor to the north.

American citizens had imposed a self-inflicted ban on visiting the island. All trade was also banned. There was an embargo. Any American citizen caught doing business with the Cubans would be jailed and his assets confiscated. This would punish the Cubans, the thinking went—the out-of-date thinking that kept American tourists from visiting the communist country. What a shame, to be so close to this island paradise and not be able to enjoy it. While the Cuban tourism industry did not miss the self-absorbed American tourists themselves, they sorely missed their dollar.

At twenty miles out, Joe banked 180 and circled around. Hawk and Bohr enjoyed being along for the ride. Joe headed back toward the island. Minutes before, as they were passing over the land, the three had observed some military installations, but these flew by so quickly that nothing made sense.

There was, in fact, a substantial buildup of military armament. But Cuba's military power was primarily aimed at defense, not offense. They were paranoid about an impending U.S. invasion. Castro did his best to keep the patriotic fires glowing about this perpetual impending crisis to take the citizens' minds off their impoverished existence.

There were no missile silos anymore. It had been twenty years since the Cuban Missile Crisis of October, 1962. During the crisis, the Soviets had sworn that there were no missiles in Cuba. But the U.S. had pictures of Soviet missiles in Cuba. So the Soviets changed their story, and Foreign Minister Andrei Gromyko explained that Soviet military assistance was being provided to help Cuba defend against a possible U.S. invasion. The U.S. had, in fact, planned such an invasion.

Kennedy blockaded Cuba. Fourteen thousand U.S. troops were called up, and Florida resembled a war zone. Then Cuba began shooting at anything that moved in their air space, including commercial flights. American pilot Rudolf Anderson's U-2 spy plane was downed, and he was killed. A nuclear war was averted when Prime Minister Khrushchev stood down and ordered the SSI missiles removed from Cuba. While it seemed much longer to those who lived on the brink of a nuclear holocaust, the crisis was over in thirteen days.

It may not have been a good idea for the trio to invade Cuba's sovereign air space, even if it was twenty years later and even if their motives were innocent. Tensions remained high between the Soviets and the U.S. The American public was never fully aware of the extent of Cuban military preparedness.

So, quite reasonably, Joe had no idea how well equipped the Cuban military was, thanks to Cuba's continued relationship with the Soviets. With extensive funds, equipment, and advice provided by the Soviet Union between 1978 and 1982, Cuba had built a modern air force, navy, and army with offensive interdiction capabilities. The Cuban Air Force's inventory of over two hundred Soviet jet fighter-bombers and interceptors far surpassed other air forces in the Caribbean Basin region. If Joe had known, he may not have been so cavalier in his buzzing of their military defense installations.

The three on the spaceship did not realize that the Cuban Air Force had been scrambled when their craft began its foray into Cuban air space well out over the Atlantic. The SKS 11, a Koni-class submarine warfare frigate, had identified the spaceship on radar. One of Cuba's three squadrons of MiG-23s was urgently scrambled, as the initial speed of the incoming craft was determined to exceed all known military aircraft. It was thought to be a missile, yet the size and shape were wrong. Perhaps it was an American spy plane. This possibility caused a huge stir on shore. The Soviets were alerted through their island embassy. News reached them about an attack by an airplane shaped like a wing and going tremendously fast.

As Joe banked the craft to the west of the island, he looked down and saw the small shape of a gray-and-white boat below. He didn't know it, but it was a new missile-equipped patrol boat. The boat was a Styx and Malakhit Osa-I-class torpedo hydrofoil. And the seasoned captain of the boat had the spaceship in its sights. The two were so close you could shake hands. Joe did not understand the gravity of the situation, and swooped casually away from the boat and back toward the island for another tourist flight.

A token attempt to hail the spaceship was met with radio silence. Of course, Joe was not monitoring his radio; there was no radio aboard the spaceship. The Cubans had followed the correct international radio frequency protocol.

"Captain," the radioing officer said in Spanish, "the aircraft is heading back to Cuba."

"We cannot allow that," said the captain. "It has invaded our airspace once. We would be idiots to allow this indiscretion again."

"Sir, we need an immediate decision before it gets out of range."

"We must assume it is hostile." After a brief conversation with his superior on the Sea/Land telephone, the captain asked the officer, "Do you have a fix?"

"Yes, Captain. Have had for some time."

"Prepare to launch One and Three MALs."

"Ready One and Three."

"Launch!" the captain ordered.

The patrol boat fired two modified Soviet Malakhit ship-to-air missiles at the retreating spaceship.

Joe was alerted to the missile attack as he was approaching the most westerly reef off the Island's coast. The ship gave a warning alert signal, and the main screen opened a window with a view of a magnified missile rapidly approaching the ship's tail.

Hawk jumped from his seat. "Joe! A missile!" Then he and Bohr shouted, simultaneously: "Incoming!"

"I see it. I see it!" Joe said. "Just when we were starting to have fun."

Bohr frowned. "Causing a war is not exactly what I had in mind, boys. We're in enough trouble as it is."

Joe snapped a sharp right to the south. The ship stood on its wing.

Their turning radius was fifty feet, altitude gain was a thousand feet per second, and speed gain was a stunning Mach 1 per second. Everything seemed to be happening at once.

The missile altered its trajectory. It rocketed toward the spaceship along the hypotenuse of the triangle formed by the relative trajectories of both crafts.

"Still coming fast!" Hawk shouted. "Gun it, Joe!"

Joe accelerated and gained altitude at the same time. He rose to twenty thousand feet and reached Mach 3. The gravity-bound Malakhit missile's speed bled down from seven hundred and fifty miles per hour to four hundred miles per hour in trying to attain the same altitude. Joe climbed to forty thousand feet, then performed a white-knuckled loop back down to eight hundred feet above sea level heading back over the island. The missiles lost their target lock and continued out to sea. They later crashed harmlessly into the ocean and sank.

The Styx Captain watched in a calm perplexity that only trained soldiers can aspire to. While those about him were gawking in disbelief and shouting, he calmly observed the maneuvers of the craft. He reported what he had observed by sea phone. Their ship's role was done.

As Joe was setting up for a final pass over Cuba, there was a collective groan from all three crewmembers as they looked back.

"I don't believe this!" Joe fumed.

"Joe, who have you managed to piss off this quickly? Usually you take longer!"

"Very funny, Hawk."

Right on their tail, half a mile back, was a pack of four tightly flying MiG-23s. Their formation was admirable as the aircraft flew at about forty feet apart. The sun hardly reflected off their gray-and-yellow camouflage paint job. If planes could smile, these would be grinning from ear to ear at their smooth pickup of this intruder. It was a textbook attack: 180, right on the tail. They fanned out to cut off any safe retreat for the intruding craft.

Bohr shook his head. "You've had this machine for less than a day, and already you're engaged in a dogfight with a hostile foreign power! The Cubans no less! The political fallout ... I can't imagine."

"David, I had no idea ..."

"Joe, try not to start a Third World War, OK?" Hawk said. "This isn't funny anymore. Let's cut bait and leave."

"Hawk, these planes can't hurt us. We have alien space technology."

"Don't bet the house on it."

A soft voice from the ship's computer interrupted with a warning. The lead MiG had fired a volley of bullets. Without Joe's even having to touch any controls, the ship projected a light-green cocoon of magnetic flux that repelled the metal projectiles.

"See that, Hawk? This spaceship has a brain. It can think and protect itself. I did nothing. It put up a shield on its own."

"Impressive," Bohr said. "Joe, these MiGs probably have onboard nose cameras to record kills. That means they may be able to record our image as well."

"By our image you mean that they can take a picture of our spaceship, right?"

"Exactly. Joe, you don't want this."

"You're right. Time to go!" Joe's arm flew over the control panel. A soft computer voice confirmed the command.

The spaceship disappeared from the radar screen of the entire Cuban military. It was that simple. It was that fast.

The MiGs were a mere two hundred yards astern when the silver craft on their noses blurred for a nanosecond and then disappeared from view. The orange dot image on their onboard radar flicked out.

The ping was gone; the lock was gone. The sky was an empty blue.

On-ground tracking was the same story. Every radar contact was lost in the blink of an eye. There had been a triangular lock between the ground base, the MiGs, and a Foxtrot-class submarine two miles off shore. It, too, was gone. For the operators, it was as if there had either been a huge equipment malfunction, or the silver craft was never there at all.

Some good luck, though, for the Cuban military. The lead MiG pilot got a good picture. Bohr had been right; there was a nose camera. It had captured a clear image of an extraterrestrial spaceship.

Bohr stared down at the lush forests and sparkling lakes below the ship. It was an endless slideshow of Earth's beauty on this cloudless day.

"We need time to collect our thoughts," he said. "We can't fly around willy-nilly for much longer. We've been spotted once before. We don't want more air force jets from God knows what country scrambled to intercept us."

"They could never come close to us," Hawk said.

"Perhaps not, but why cause more attention than need be?"

"Hawk, he's right," Joe said. "Whoever is after us might be grateful to know where we are. Why advertise anymore? I think we're over Chile. Let's look for a place to land."

Adjusting his cardigan, Bohr said, "Before you land, I was wondering if … well … I know this sounds childish, but …"

The two brothers turned and looked at him. "What?"

Bohr took a deep breath, and the thought gushed out. "I'd like to fly the spacecraft. Just this once. So I know what it's like to fly it. I put one together once, but I never knew the feeling of controlling one.'

The brothers were hesitant. "You know nothing about how to operate this vessel," Joe said.

Bohr nodded, eyes downcast.

"Oh, don't be like that. Is it really that important to you?"

"It's a once-in-a-lifetime opportunity," Bohr said.

Joe ran his tongue over his teeth in thought. "How about this. You pilot and I co-pilot, like a civil aviation training exercise."

Bohr smiled broadly. "Like my pilot's license?"

"Something like that," Joe said.

"A crash course," Hawk said.

The other two looked at him sternly.

"Sorry."

"Let's go over the basics," Joe began. "You never know—you may have picked up something subconsciously in the Learning Stall."

"I can't remember," Bohr said.

"First, we stop and hover. Watch the monitors."

The craft stopped instantly and remained motionless.

"Next we ID you with the ship so that it recognizes you." Joe motioned for Bohr to approach the instrument panel. "Computer, scan and identify the occupants on the bridge."

The computer replied. "Three humans: Joe Grayer, Harry Grayer, and other human."

"Other is called David Bohr."

"David Bohr has already been scanned. He was in the chamber. He is known."

"Good. David will be the pilot in command until that order is rescinded."

"Understood."

"David has no experience piloting this craft."

"The pilot must be trained before assuming command."

"Yes, ordinarily, but there is no time."

"Understood."

"Now, David, place both your hands about a yard apart on the console."

Bohr did so. The panel glowed in several multicolored light streams, each swirling slowly in a perfect circle in front of him.

"What colors do you see?" Joe asked.

"Mostly gray and orange."

"Look closer."

Bohr smiled broadly. "Oh my, I can see many other colors, now that I'm concentrating."

"Good, very good. It seems that your experience in the Learning Stall has broadened your light spectrum sensitivity and recognition." Joe was pleased. "The craft responds to your body language more than your touching the control panel. The lights on the panel are for elementary shifts in speed and height. Directional changes are subjective rather than directive."

"What do you mean?"

"The computer interpolates minuscule changes in body language as direction commands. It's faster than you can think or act. If you want to turn left and fly up, you think about it and the computer reads your eyes and subtle body movements, and obeys instantly. Understood?"

"I think so."

"OK, then. You have command."

Bohr's eyes flew open. "That's it?"

"Yup, I just told the computer to obey you. Take it slow and easy. The circle of green controls speed, and the circle of red controls height."

"What about all the other colors?"

"Not important right now. Tell us what you plan to do, and we will see how you fly."

"I plan a slow turn to the left and a swooping descent."

Nothing happened.

"What must I do?" Bohr asked, a little frustrated.

"My fault. Not much of a teacher. Place one hand on the green circle and the other on the red circle. In the green area, press downwards and push forwards very slowly to accelerate. In the red lighted area, push down and slowly draw your whole palm down toward your stomach."

At first there was nothing. Bohr shifted his body dramatically in a half-pirouette.

"Tiny movements only!" Joe managed to yell before the ship suddenly broke its hover and soared, spinning, down toward the planet's surface. The gentle arc became a mind-numbing spiral dive. The three were thrown up and over the control panel. Their faces were plastered against the view screen. The ship plummeted toward the ground. It sucked the air right out of their lungs. Bohr began slapping the control panel randomly, screaming, "Oh my! Oh my! What have I done?"

At about five hundred feet above the surface, the ship came to an abrupt stop and hovered. The computer had regained control. The trio were thrown forward and then backwards into their respective command chairs.

"Whew! What a ride," Hawk said with a laugh.

Shaken, Bohr asked, "What did I do wrong?"

"A few things, such as disengaging the anti-grav," Joe said, rubbing his shoulder. "My fault. I should have told you. Let's take it a little slower next time."

"Next time? You mean I can try again?"

"Until you get it right."

The next few hours were dedicated to David Bohr and his piloting skills. And, in the end, he did get it right. Or, close enough.

They waited until late in the afternoon to avoid detection, and then Joe brought the ship down for a landing. At random, they hovered over a clear mountain lake. There was no wake or surface disruption—unlike a helicopter, the ship created no air disturbance. Joe plunked the craft clumsily on the surface of the water.

"Joe, you land on water like you play a water hazard in golf."

"Quiet, Hawk. I'm still learning."

"It might sink."

"Might. Then what?"

"Dunno," Hawk said, as he stood up from his chair. There was no visible floor. It was a transparent deck. He placed a tentative step outwards and began to walk in a short circle. His eyes were glued to the water directly below his feet. "It's like walking on water. Now I know how Jesus felt."

Bohr got up from his chair and followed suit. "It is an unnerving experience all right. Reminds me of those glass-bottom boats in the Caribbean."

Joe diminished the gravity dampers to allow for a more natural feel on the water. The small waves caused a slight roll to the craft that was felt inside.

Joe had landed the ship in the region of Chile known as the Futaleufu Valley. They sat in the middle of Lago Espolón, a beautiful alpine lake. Across the lake was the small village of Espolón. The people of the village still used horses and oxcarts as their primary mode of transportation. No vehicles or electricity could be found here. No prying eyes.

"Joe, I have some U.S. currency," Bohr said. "Let's go ashore and see if we can get you some first aid and some clothes."

"And some food!" Hawk said. "I'm starving."

"Yes, some food," Bohr said with a laugh.

Joe piloted the craft toward shore. "You two go ahead. I'll stay with the ship."

The ship glided gracefully at about a foot above the water line. There was a substantial wake as the craft flew across the lake like a gigantic skipping-stone. They pulled up silently onto the grassy shore and ground to a halt a few yards from the water.

Joe led the way, opening the portal. He had a slight misgiving for a moment before stepping outside, but it felt good to be on terra firma. The lush humidity and sweet scents of exotic flora hit him like a face slap.

"Come on, Hawk. Let's go!" Bohr said, he descended from the ship. "I figure we're only about a quarter of a mile from the village."

"Here, take this." Joe handed Bohr a flashlight. "It'll be dark by the time you get back. Signal me from shore when you want to be picked up."

Bohr nodded and ruffled Joe's hair, and then he and Hawk disappeared into the dusk.

Lago Espolón, Chile

Joe piloted the craft backwards toward the water. He made a slow 180 and headed to deeper water. Then he tipped the ship suddenly and it slipped below the waves, slicing through the cool Chilean waters. The water blackened quickly, but Joe felt he should not illuminate the ship for fear of discovery from shore. He hovered at thirty feet below water level and stabilized the craft. Once it was secured, he left the control room to explore for water leakage, if any. He knew it could be hours before the pair came back from the village.

Normally, he would not have been the least concerned about how watertight the ship was, but the force of the car crash could have caused damage that would lead to a leak under pressure. As he left the bridge, he turned and hesitated a second. Maybe he should run a general diagnostic before checking around. He decided against it for now; he would do it when he got back. He wanted to see for himself if there was a problem on board.

He walked down a few corridors before reaching the door. He inspected all around the opening and found no evidence of leakage. He felt relieved. He began a less urgent inspection around the outer bulkhead, taking an indirect route back to the control room.

As he rounded a sharp turn, his instincts jarred him with a feeling of danger. He heard a rustling sound behind him. He spun around but not fast enough. His eyes caught movement, and then there was a terrific blow to the side of his head. He felt hot pain bursting in his skull. His vision went black, then filled with stars before blurring to a bright white. Then nothing. He slipped to his knees, unconscious, and fell forward with a dull thump, his arms limply at his side. His face slammed against the floor, breaking some smaller blood vessels in his nose. Blood poured from his nostrils onto the deck.

When Joe awoke, he was bound to one of the control room chairs. His wrists were tied at the back and his ankles were bound to the base. His head was hurting bad. He had suffered a mild concussion. His mouth tasted coppery. The pain was centered right behind his eyes. It was too painful to open them. His nose also hurt like mad. Tears of throbbing pain filled his eyes. He half sobbed, half moaned.

A middle-aged man with a military haircut and a polyester-wool blend blue suit was staring at him. His M-1911 pistol was clearly visible nestled in his brown-leather shoulder holster. The large, gray steel weapon made the holster appear too small.

"You OK, kid?" the man asked sounding more curious than concerned.

"I'm going to throw up," Joe said weakly.

"Use your powers and repair the damage," he suggested. "It's probably a concussion."

"What?"

"You heard me. You can repair the damage. It's not serious."

Joe screwed up his face. "I don't understand. I have no powers," he said weakly. "I'm going to throw up."

"Hold on. I don't want you puking."

"Why did you hit me?"

"Couldn't take a chance that you'd turn your powers on me."

"What 'powers'? What are you talking about?"

"Don't know. That's just it. I don't know what you can do."

"I can puke."

"No special powers?"

"None."

The stranger nodded reluctantly in agreement. "Probably not. I don't sense any Signature from you. You seem to be just a normal Earth kid. Aren't you Frank's kid? God, has someone made a mistake here?"

Joe grimaced and started to dry heave and bleed from the nose. His head hung low against his chest. "Help me. The pain …"

The stranger wasted no time. Realizing there was no trickery involved, he quickly untied Joe and half dragged, half lifted him down the corridor. His orders did not involve fatalities. He awkwardly shoved Joe into the Learning Stall.

"Get in there. The medic program will repair your injury and correct your chemical trauma. Lean against the wall." He held Joe up with one arm, then reached in past him and touched various lights against the far wall. Then he withdrew his arm quickly. Before Joe had a chance to sag against the wall, the door shut and the chamber flooded.

Ten minutes passed before the door flew open. The stranger had his weapon aimed at Joe's face.

"Whoa. Easy, buddy."

"Now how do you feel?"

"Fine. I feel fine," Joe answered, cornered in the small stall. "Can I get out of here?"

The man stepped back, not taking his eyes from Joe and not lowering his pistol. "Head toward the bridge. I assume you know where that is. If I see even the hint of a shield come up, I'll shoot. Understood?"

"Understood."

"Good."

"What's a shield anyway?"

"I thought you said you understood."

"I did, sort of. Except for the part about the shield."

"Don't mess with me, OK kid? Just move."

Joe turned and walked in front of the man. He turned slightly and asked, "Now that you have assaulted me, I wonder if I might ask a question?"

"Depends."

"Who are you and why did you slug me?"

The man hesitated a moment, as if weighing the risk of divulging any information, then answered. "My name is Cringen, DIA. I am with the Directorate of Operations. The reason I slugged you, as you so eloquently put it, is because I didn't know what your strength was. I figured you had your father's powers."

"Father's powers ... what are you talking —?"

"You and your brother have stolen government property," Cringen said.

"What, *this*?" he said. Joe gestured grandly to the walls as he walked ahead. "This is not government property!"

"I didn't say which government," Cringen said, half to himself.

They reached the control room. "Sit down. What's your name?"

"Joe Grayer. Frank is my dad."

"Then you *are* Frank's kid."

"He's a senior White House person. He works for the Department of Defense. You and your friends are in trouble."

Cringen laughed. "Your father is interfering with an approved government operation. He's the one who's in trouble, not us."

"I don't believe you!"

"Never mind that, kid. Where are your friends? When are they coming back?"

"Why should I tell you anything?"

"True. You don't have to tell me squat. On the other hand, I can easily find them and incinerate them as they walk back to shore. Want that?"

Joe decided he didn't like that option. "They're on shore waiting to be picked up." He glanced at his watch.

"How do you know when to pick them up?"

"They have a flashlight. They're going to signal with it."

Cringen pointed to a control chair. "Sit down and put your hands behind your back."

Cringen moved behind Joe and bound his hands tightly. Then he tied his ankles to the chair. "Comfy?"

Joe just glared back at him. "And just *who* is going to fly this ship?"

"I am," was the calm reply.

"You!" Joe laughed. "What do you know about flying spacecraft?"

"I know enough," Cringen said. "I *am* a flight officer, and I once served aboard this ship. It knows me and will follow my every command. I can easily override your lock-out commands, for instance." He looked over at Joe. "You could learn a lot from me, kid. But I'm not in the mood for teaching."

Cringen walked casually over to the control panel. A voice, in some foreign language, greeted the man. Cringen smiled arrogantly and looked over at Joe. "English for our young friend here."

The computer responded in English. Then Cringen passed his hands expertly over the panel surface and issued a voice command. There was immediate movement upward. The craft bobbed to the surface. It was dark outside. All the side screens were activated. The only thing they could see were the village lamps in the distance. Hawk and Bohr had not returned yet. A few minutes later they saw short bursts of light from the shore.

"I think your friends have arrived. Let's pick them up, shall we?"

Cringen guided the craft toward the shore. As the ship approached the light signal, it slowed and stopped a few feet from Bohr and Hawk. There was a moment's hesitation and then the portal door opened. The ship seemed foreboding.

Hawk turned to Bohr. "Where's Joe?" he asked.

The pair entered.

"Joe?" Hawk called out.

"That's funny," Bohr said. "You'd think he would be here to greet us explorers."

"From a strange and hostile land," Hawk said with a laugh.

"Hostile? Don't be silly. These people were nothing but helpful and friendly."

"Joe, where are you?" Hawk began to feel the pin pricks of unease.

The portal door closed without a sound behind them.

"Let's go straight to the bridge," Bohr said.

The craft lifted off the ground again and began to gain altitude. This alarmed Bohr, because the plan had been to lie low for a while. They began to run.

As the pair burst into the control room, Bohr said, "Joe, I thought we agreed to stay put for a while. What are you doing?"

"I'm tied up!" Joe said gloomily.

"Easy does it, fellas," Cringen said from behind.

They spun around and stared into the dull gray muzzle of Cringen's M-1911. Bohr and Hawk exchanged glances.

"Don't even think about it!" Cringen said. Then he motioned

toward the chairs. "Kindly sit down next to the young man."

He threw Bohr a strand of transparent thin material that resembled Scotch tape. "Bind the other kid, will ya, Pops?"

Bohr did as he was told. Then Cringen tied Bohr up. He walked behind the trio and tested the bindings.

"Joe needs medical attention," Bohr said, nodding toward the bags on the ground. "We bought some supplies in town."

"Take a look at him. He's all better now, aren't you, Joe?"

They looked at Joe and it was true. No bloodstains, no cuts or scrapes. He looked perfectly normal.

"It's true. I feel fine. He put me into the Learning Stall after he bushwhacked me. I'm not sure what goes on in there exactly, but my injuries are all better."

"Bushwhacked? Joe, who the hell is this guy?" Hawk said.

"He must have hidden on board. Probably when the car had forced the door open."

"That's right, kid. I slipped in before the portal closed back up."

"Then he lay low until you guys left. I went on an inspection round and he slugged me from behind."

"He's monkey man!" Hawk said.

"The Learning Stall," Cringen sneered. "Is that what you call it? That's infantile."

"That's what we call it. What do you call it?"

"It's not important. There's no translation into English anyway." He was paying attention to flying the spacecraft. He ascended and leveled at seventy thousand feet.

Beneath, the coast of South America was visible in the pale lights of the coastal cities and towns that dotted the shoreline. To the west, there was the faint glow of a sun long since set. To the east, there was the faintest hint of a new day, as black night skies surrendered to gray interlaced with wisps of pink.

The trio, bound hand and foot, watched as Cringen guided the spaceship north through the night sky. Ahead, on the far horizon, was the glow of big-city lights that illuminated the U.S.

Cringen gave a voice command, and the flight deck of another, identical ship flicked into view in a separate viewing window. The chairs were empty, the bridge deserted.

"This is Cringen reporting in. I have successfully captured the ship. I am en route to the desert. ETA two hours. Please advise further." He signed off and the view window dissolved.

CHAPTER 24

Washington, D.C.

When Frank Grayer arrived back in Washington, he found himself in a bit of a moral quandary. On the one hand, he felt obligated to keep the Defense Department up to date on the status of the newly discovered spaceship. On the other hand, he felt reluctant to discuss his sons' involvement in the ship's disappearance. He sat at his desk and began to make inquiries about a few of the men that he had encountered in Canada.

He pulled the dossier on Corey Wixon first. It was no surprise to him that Stell had risen through the ranks so fast. Although he wasn't qualified through education, he became a senior officer at the National Military Joint Intelligence Center. He was now second in command to H.

"Jeez. He still works for H," Grayer whispered to himself. After their chance meeting in 1977, he had run a file check on Wixon. The file showed that Wixon had run a check on him, too.

Grayer read on. Wixon's file was thicker than the last time he reviewed it. There were references to relationships in other departments. There were field operations that he'd had a hand in. Grayer flipped through the pages. There was a report that listed all the reports Wixon had requested since 1977.

It was clear that Stell was searching for something. His search arena was vast—it spanned the globe. His search methods included ultrasonic sound impulses and infrared satellite high-resolution photos. He had also performed magnetic anomaly searches along with antimatter radiation tracing. Grayer took special note of those. Clearly Stell was searching for the missing spaceship, or parts of it, just as he was.

He fingered through the files one by one. Wixon had had several classified meetings with a handful of DIA people over the years. The file did not disclose the itinerary or the subject of those meetings. That was somewhat unusual—interdepartmental meetings almost always had an official itinerary. Grayer noted that the meetings were usually with the same people. Another curious item was that Wixon usually met with people who were at a lower security level than he was. There was no mention of their respective department heads clearing the meetings or being aware of them.

Grayer was looking for a pattern, and he gradually saw that pattern emerging. He was suspicious that Stell had planted his crewmembers among government employees in sensitive areas of intelligence. It looked as if Stell had recruited senior members of the DIA into his inner circle of trusted associates. Smart move, because the DIA had access to the fastest computers and latest intelligence.

Wixon's bosses no doubt believed that he was looking for intelligence on Soviet espionage or terror groups—and they were right. But as Grayer knew, Stell was really focusing on his search for the remains of the missing spaceship.

Grayer turned to the computer screen. While the computer was quite an antique by Kor's standards, the device and its operating methodology were somehow comforting to use. Kor's experience with intelligent computing devices on his planet had been limited to voice, situation, or body-language commands. These 1982 Earth machines were literally more hands-on, and that gave Grayer reassurance. These machines were metal and plastic, with oscillating electrical currents flowing through a circuit board.

Kor had been used to integrated bioelectronics; that is, biological machines that worked like the human brain. On his home planet these devices were taken for granted, not unlike humans turning on a faucet for a drink of water. Research and progress in computing, as humans understand it, had ended millennia before Kor's lifetime. Their species had other areas of importance on which to focus their energy.

The Internet was still a fairly new method of global human communication back in 1982. The DoD was one of the first government agencies to adopt this—by Earth standards—quick and very efficient method of communication. It made it easier for the Agency to keep in touch with field operatives. Audit trails were instantaneous and snail mail was eliminated. Because of logon protocols, messages were never intercepted by hostile governments. Kor understood the theory of the Internet. He liked it. He liked the thought of humans communicating freely with one another. Even though its operations were primitive, the results were acceptable.

Grayer logged on to a highly secretive intra-government dial-up connection. Soon he was into the secret files of the DIA and CIA. His logon code gave him the highest clearance there was. No data was denied him. It did not take him long to understand that there was an unusual amount of communication between Stell and other members of the DIA.

Grayer discovered that Stell had redirected the priorities of several agencies. Stell had slowly prioritized his singular interest: the recovery of the missing spaceship. Certain names began to reappear frequently. They were James Cringen, Steve O'Sullivan, Hunter, and Connelly. Grayer pulled the file on Cringen first.

James K. Cringen
Career began right out of university, Ohio State
Recruited initially for the FBI
Trained out of Chicago
Bumped to DIA (his request)
Has done some wet work involving organized crime
Career took off a few years ago

Grayer pulled O'Sullivan's dossier. Similar pattern. His career had also skyrocketed a few years before. Made some smart political moves, no doubt assisted by Stell's behind-the-scenes manipulations, he suspected.

Cringen and O'Sullivan were now high-level bureaucrats. They were most likely original shipmates of Stell's who had taken over human bodies. The other two, Hunter and Connelly, were lower-level ops who did as they were told. They were probably human.

Cringen and O'Sullivan were dangerous, because they had the power to eliminate any opposition at will. Really dangerous, because they were probably from Stell's original spacecraft. Like Stell, they would have recourse to special powers. So did Grayer, of course, but Stell and his team outnumbered him severely. And except for their tell-tale Signature auras, their difference was almost impossible to detect. He tried to recall if he had met these men, but of course he hadn't— he would have seen their Signatures immediately. They had cleverly dodged face-to-face meetings with him throughout the years.

Grayer had read enough. He rang up the Secretary of Defense, Dwight Gerst, and requested a return call. The Secretary wasn't in, so he left a message emphasizing the importance. He shut down the computer and got up to stretch his legs.

He strolled to his Spartan office's en suite bathroom and glanced in the mirror. He wondered how long it would take for a return call from Gerst. He absently ran his fingers through his black hair. At his age, his hair should have been streaked with white. His skin should have been wrinkled. It wasn't. His alien genetic code was able to override the human genes within his human body. The alien genes realigned their human counterparts. Attaching themselves to the human genes like a friendly parasite, they corrected most, but not all, of the evolutionary flaws that were the cause of cell degeneration. In other words, the alien presence in the body helped guide its human host cells to delay aging.

Grayer had no idea how long he would stay alive. There was no precedent, but his best guess was about two hundred years.

Gerst was one of the few people who knew that Kor was an alien residing within a human host called Frank Grayer. Grayer smiled back at his image in the mirror, recalling the first time Gerst had been briefed by his predecessor. Dwight could hardly believe that Grayer was from another world. He stared and stared as if he was trying to see some horrific monster within.

His unease disappeared as Grayer's peaceful mission to Earth was disclosed. Once that became clear, many resources within the intelligence community were put at his disposal. Grayer's origins were a closely held secret. Only a select few knew about him. The President knew. As the Democrats and Republicans traded the Oval Office, each was briefed about the alien in their midst.

In 1977, Grayer had reported that Stell was among them and that in his capacity as Wixon, number two to H, he had access to high-level security. The Secretary decided not to take action against Stell because of the Government's satisfaction with his performance. He did agree, however, to keep Stell's activities under surveillance. With H's cooperation, Grayer and the Joint Chiefs of Staff had kept him on a short leash since 1977. What no one knew at that time was to what degree Stell and his crew had already infiltrated the U.S. military-industrial complex.

Looking back at these events, Grayer thought about why the military had not gotten rid of Stell immediately because of the risks he posed. It was pretty clear to him.

First, the military were not completely confident about Grayer himself. What if Stell/Wixon was in fact "the good guy" and Kor/Grayer was "the bad guy"?

Second, since Stell knew that Grayer knew who he was, he was able to leverage his worth to the U.S. Stell began to share bits of low-level alien technical know-how with the U.S. military. This enabled the U.S. to leap ahead of its perceived enemies in the arms and intelligence race.

Third, no one knew who was aligned with Stell. Every good intelligence operator knows the importance of patience when involved in counterintelligence. The Government began covertly gathering information on Stell and his circle of friends in order to get a clearer picture of whom they were dealing with.

While Gerst never pushed Grayer to feed him shreds of advanced alien technology, he hinted broadly at the idea from time to time. Both he and Grayer knew that Stell was supplying information to H. However, Grayer felt that he should not interfere with the evolutionary technical development of his human hosts. Kor's time on Earth had taught him that his hosts were an astoundingly immature and violent species.

Grayer felt that humans would do the smallest amount of harm if they were confined to elementary weapons. He watched Stell feed biometrics and genome technology to the humans. Not weapons. He watched as he guided the humans with advanced computer technology. Not weapons, not yet. He kept watching.

The phone rang, breaking into his thoughts.

It was the Secretary. "Frank, I got your message to call."

"Thanks for returning my call, Dwight. Let me get straight to it. As you know, I went under deep cover to find the lair of Stell and his crew. I also wanted to protect my two sons."

"And something has happened?"

"Yes. I tracked Stell to Sudbury in Canada. Two young men reported finding a buried UFO. It turned out that the report was genuine. Stell had a select group of men investigate. It seems reasonable that these handpicked men must be part of his original crew. They discovered that the craft was airworthy. Stell and his men tried to take possession of the ship, but the young men who discovered the craft decided to take the ship themselves. They escaped in the spaceship. That was several hours ago."

Grayer explained in brief the events of the last two days in Canada.

"What about Wixon and his men?"

"Don't know. Those two young men ..."

"Yes ...?"

"They are my sons."

The Secretary groaned. "Why did I know you were going to say that?"

"I want them back safe and sound," Grayer said. "If Wixon and his men catch up to them, I am afraid he will harm them, possibly kill them."

"Why?"

"The short answer is simply that they are my sons conceived here on Earth with an Earth mother. They are unique. They have the genes of two species. They pose a potential threat because nobody knows what alien-developed genes they possess. In other words, nobody knows their evolutionary powers. Even more problematic for Stell is that my sons are my heirs. They are princes of the House of Narok, the ruling family back home on our planet. On our planet all people were automatically vassals to our family. Thus Stell would be a vassal of my sons.

"No doubt he sees my sons as half-breeds and is not willing to subjugate himself to them. He has already revolted against our House because he has turned against me. But those reasons are more complex than I can go into at the moment. Suffice it to say that we have to get Stell under control, or out from under foot. One or the other."

The Secretary let out a long sigh.

"Stell needs me out of the way to accomplish his goals," Grayer said. "You are aware of his goals. He never could have figured on my having children. He sees them as an extension of me. Get rid of me, get rid of them."

"And the long answer?"

Grayer smiled. "Takes too long. Basically it has to do with our original space flight mission and two feuding families back home."

"We have received reports of UFO activity on the east coast. We also intercepted transmissions from Cuba to Mother Russia regarding possible missile or air attacks. Could be your sons buzzing Cuba."

"Could be. I've been looking at the same intell. I think you're right. It's an unlikely coincidence. The reports are following a route, a pattern of sightings heading south. I am confident that this is the route of the spaceship."

"They've got to try to make contact with us," Gerst said with concern.

"Us? Us who? Think about it. They were attacked by our own Government agents. Who can they trust?"

"We should have shut down Wixon and his people long ago,"

Gerst said angrily. "This would never have happened."

"True. But think about it, Dwight. We have now flushed out all of Wixon's people. That's one accomplishment. I have a short list of names that I believe are Stell and his crew."

"Let's hear it. Anyone I know?"

"These names won't be a surprise. They've all been named by our counterespionage operatives. There's Wixon and James Cringen, both DIA, working out of Agency headquarters at the Pentagon. Another, named Steve O'Sullivan, works at the Missile and Space Intelligence Center at Redstone Arsenal, Huntsville. There are two others who we suspect may also be his men. They are Max Pulman, who works for the CIA as the personal assistant to the Director of Central Intelligence, and Jao Wang, also CIA, who works in research."

"Are they back from Canada yet?"

"Unknown."

"Doesn't matter where they are. We'll have them brought in for questioning, Frank."

"Let me know if and when you have any of them. I can be of help. Our species gives off a distinct aura. We call it our Signature. If they are aliens assimilated into human bodies, I'll be able to detect it. I'm going to continue tracking the ship as best I can. If you could try to round up these people, we could narrow down our field. Thanks for your help, Dwight."

"No, thank *you*, Frank. Someday the world will thank you, too. We have a daunting challenge ahead. I'm concerned that Wixon may be more of a serious obstacle than we first thought."

As Gerst said goodbye and hung up, there was another call on hold, waiting for Grayer to pick up.

"Frank, we have another verified sighting," the voice said. "This time off the coast of Chile. Several confirms. Seems to be heading north."

Grayer thanked his caller and turned to his map of North and South America. He reached over, picked up the bright red tack from his desktop, and stuck it into the map about halfway up the coast of Chile. He stood back and examined the map. There were about twenty red tacks in all, beginning in Canada, near Sudbury. Then the trail went east to the Atlantic Ocean, south to Cuba, and finally followed a haphazard pattern through the northern part of South America and into Chile.

Sometime later, the caller rang Grayer again. "They're leaving Chile, heading north up the west coast. Present position is just north of Chile."

"Any attempt from my sons to contact me?"

"No, sir."

Twenty minutes later, Grayer received another call. The craft was now over Mexico's west coast. Still heading north. Ten minutes later the caller informed him that there had been confirmed sightings in U.S. airspace near the southern part of New Mexico.

After Grayer had pushed in the last tack, he stood back and observed a pattern. The craft had meandered during the initial stages of its flight, but after Chile there seemed to be a heading that was being held steady. The craft was coming back to the U.S. Southern New Mexico was their last known position. Grayer had an intuition that this was the final destination. It was too much of a coincidence that the original crash site was in New Mexico.

Grayer picked up the phone. "Get me a small commuter jet. A Bombardier? Perfect. And a fresh pilot to get me to Albuquerque ASAP. Call Secretary Gerst and let him know my itinerary. Arrange for an air-to-ground telephone link on board so I can keep up with the latest developments. Oh yes, and have a set of Air Force jump-suit fatigues waiting for me on board the jet. I will need to be armed; side arm, good knife, that sort of thing."

"Will do. Yessir. That's odd—our latest sighting is from just outside of Albuquerque."

"What a coincidence."

"Coincidence. Yessir. I will have a car waiting for you by the time you reach the front door."

Grayer flew to New Mexico that night. There had been one subsequent report of a sighting since he boarded. It was near Roswell, New Mexico. He was not surprised. Grayer had long surmised that Stell's craft was hidden somewhere in the New Mexico desert. What better place to hide a UFO than where there were UFO nuts around always reporting UFOs? Stell must have a cave or abandoned hangar nearby.

His worst fears were about to be realized. For some time he had been concerned that the boys had made no attempt to contact him. The fact that the ship appeared to have ended up back in the States seemed to point to a rendezvous. The twins would have no reason to meet up with Stell. Why head for New Mexico? They would not have gone willingly. Therefore they must have been compromised. No other explanation seemed reasonable. The question was: How were the twins doing? Had they been harmed?

About twenty-five miles out of Albuquerque, Grayer made his way to the cockpit.

"Evening, boys."

The copilot lifted his DC headset to free an ear. "Help you, sir?"

"I need a helicopter and pilot to meet me upon arrival."

"Civilian?"

"No. Air Force."

"Shouldn't be a problem, sir. Washington already made standby arrangements in case you needed a chopper."

"I'm impressed."

"Yessir. Anything else, sir?"

Grayer smiled and patted the doorframe. "Nope."

The copilot nodded and resumed his pre-landing ILS check.

After the sleek twin-engine jet had taxied and coasted to a stop on the tarmac apron in front of a discreet Government hangar, Grayer deplaned and boarded a waiting helicopter.

Grayer shook hands with the helicopter pilot after he badged him, and then put on the light-green David Clark H10-56 headset the pilot had handed him. "Good evening. I'm Frank Grayer. DoD. I'd like to do some low-level recon near Roswell."

"How low, sir?" the pilot asked.

"Depends on terrain and populated areas. You know the drill. Two hundred feet will do fine. This is a discrete op, so avoid civilian areas. Focus on old storage buildings, abandoned hangars, caves, that sort of thing. We are searching for a missing Government experimental aircraft that has been appropriated by hostile forces."

"Sir, if it's an aircraft, why are we looking on the ground?"

"It's a stolen aircraft. We have an air search already under way. We understand that the hostiles have taken refuge on the ground near Roswell to avoid detection. Their intent would probably be to move the aircraft once the coast was clear."

"Makes sense. Sir, I know this terrain pretty good. I will check out possible hiding places. How about a circular search pattern to start?"

"Sounds fine to me, I was counting on your familiarity of the area. How much air time do we have?"

"Counting our forty-five minutes' fuel reserve time, I figure we have about four hours, sir," the pilot said. "What sort of detection equipment have you got?"

Grayer thought for a moment. In truth, there was no equipment at all. *He* was the detection device, because he could sense the Signatures of his quarry. Then he had an idea. He removed a small handset from his pocket. It was a prototype GPS-radio combination for him to use in remote areas where direction and position were important for survival.

"This unit can detect a homing signal from the aircraft. Much like an ELT,*" Grayer said.

"Impressive," the pilot said.

"You have no idea," Grayer said.

The search for the missing spaceship and his sons began.

* ELECTRONIC LOCATOR TRANSMITTER

CHAPTER 25

West coast of Central America

One hour earlier, over Central America, a pop-up window suddenly flicked on in the main forward view screen. A super-large image of Wixon appeared on the screen. It was evident that he could see into their control room. His eyes narrowed as he looked in on them.

"My, my, Cringen. You have done well."

"Thank you, my Liege."

"And you have friends with you. Good evening, Dr. Bohr. How on earth did you manage to get aboard? Don't bother answering," he said in a bored tone. "The question was rhetorical anyway. And who are your young friends?"

"You know who we are," Joe said.

"Frank Grayer's sons. Joe and Harry. Correct?"

"Hawk. I'm Hawk, don't call me Harry."

Bohr glared at Hawk, signaling him with his eyes to keep quiet.

The less these people knew, the better.

"You're in a bit of a jam, by the look of things."

The three prisoners merely glared back at the screen. It was evident that they were tied to their chairs.

"Cringen, how did you manage to get inside the ship? We never could figure out what became of you after the arena explosion," Stell said. "Good work. You have saved us a lot of trouble."

"Thank you. As for gaining entry, I was the flight engineer for a while aboard this vessel before it was rigged for intergalactic flight. It remembered my Signature and opened the front portal for me. By the way, I ran a diagnostic and the ship is in fine shape. I have not run a weapons check yet, though, because I don't want to alert any Earth tracking devices."

Stell talked directly to Cringen through the screen. "It doesn't matter. You have probably been tracked since you left Canada. We have what we came for. The time for secrecy is over."

"Did you check with Washington to see if the Agency has been tracking the ship?"

"Yes I did, and the Department of Defense has a flight log on the craft," Stell said. "When I tried to dig further, I sensed something wrong there. When I contacted my office, I was told to come in ASAP, orders from H. But I couldn't get a hold of H personally. That has never happened before. I was suspicious, so I called an agent I know, and he began asking me what the trouble was all about. Something big is going on at the DoD, and it involves all of our little group. I'm afraid that they have figured out who we are because they are searching for you, me, and O'Sullivan. I called CIA and pulled Max Pulman out. He was sure to be on the list."

"As you say, it doesn't matter. We have the two remaining ships. Time to contact the fleet?"

"Never mind that," Stell said. "We have more immediate matters.

254 JAMES T. HARRIS

We have to deal with Kor. Fly to the old hangar. We will be waiting for you."

"See you shortly," Cringen said, and the view window disappeared.

Within minutes the spacecraft was soaring over the New Mexican desert. They had bled off most of their altitude. It was a dark cloudless night. Moonlight bathed the ground in a milky white glow. The ship passed over a small cluster of abandoned USAF hangars. The runways had been torn up long before to discourage civilian aircraft from landing at the deserted outpost. There were no maintained roads into the site. The one tired dirt road that led into the area was barricaded with a barbed wire fence. It was all Government land that had been rezoned as "environmentally sensitive."

The craft banked sharply, then hovered in front of a rusted corrugated-steel hangar. The hangar was half-moon shaped. The corrugated steel was ribbed every fourteen inches for structural support. The ship flashed a brief signal to the ground. Two giant wooden doors creaked open. The vessel nosed down toward the opening and flew gracefully inside.

Cringen flew the ship slow because it was designed more for interstellar travel than planetary flight. It was a star ship, not an airship. It did not maneuver well in confined spaces, such as when taxiing into a hangar—especially a hangar already crowded with another, identical, spacecraft.

The ship made a whisper-quiet landing a few feet in front of the other craft, blocking the entranceway. A Honda diesel generator provided power for dozens of old, incandescent, overhead light fixtures with large green shades. The 1940s illumination was woefully inadequate, and yet there was enough light to see all but the farthest corners of the building. There was a small adjutant's office in the corner by the hangar doors. It too was sparsely lit. Inside was Stell.

The portal opened and Cringen emerged. "The missing ship, delivered," he said with a laugh, but his face didn't change expression.

Stell joined O'Sullivan in greeting Cringen, then ushered him into the dusty old adjutant's office.

The trio were still bound tightly to their chairs back inside the ship, feeling sorry for themselves. The ship was locked down, and all the view areas had reverted to blank, gray walls. A pale green glow remained in the dull walls and floor.

"Sorry I couldn't warn you about the trap," Joe said. "That guy got the drop on me and slugged me out cold."

Bohr shook his head back and forth like an old grandmother. "Shush, Joe. Not your fault at all."

"David's right, Joe. We should have searched the ship better once that car wreck was yanked from the door back at the arena."

"That fellow who flew us here, Cringen, was known to the ship," Bohr said. "He knows this craft because he was the flight officer. Most probably he dampened the intruder alert and homing mechanism because he knew some code or bio-identification that allowed him to subvert the system."

"So that's how he shipped with us like a stowaway right from the start," Hawk said.

"Exactly. The ship didn't warn us because it recognized Cringen as a legitimate crew member."

"Still, it's amazing how he must have climbed up the tow rope, then hung on to something as the car was ripped out of the fuselage."

"Not entirely human."

"Obviously not," Joe said. "And, I don't know if anyone has noticed, but there's another spaceship exactly like ours parked a few feet away. What is going on here?"

"And government agents who can fly spaceships," Hawk said.

In sheer desperation, the three began trying to free themselves.

Bohr's face was flushed from the exertion. He was becoming very worried about his future prospects. He served no purpose and his life was forfeit. They had no reason to free him. He was baggage. No, worse than that, not only did he have serious government links, he was a professor of stature. His position and influence could expose them to the world. He was a threat.

Droplets of blood were slowly dripping down his wrist and collecting at his fingertips. "I can't seem to budge these bindings," he said.

"Me neither," said the other two at once.

"David, I've been meaning to ask you about what's happened in the last few days," Joe said. "What I mean is, how come there are people in the government, you know, the 'Agency,' who know how to fly a spaceship? Like this Cringen guy, a flight engineer? He knew how to fly a spaceship. God! How many flight engineers fly spaceships?"

"Joe, I am just as surprised as you," Bohr said.

"Joe's right. Something doesn't add up," Hawk said. "After we reported the discovery of the ship, how come you showed up, and Major Connelly? I remember that you and the Major worked together on a secret project in Los Alamos. Is that true?"

"Yes," Bohr answered cautiously.

"You're right, Hawk, I see where you're going," Joe said. "Didn't you and Dad work on that same project together, David?"

Bohr sighed. "Your father and I worked on a very secret project in Los Alamos, that's right."

"Suddenly, all you guys show up at our doorstep at once," Hawk said.

"Right," Joe said. "I'm betting that there's a connection between our finding the crashed spaceship and Los Alamos. Am I right?"

Bohr sighed. "You are correct, both of you." He looked from twin to twin. "I should have told you this from the outset. The Los Alamos job was a secret Government project. It involved the reconstruction and research of a crashed spaceship that was nearly totally destroyed. A ship identical to the one that you found intact."

The boys looked at each other with "I told you so" expressions.

Bohr went on. "We were told that there were others also. Two other spaceships crashed into Earth at the same time."

"These two?"

"Right."

"Why did they crash?" Joe asked.

"Who told you about the other two?" Hawk asked at the same time.

"No one knows with certainty why they crashed." Bohr looked up, hesitant to continue, searching for the right words. "The crew was in a state of … a state of suspended animation. They were not awake and therefore could not have prevented the collision with our planet."

"Why three ships?" Hawk asked.

"I have often thought about that myself. My theory is that this was a scouting squadron of some sort. An advance guard, perhaps."

"Advance guard for what?" Joe asked.

"Whom. For whom. Others of the same species, I suspect."

The twins pondered this for a while.

"How was Dad involved in all this?" Hawk asked.

"Your father's job initially was to assist in the field research of the wreck. As we gained more and more knowledge about the aliens, his job shifted to locating the two other missing craft."

"How did you know about the missing ships?" Hawk asked.

"Your father knew. He told me."

"How did he know?" Joe asked.

"Weren't you and Dad and Major Connelly on the same side?" Hawk asked. "Didn't you all work for the U.S. Government? So what happened? Why is our Government hunting us?"

Hawk turned to his brother. "We would have been cooperative if it hadn't been for their weird behavior, right, Joe?"

"Yeah, and why are we here now with our hands tied behind our backs like prisoners? These are our own Government people."

Bohr looked hard at Joe and pursed his lips. "Maybe not. I am convinced only your dad is truly working for the government."

"Who would they be working for then?"

"Hard to say." Bohr continued to be somewhat evasive. He wondered aloud, "How could Cringen possibly know how to fly this ship? A human could not. It's not possible."

"I did," Joe said.

"I know *you* did, Joe. But you were trained in that chamber for a period of time. Cringen was not."

"David's right, Joe. Cringen said he knew how to fly this particular craft. Only an alien would know what he knows."

"He doesn't look like an alien," Joe said.

"What does an alien look like?" Hawk asked.

"I don't know for sure."

"I think that the bunch of them are aliens," Hawk said. "Didn't you overhear them talking about the other guys and how the Government was on to them?"

"I agree," Bohr said. "They must have been aboard the second spacecraft that we couldn't find, the one that's right beside us. I believe that all three ships were manned by a small crew of four or five aliens. They may look human, but I think several of them are imposters who have assumed human form and infiltrated some key Government agencies, such as the DIA."

"Yes, but we searched the ship," Hawk said. "There were no aliens on board this craft."

"We searched the ship and never found that Cringen guy, either," Joe pointed out.

"If all the ships are the same, then there are no aliens on any of them," Hawk said. "We found no quarters for them. No food. No clothes. No toilet. Nothing. I'm afraid your theory is wrong. The ships came here empty. Why would there be space travelers on one ship and none on another?"

"Boys, think about it. Why would an alien culture send a star ship millions of miles, empty? A drone? For what possible purpose? No— the crew was hibernating in a hidden place. A place you would have never thought to look."

"I wonder why a hidden place?"

"Probably to avoid what happened here. Probably to escape detection if the ship crash-landed."

"I've run a diagnostic layout plan of this entire ship," Joe said. "There are no crew quarters. There are no life signs or infrared heat signs, or anything on this ship that indicates someone is alive. Period."

"I know with certainty not only that the ships are manned, but how it is done," Bohr said.

"You do?" Hawk said.

"Yes, I do. Maybe it's about time you knew a bit more than I have told you to date. In case this goes wrong here. In case I don't make it."

The boys laughed nervously. "You're nuts. Don't talk crazy," Joe said.

Bohr smiled wryly. "Boys, look at us. Look at our situation. I don't know exactly what's going on here, but the stakes are huge. Our lives could simply be collateral damage."

The twins wriggled in their chairs uncomfortably.

Bohr continued. "It all began with the discovery of a wrecked UFO in the desert. I assembled a team to attempt to reconstruct the craft, to learn as much as we could to help the Cold War effort. Your father was a test pilot at that time. He was also a graduate engineer in aerodynamics. He volunteered to help on the aerodynamics questions that we encountered."

Bohr went on to tell the twins all that had happened many years before. He told the boys how Grayer had volunteered to go into the rickety Learning Stall. He explained in rudimentary language how the principle of the transition worked. Frank Grayer, the human, had gone into the room, and two beings came out—as one. Bohr disclosed how Grayer and Kor had become two entities sharing the same body.

"It was a symbiotic relationship," he told them, "using the human as the host. In order for the aliens to travel great distances over extended periods of time, the matter of their bodies was disposed of and replaced by bioelectrical spheres that held their every thought, their every memory, and all their accumulated knowledge. Their brain, their ego, their essential memory and thinking data were stored in a sphere called a crypt-orb. Their *Being* was coaxed to exist within or in close proximity to the sphere.

"The alien Being," he continued, "does not consist of physical matter. The Being is free to drift wherever it wishes. Over many centuries, your father's people had done experiments that showed that most Beings remained in close proximity to the living human body until it expired, regardless of how the mind was encapsulated. By encapsulated I mean whether it was held in a flesh body or in an artificial container."

Bohr checked to see if the twins were still with him. They were.

"Thus the Beings of your father's people were able to exist aboard a spaceship traveling at a speed approaching light and never feel the effects of time. They did not age because the body, which ages and is mortal, was no longer hosting the mind. This is how your father explained it to me many years ago. I am not sure if that's an adequate explanation, but that's how I understand this complex situation."

Bohr went on to say that the alien's Being and Mind *both* occupied space within and around the body. Both, together, became the definition of a complete human Being. After transitioning, both minds are joined in one organic brain. The minds of the two species share the organic brain of the human host. The human host seems content with this situation because he becomes aware of truths eons more advanced than those available to him in the present. A wondrous, complex, complete, and alien world would be revealed to them—a revealed future world of evolved civilization, what could and might be.

Bohr gave the twins little time to digest all this information. "There is so much to tell you, and so little time. How do I summarize this? Let me see. All living creatures share a biorhythm where one interacts with the other. This rhythm is sometimes explained as music. There are universal frequencies and tonal modulations that all creatures throughout the universe relate to, well, universally. We call it music but it is much more complex than that. It is the pulse of the universe. It is the song of the universe.

"For example, how do we distinguish bad music from good music? It isn't only a matter of taste, it is related to our biorhythm, even our health. Ugly and hateful music makes us feel anxious, negative, sad, resentful, and pitiful. Beautiful and heavenly sounds make us feel peaceful, happy, joyous, and good. Mere sounds can cause all living creatures to respond either positively or negatively. We all have this sense of it. It is the universal code of Life's Song."

He went on to tell them of a planet hundreds of light years away, a dying planet on the outer part of the galaxy, millions of years older than Earth. Their sun, he explained, had grown too old to sustain life on their planet. Living creatures and vegetation were rapidly dying because of the excessive heat as the sun grew larger and larger. The sun would eventually go supernova and explode. The race knew that no life could live on the planet once their sun reached a certain size. In order to save future generations, and their own future, intergalactic spaceships were built to roam the universe and select a new home for their civilization.

"Our Earth was an option, but not the intended final destination." Bohr said. "The plan was to check out Earth before moving on to the ideal candidate planet. Kor and Stell were part of a three-ship recon team attempting to establish suitability."

The twins were most surprised by what Bohr told them about their human mother and how Frank had loved her. He talked briefly about the car crash and their mother's death. He described his own role as their guardian within this new context, explaining that he had helped raise them over the years as their father traveled the globe hunting for the missing spaceships and his own people.

The control room became quiet, as each of the three was lost in his own thoughts. Joe and Hawk were now aware of their origins. Their father was part alien. They were some anomalous form of half-breed. Who knew for sure?

Unbeknownst to them, there was confusion outside. Stell and the other two rushed from the shed and went outside. They stared up at the sky. There were no stars, only an overcast canopy.

"He's found us!" O'Sullivan shouted, as the sound of the Government helicopter came closer to the hangar.

"Get to the ships. Cringen, with me. Now!" Stell yelled as he ran back into the hangar.

Stell and his men split up and dashed inside their respective crafts.

Stell and Cringen burst into the control room where Bohr and the boys were bound, and the main viewer sprang to life. Cringen spoke to the panel, and a small picture of the sister ship's controls came into view. O'Sullivan was in front of its panel.

Stell watched as Cringen took control of the situation. He seemed pleased with how he handled the ship.

"Follow me out. We will fire when we have a clear line of sight," Cringen told O'Sullivan.

The ship rose a few feet off the hangar floor on his command. It slowly exited the open hangar doors backwards. Its sister ship followed close behind.

"On my signal, aim at the helicopter when it comes into view," Cringen commanded. The image of the approaching helicopter was now visible on the screen. "Say goodbye to Daddy!" he said to the twins, with no show of emotion.

Suddenly, the helicopter slowed, and then hovered nearby, its searchlight panning across the area ahead.

Cringen held a hand to his head. "I can feel him probing, my Liege."

Stell answered, "Me, too. He's got a fix on us. He knows we're here!"

The helicopter jerked suddenly skyward away from the hangar.

"Fire now!" Cringen slammed one hand on the panel and delicately touched the controls with the other. A burst of white energy shot from the craft. There was an almost unperceivable shudder of energy-recoil. Almost immediately, a second line of white lightning from the other ship joined the first. The two bolts intersected at the helicopter.

The chopper exploded into shards of white flame. Pieces of the machine flew in all directions at once. A flaming ball of aviation fuel hung where the helicopter had been. A fiery ball of debris plummeted to earth, leaving a huge black trail of dense smoke swirling downward. It hit the desert floor and exploded again. Finally the embers glowed dimmer and dimmer as the fuel burned down.

Joe squeezed his eyes shut. It can't be! he thought. It can't be our father out there. He couldn't have been on that doomed helicopter.

The ships retracted majestically into the hangar.

Cringen looked at his captives. "Now that he's taken care of, I'm not sure we need to keep you around any longer."

CHAPTER 26

South of Roswell, New Mexico

Moments before his helicopter was blown out of the sky, Frank Grayer was peering suspiciously at an old rusted aircraft hangar a mile or so ahead on an abandoned USAF base. He trained a powerful spotlight on the building. He focused his senses on the hangar below. He felt the presence of various Signatures.

He had found their lair. He *pushed* and felt for Stell's Signature. He found it easily. Grayer knew that Stell knew he had been spotted. His Aura darkened and became threatening. Grayer was aware that an attack was imminent.

He grabbed the right seat stick and applied full throttle to the dual diesel engines simultaneously. He arched the helicopter away from the hangar toward the open desert. He guessed it was too little too late. The attack was coming. His defensive shield was the only option.

With a flick of his hand, Grayer released his seatbelt and shoulder harness. In a flash, he leapt from his seat, grabbed the pilot by the lapel, and pulled himself close to the pilot's body. Grayer focused his will on a full-body protection aura that would encapsulate the pilot and protect them both. At that exact instant, the beams hit the craft and it exploded as the fuel ignited. Grayer and the pilot began to tumble earthward.

Grayer knew he had little time. The pilot's seat was aflame and dragging both of them down. Enveloping both of the bodies and the burning seat was using too much of his aura. He would have to jettison the seat. He reached down to the leg of his flight suit and slipped out his knife. He flicked it open and slashed the shoulder harness in one motion. The seat flew away in a ball of flaming sparks.

Grayer was then able to envelop the pilot completely, just before the pair struck the desert floor. Their two bodies were encapsulated within a shimmering green ball that bounced once and rolled to the edge of the flaming wreck. The entire event was hidden from view by the flaming ball of debris from the wrecked helicopter. Stell didn't see them escape death.

The force of the fall broke both the pilot's legs. Grayer fared better because he braced for impact. Back on his home planet, Kor had trained his whole life for an event like this.

The pilot screamed in agony. Grayer could not tell how badly he was hurt. He was uncertain if there was internal damage to the pilot's organs as well.

He couldn't sustain the present level of protective cowling indefinitely. He decided to conserve energy for Stell's next attack. The green aura diminished and was evident only on the one side where it protected the two from the flaming wreck. It looked like a six-foot-tall transparent green umbrella lying on its side.

The injured pilot was crying out in agony, oblivious to his surroundings. Grayer cupped the pilot's face in his hands and looked into his eyes. The mesmerized pilot went silent, and Grayer sent him to sleep with a few singsong words. He caught the comatose pilot in his arms and gently placed him on the desert floor.

He didn't want to move him for fear of aggravating his injuries. Grayer sat on his haunches and prepared for his adversaries to come and attempt to finish him off. He cloaked his Signature using a kind of self-hypnosis and simply waited for an attack, watching the sputtering embers from the explosion slowly die down.

After waiting about half an hour, it became evident that the follow-up attack would not come. They must think we're finished, he thought—that we were killed in the explosion.

He foraged around in the pockets of his flight suit until he found the small satellite telephone given to him before he left. He punched the preprogrammed telephone number and waited. After several rings, an adjutant answered. Grayer identified himself.

"We've encountered a situation here," he yelled into the small phone. "I need ground evacuation for my injured pilot. Not sure of the coordinates, so please home in on my transmission signal."

"Acknowledged. Please stand by, sir." There was an extended delay. "Sir, we confirm a lock on your present location. Expect ground evacuation by 0500."

Grayer looked at his watch. "That long?"

"Yes, sir. If you'd rather we air-evac, that would be much quicker."

"No. Too risky a pickup. We'll wait. Have them bring a medic. Out."

Inside the ship, Stell left the control room, with a nod to Cringen to follow.

Out of the captives' earshot, Cringen turned to Stell. "I believe we should terminate our hostages. Prince Kor is dead. No one could have survived that attack and explosion. I see no reason to keep them alive. His spawn may have inherited his powers."

His words were a prod to Stell's indecisiveness. Whatever his ambitions, he was not a murderer.

"Is there any evidence that Kor is dead?" Stell asked.

"Not yet. It might be prudent to visit the crash site and confirm the kill."

Stell pondered the suggestion. "You're right. Never assume." He motioned back to the control room. "Let's finish here first."

After the trio's bindings were cut, Cringen barked. "Outside."

"I don't like the looks of this," Joe whispered to Hawk.

The captives were marched out of the control room and walked off the ship and onto the dusty hangar floor.

Bohr looked steadily at Stell and then at Cringen. "We know who you are. You must be rogue agents. The Government will hunt you down."

Cringen looked at Bohr. "Oh, don't count on that, old man."

Without warning, Cringen calmly raised his pistol and shot Bohr at point-blank range. The bullet exploded into his chest, puncturing a lung and severing several arteries.

Bohr clutched his body and began to sag. Cringen fired again. This time the bullet blew through his heart and exited out the back of his ribcage. Bohr's body flew backwards, but Hawk caught him before he hit the ground. Both boys screamed in rage.

Stell grabbed Cringen's gun away from him and struck him across the face with the barrel. "Was that necessary? I never gave the order to kill."

Cringen spit out blood in defiance.

Hawk cradled Bohr's twitching body. Joe rushed to his side, his eyes wide with shock and sorrow. The twins watched the life ooze out of their friend and surrogate father. Bohr's sightless eyes went stony and cloudy as death embraced him. The hangar was silent after the rolling echoes of the pistol shots had ended.

"Get up, you two," Stell said.

The boys held the body of their dear old friend, ignoring Stell. This was the first time they had encountered death first-hand.

The air became charged with energy—from out of nowhere, it seemed. Joe began to tremble. Hawk glanced at his brother and his jaw dropped. Joe, the teenager of eighteen, was gone. In his place was an enraged man who no longer even looked human. Colors began to swirl in Joe's eyes like sparks.

Stell seemed not to notice the charged atmosphere. "I said get up!" he bellowed. "We're not going to hurt you. But we have to leave, and I have to take you with me for insurance."

Like some horrible zombie from a B-movie, Joe slowly started to rise. He began to emit a growling noise. The pitch of the growl rose and rose until the sound began to pierce the walls of the hangar. His hands were limp at his side. Wisps of lightning arched from his fingertips and snapped at the ground with an explosive crackling. In an instant, his entire body was encased in a transparent green canopy.

Cringen grabbed Stell by the arm. "He has *the power*! Just like his father."

Stell shook him off and made a motion toward Joe. Cringen, sensing the danger from the boy, grabbed the pistol from Stell and fired at Joe. The bullets ricocheted off the green shield and clattered to the ground.

Joe's fury was all encompassing. The volume of his shriek was deafening. Cringen held his hands over his ears and began to stumble backwards. Joe reached out a hand and Hawk took it automatically. The two twins stood side by side, now both protected by the aura.

The green aura gained strength and began to pulsate. The brothers, guided by some instinct, stared straight ahead at Stell and Cringen. The hair began to rise from their skulls, as if a secret wind was blowing.

Instinctively Joe knew what to do. He nodded his head forward slightly and began to *push*.

Cringen, not as well trained as Stell mentally, grabbed at his head and screamed in agony. His gun was still aimed at the twins, but his resolve had wavered. Stell grabbed him by the shirtsleeve and dragged him away from the boys. Both men stumbled backwards as the mental assault from the twins increased in intensity. Cringen fired a few rounds in futile frustration.

Stell and Cringen ran toward the second spacecraft holding their skulls in pain. Inside the control room, Stell barked at O'Sullivan, "Get us out of here, now!"

"But their ship blocks the door!" O'Sullivan said.

Stell leapt to the control panel and shoved him aside. "This is a spaceship, for God's sake. We don't need doors!"

Stell applied energy and the ship rose swiftly. It made a half-turn, then crashed through the flimsy corrugated-steel roof. Pieces of roofing material and rusted girders rained down onto the hangar floor. There was a tremendous clatter and clanging, and then the hangar was silent. Stell was gone.

Hawk let go of Joe's hand and turned and touched the body of Bohr as if that very act could bring him back to life. It didn't. Bohr lay slumped in a pool of dark red blood, his eyes staring back at them in cloudy indifference.

Hawk went down on one knee and wrapped a sympathetic arm around Joe's quivering shoulders. Joe was crouched down hugging both of his legs, his chin resting on his kneecaps, staring at Bohr.

They were unsure of what to do next—and also unsure of what had just transpired with their strange show of power. They mourned their loss of Bohr. They mourned their loss of innocence.

After some time, Hawk stood up and said softly, "Help me inside with him, will you, Joe?"

Joe nodded absently and grabbed Bohr's body under one armpit. Hawk took the other. Together they re-entered the craft. Bohr's shirt was wet with his blood. The twins gently placed him in a small room, then proceeded to the bridge together.

Back in the control room, the pair discussed their options.

"I say we go to the crash site," Hawk said. "If it was Dad in that helicopter, he may need help."

"If it was Dad, he's probably dead," Joe said. "You saw the helicopter explode and crash. I'm not sure I can handle any more deaths right now."

Hawk let the statement linger for a moment. "You know we have to go and see for ourselves, Joe. You know we have to."

Joe nodded and turned toward the control panel. He backed the ship slowly out of the hangar. There was a pool of dark red blood where Bohr had died. In the distance Joe saw the remaining fragments of the crash still smoldering in the desert. Joe approached the site and applied spotlights to the immediate area. Their ship slowly passed over the smoldering debris scattered over the ground.

There was nothing. Joe extinguished the lights and prepared to abandon the area.

Suddenly, Hawk called out, "Over there, Joe. It's a green glow. See it?"

Joe saw it, about a hundred yards. He trained the spots on the area and proceeded to fly there cautiously.

When they arrived, he flicked the lights back on to reveal a strange but welcome sight. Their father was tending to an injured man. He squinted up into the bright searchlights and waved.

Joe extinguished the lights. "He's alive! Hawk, he's alive!"

Joe clumsily landed the craft, its nose plowing into the desert gravel. They both exited the control room and ran to their father.

Their silent but hearty embrace lasted for several moments.

But something was muting the twins' exuberance, and Grayer could feel it. He pulled back and looked from Hawk's face to Joe's.

"What is it? What's wrong?" he asked.

That opened a floodgate of grief as the boys described the murder of Bohr and the trauma of the past few hours. Grayer clenched his hands in anger.

"Show me his body. Help me bring in the pilot, too."

The twins rushed to help their father. They held the pilot up by his armpits and, lifting him off the ground, took him into the space-craft. A sad moan escaped from Grayer as he spotted the body of Bohr slumped in a heap. The first human that Kor had ever known was now a victim of Kor's past. He held his old friend up and gestured to Joe to help lift Bohr up.

Grayer cradled Bohr's lifeless corpse along the corridor. "Follow me to the Chamber," Grayer told his sons.

"He has been here already. It's not going to help him," Hawk said. "He's dead."

"Since he has been exposed to the power of the chamber, it may well save his life. With luck there has been a subtle metabolic change and we're not too late."

As the group reached the door of the stall, Grayer eased Bohr's body inside. He gestured for the boys to place the still-mesmerized pilot inside, too. It was a tight fit. The Learning Room was a sorry sight. It resembled a field hospital where interns carry the wounded down the aisles to surgery. In a way, that's exactly what was happening.

Grayer voiced some instructions and slipped out the door as it closed. He led his sons to the bridge.

The view screens were already activated when they entered. Grayer went to the control panel and spoke softly. The middle screen switched to a view of the Learning Stall. They could see the two men immersed in a greenish substance, their limp bodies suspended and their arms floating gently beside them.

Hawk was confused. "Dad, Bohr is dead. What are you doing?"

Grayer moved his eyes slowly away from the screen and addressed his son. "I may be able to help him return to our world, the world of the living. I am hoping his Being has lingered—out of uncertainty, perhaps, or reluctance to move on. Most times, the shock of traumatic death causes the Being to cluster around the body. Since time measurement does not exist outside of the human mind, his Being has no sense of it, and may not move on immediately."

"Wait a minute. You can bring him back to life?" Hawk asked.

Grayer answered patiently. "David's body is in need of repair. He has had exposure to the machine already. I mean, prior to the attack. He is already protected from fatal damage. If he were human, he would not have survived. Exposure in the Stall means that he may live. His organs must be rebuilt after having been starved of oxygen for so long. The brain is the most delicate. Its survival depends on how long the organ has been left to degenerate.

"In David's case we may be in luck because he hasn't been gone for too long and he has had exposure to the stall. What you call the Learning Stall is primarily a healing chamber and should be able to repair the damage to the body. If we've acted in time, body and Being will reunite into a single 'David' again."

"And if not ...?" Hawk asked, anxiously watching his father's face.

"There could be irreparable brain damage."

The brothers moaned in unison.

"Worrying won't do you any good. Let's deal with results and plan from there."

Grayer gestured to the screen. "Both of them are fine for now.

The repairs and healing will take time, especially as we are processing both at once."

He nodded to the doorway. "Come with me, there's much to do. If we're in luck, we may be able to rescue the crew. I will show you where to find their hibernation quarters. There's no time to waste."

"So there *was* a crew on board?"

The boys followed their father down a series of short corridors. Grayer halted and touched a seemingly solid wall, and a three-foot door shuttered open. Inside was a blank cell. Grayer had expected to see a case, somewhat like an egg carton, with several silver balls inside. To his shock, the tiny cell was empty.

"Dad. What is it?" Joe asked. "Where are the crew's quarters? This can't be it. This is a hole in the wall. Literally."

Grayer's voice was strained. "They have taken the crew. Stell must have taken them after he captured you."

"Dad, this is a small hole. What is this crew? Midgets?"

"The crew was safely stowed in crypt-orbs. There were five of them per ship, I believe. They are globes the size of a large softball. Stell must have them now. I am afraid that he will recruit them to his side after transitioning them." Grayer's shoulders sagged noticeably. "I needed them to even the odds against him."

Grayer rubbed his chin thoughtfully, still staring at the gaping hole. He passed his hand over the wall and the cabinet door shut, soundlessly, disappearing once more into the wall. The twins followed him to the bridge.

On the way, Grayer explained the necessity of the crypt-orbs. He began by describing how his race had evolved a method of extended space travel. Long periods of travel time—hundreds of years—necessitated that their bodies be reconfigured to last the length of the journey without deterioration. None of their initial attempts to accomplish such a reconfiguration had worked at all.

In the end, over the course of thousands of years of experimentation and refinement, they were able to separate the body from the Mind. Kor's race had learned how to digitally transfer the complete contents of the Mind into spherical globes called crypt-orbs. Each of these eight-inch silver globes contained the entire essence of an individual's Mind.

The most important and fortuitous discovery was that—once the Mind had been transferred to the tiny globe—the Being accompanied the mind in close proximity. Since the Being is a *force* and not comprised of matter, it exists outside—or, arguably, *inside*—the world of matter. It was almost always the choice of the Being to accompany the Mind's essence on the journey through space by occupying the same space as the crypt-orb.

On prior test journeys, the astronauts' bodies had been thawed and reunited with the Mind and Being using the technology in the Learning Stall. This very long distant space journey was different. It was a prototype for travel without any body recovery. The flesh bodies would be acquired from the resident population. The main reason for choosing this method was that scientists had no idea what immunity from disease would be necessary to survive alongside existing creatures on an unknown planet.

It was likely that the resident race of people would have viruses that might prove fatal to the travelers. And vice versa. What if the travelers carried a virus that wiped out the entire race of native peoples on the new planet? And, of course, traveling without bodies would allow vast numbers of people to make a long journey in a small number of spaceships.

Kor went on to describe how his race could assimilate with another person and share their body. It is understood, he explained, that all Beings share a celestial commonality. In other words, we are all Beings together sharing a bountiful space. He also explained that the brain was considered an organ of the body—the most important organ, maybe, but an organ nonetheless, and not synonymous with the Mind. The two Beings and two Minds would share the one body together as if it were a totally natural state of existence. It was a joyful state of Being.

Joe spoke first. "So you are really two people coexisting in one body. Have I got that right?"

Grayer smiled. "Yes, you do. We—the human Grayer, and Kor—are one co-joined entity. All that was Grayer, and all that was Kor, are now one new entity."

"Can you be separated back into your, er, parts again?" Hawk asked.

"You know, Hawk, that's a good question. I don't really know. We would feel a tremendous loss to be separated, now that we have grown together as one. I see us as inseparable now."

Grayer went on to describe in detail how in the beginning, many years before, he had been a military volunteer working with Bohr. He volunteered for a test and was merged with Kor using the Learning Stall. Unfortunately, the Stall was destroyed during the transfer, and none of the other crew made it through.

"So the rest of your crew is still trapped aboard your wrecked spaceship?" Joe asked.

"All the recovered pieces from the wreck were buried to avoid discovery. The crew's crypt-orbs included. No one who saw them would ever guess what the globes were really for. Well, David did, but he kept it a secret. There is the real possibility that their Beings may have abandoned their Minds if they felt a need to move on, or if the globes had been damaged during the crash."

"Were they damaged?" Joe asked.

"I'm not sure. They appeared scorched on the surface, but that wouldn't have fatally damaged them. They looked pretty beat-up and tarnished when I saw them. Their luster was gone. They looked gray.

I'm not sure about the integrity of their Mind and memories."

Suddenly, he slapped his hand down soundly on the control panel. "You boys have given me a great idea."

"What's that?" Hawk asked.

"We can recover the hidden crypt-orbs from my old ship and try to transition them with other humans. That might even up the odds for us if or when we do battle with Stell. If I know Stell, he has grand plans for this planet as his fiefdom. If we could rescue my crew and use them to fight Stell, we could stand a chance to stop him. Otherwise I am afraid we are doomed."

"Doomed? Why doomed?" Hawk asked.

"Well, what are we waiting for?" Joe said, ignoring Hawk.

"Can you find them?" Hawk asked.

"I know where the crew are," Grayer said, he turned to the control panel. "They are part of the wreck, and it's in storage underground. I just don't know what condition they're in. Now, with this ship, I may now be able to restore my crew. My crew! My mission! Boys, we have a chance."

Just then, they all spotted a small convoy of military vehicles. "I forgot about them," Grayer said. "I radioed for help after the attack on the helicopter."

The convoy was a few hundred yards away. The twins looked to their father for a course of action. He shook his head, admonishing himself for his lapse of focus. An immediate decision had to be made. "I'm going to have to launch. Unfortunately, the convoy is going to be a witness."

"Dad, we have no choice!" Hawk said.

"You're right. We're out of time, Hawk." With that, Grayer spoke a command to the panel and the silver ship disappeared.

Or seemed to, in front of the astonished eyes of the men driving the convoy trucks. One minute a strange craft was in front of them, and the next second they were looking at empty desert.

The lead vehicle ground to a halt, and a camouflaged soldier jumped from the truck. With his hands planted firmly on his hips, he looked all around him. There was nothing but the charred remains of a military helicopter in front of him. The sky was a stark black, with only twinkling stars interrupting the inky nothingness. There was no ship. The silver airship that had been no more than yards away from him had simply vanished before his eyes. He had seen his first flying saucer. He knew that a close-encounter report would have to be filed. Of course, he dreaded the jokes and laughter he'd face.

Out of the corner of his eye, he spotted his driver. He too was in awe. The soldier wasn't the only one to have seen it. The whole convoy must have seen it, too. Maybe the smirks would not be forthcoming this time.

CHAPTER 27

Groom Lake, Near Mexico

Once airborne, the craft streaked through the sky.

"Only minutes away," Grayer said. "I've been meaning to ask you—how did you escape from Stell?"

The twins began to fidget and look uncomfortable.

Joe ventured in. "I guess it was me at first. They had shot David. I went ... well ... nuts! I forget what happened exactly, but they were going to shoot Hawk and me, too. I guess I lost it. Some weird feeling came over me. It was as if I knew what to do to protect Hawk and me from danger. It was instinct more than anything. There was this green sort of wobbly clear flux that acted as a shield for us. Lightning sort of started coming out my fingers, too."

The guy they called Cringen shot at us," Hawk said. "We were scared at first. Then we got really mad. Well, Joe got really mad. He made this weird loud-pitched noise. He projected it, and they backed off a bit.

Well, then I joined Joe and together we *pushed* them hard, really hard. We thought unpleasant thoughts, like nasty attack thoughts, and *pushed* them at Cringen and another guy."

Joe chuckled. "Then they ran away covering their ears."

"Thought and sound as weapons," Grayer said. "It's a learned skill that takes millennia to develop. Humans need thousands of years of evolution before they learn these skills and then genetically pass them on to their offspring. And yet, you have this skill."

The twins looked at him curiously.

"What you describe is a psychic weapon that evolves with the slow evolution of the brain and an intuitive comprehension of some of the secrets of sound modulation. We can harmonically fluctuate the airwaves to create sounds that the human ear cannot detect. Our primal instinct is to flee, but over time we evolved the option of utilizing these harmonics to immobilize or mesmerize attackers. You must have genetically acquired these skills as part of a hybrid mutation of your mother and me."

"Are you telling us we're mutants?" Hawk asked.

"No, Hawk. I am telling you that you and Joe have jumped a genetic chasm that has propelled you hundreds of generations ahead of your fellow humans. By pairing our two species, I may have begun a genetic process that has accelerated human evolution as much as half a million years. When you mate …"

"What?" Joe blurted out. "Whoa, Dad. Give me a break. I'm eighteen and normal. I'm not some bug-eyed alien!"

Grayer studied the pair in a new, more scientific light. "You're right, Joe. You're not alien; you're human. You and Hawk don't look like my Kor body. I was evolved a million years beyond where human bodies are today. However, my ancient ancestors *did* resemble humans as they look here, today. You may look normal, but you have the evolutionary power and skill of a human being far into Earth's future."

"You mean all humans will evolve into a people who have advanced powers, like the one we used on Stell?" Hawk asked.

"There's no doubt that some will," Grayer said, watching the monitor as they flew along. "There is something strange, though."

"What's that?" the twins asked.

"Few of our race ever acquired true psychokinetic power—what you called *push*: the movement of thought waves through space or air to make contact with another person. Or, in your case, to actually attack another."

Grayer turned from the panel and looked at his sons. "You seem to have this power. And, I suspect, other talents we have yet to learn. My special skill is the power of suggestion using sound waves. People cannot resist this power. On my home planet, we called this the power of the Song.

"Our race, all races actually, are governed by the Song. That is the rule of music and sound. Why do you think humans love music? It is the rudimentary element of the universe. Sound, frequency, pulse, beat, tone, are all, each and every one, the singular link to all others in the universe. We are not alone. We are linked. We are linked as a planet. We are linked as an interplanetary system. We are linked as a galaxy. We are one as a universe. We are one with God."

Both boys looked at their father, speechless. "God?" they said. "You've never mentioned God before. We always thought you were, you know, sort of non-religious."

Grayer looked puzzled. "I am. Of course. Religions are the creation of Man. They are contrived. We, too, had organized religion as a form of idol worship for many millennia."

"Then what happened?" Hawk asked.

"We discovered that God truly does exist, of course," Grayer said nonchalantly. "So we did not need superstitious beliefs, prophets, or idols to prop up our insecurities any longer."

"But all religions believe in God, or *a* god."

"None that I have studied here on Earth truly believe in a non-human-like god. Most believe in a Santa-Claus-looking humanoid god. They talk about belief in God and in God's 'messengers' as a *road* to salvation. Belief in God is the *destination* discovered. If you truly believe and understand God, you *are* there."

Religions worship religion itself. Worshipping a religion becomes the end unto itself. Mortals created religion. God didn't. Why would He have to create religion? He is God. God does not care if anyone believes in God.

"We humans exist throughout the universe. My home species of human exists. That is all that matters. If we are, they are, and God is. How much simpler can it be?"

His sons simply smiled blankly.

"Uh, Dad? Can we get back to the mutant bit?" Hawk asked. "Joe and I don't know what happened exactly, but calling us alien mutants sort of freaks me."

"Me, too," Joe said. "I don't feel like some weird mutant, Dad."

"There are certain things my original race can do because of evolution," Grayer said. "They may seem like magic, but the science is simple. The most common is using the power of the Song to mesmerize people into doing what you wish. It's rarely against their will. It's the power of suggestion."

Grayer looked at the screen. He was working on some program with the computer while he was talking. "What you boys did today was go to a new plane where you attacked your adversary with the power of your Mind and your Song combined."

Before the boys could say anything, Grayer said, "We're here.

We'll talk more about this later. Time to rescue my crew."

"We have company," Joe said, pointing to a gleaming spaceship about a mile away on the ground.

Grayer cursed his bad luck. However, he had not picked up any Signatures yet. He masked his aura as best he could and set the craft down outside the range of the other ship.

"Joe. Hawk. Stell has beaten us to the remains of my ship. He's landed at the spot where the remnants of the wreck were buried underground in 1977. This is as close as I can get without alerting them to my presence. You two must go in my place. They won't sense you because your human aura is minimal. Ordinarily I wouldn't ask you to risk yourselves, but it's too important not to try."

"What do you want us to do?" Joe asked.

"Less than a mile away, exactly where their ship is, there's a secret government burial site for top-secret objects and such things. Things that the government believes would not be in the best interests of the population to know about. What's left of my original spaceship, and my crew, is buried in a fifty-foot container below ground. The container is rust colored and has the serial number LA2423 on the side. The container is stored on Level 5."

"2423, Level 5," Hawk repeated.

"I need you to take the Bot and go quickly to the site. Use the element of surprise and go inside and retrieve the crew crypt-orbs. They're in a black metal box inside the container. Don't allow these government men to leave with my crew from the wreck. I'll come immediately and lend a hand if you've been compromised."

"How will you know?" Hawk asked.

"I'll know."

Grayer ushered them to the forward port door. With ghost-like stealth, a Bot appeared behind them. It hovered soundlessly. The door whispered open, letting in the desert air. "Go now. The Bot knows the coordinates."

"Never even knew we had a Bot," Hawk said.

"Wonder where it was all this time?" Joe said.

The twins stepped out and away from the craft, but their feet never touched the ground—they were grabbed by a faintly visible, green force field emanating from the Bot. They were whisked off through the desert morning in the Bot's firm clutches.

As their father had said, it was less than a mile to the entrance to the underground storage site. They flew at about a hundred miles per hour over the flat, desolate desert floor at about ten feet, high enough to clear any brush or cactus. It was exhilarating for the boys, who had a hard time wiping the grins off their faces. For Joe, who loved biking, it was exactly the sort of adrenalin rush that he relished. For Hawk, less so, but he enjoyed the speed nonetheless. It helped both of them forget the serious situation.

In less than a minute, the Bot slowed to about twenty miles per hour. Joe could see the silver spaceship glittering ahead. Seconds later, the Bot stopped and released them. They dropped to the ground indelicately. The Bot turned back toward their ship and sped away, disappearing from sight in seconds.

"Well, that Bot isn't much on etiquette, but it's fast," Hawk said.

"Sure is. Look, I see an entrance not far from their ship. It's ahead to the left."

"I see it too. It's almost invisible, even from here."

"Figures. Dad told us that this is a huge secret underground storage facility for the military. They don't want accidental visitors."

The pair trudged toward the facility, their running shoes hardly making a sound. Along the way, they observed no one and encountered no resistance. There was no lookout that they could see. Within minutes, they found themselves at the mouth of a cleverly disguised entranceway. It blended in with the desert and would have been impossible to spot from the air.

The spaceship sat quietly just yards away from the entrance. They cautiously approached the entrance to the facility. For a brief moment they hesitated—they were not armed and had no way of knowing what they might come up against. Emboldened by their newfound powers, however, they continued through the entrance.

The boys stumbled as they entered from light into darkness, losing their footing as the floor sloped down away from them. As their eyes adjusted to the lack of light, they were able to see elevator doors ahead.

"I don't want to take an elevator and walk right into their hands," Joe said.

"Look around. I don't see any stairs, Joe. Got a better idea?"

"No," he said grudgingly, and pushed the elevator button.

At first nothing happened, then the doors suddenly flew open. The boys jumped back, startled, expecting an attack. But there was no one there.

Looking left, then right, they entered the elevator. There were half a dozen buttons leading to six stories of underground storage. The doors began to close. Joe stuck his foot out and jammed it open.

"Hawk, we don't have time to search all six floors," Joe said.

"Dad said the container was on Level 5. It's a safe bet that means the number five button on the panel."

"I guess so," Joe said.

The door tried to close again but recoiled abruptly after hitting Joe's foot.

"The government agents are probably there already," Hawk said. "We're sure to run into them."

"You're right. We don't want to walk straight into a trap."

"Or worse. They get past us and escape, trapping us down there."

"Do you think they know where the container is?"

"They knew where the installation was. I'm sure they do."

The elevator door made another angry attempt to close. After a moment, Joe said, "I vote we not go down there. I think we should stay here and use the advantage of our surprise. We nab them as they leave the elevator."

"Good plan. I agree. Dad can't be more than a few minutes behind us. He can back us up."

Hawk was about to turn and leave when an alarm bell started clanging. It came from the elevator. "So much for the element of surprise! We've held the elevator too long. The damn alarm went off."

The boys jumped from the elevator, and the door closed. They heard noises from inside the elevator shaft. It was on its way down, most likely to get Stell and his men.

"Hold on, Joe, we do have a weapon! Think about it. We can *push* them. Force them really hard, you know, with our thoughts. Remember how they ran the last time?"

"You're right. We also have that shield thing we can do. I love that green force field stuff that you do. You have to admit that was cool. As for the *push*, I don't think I can just do it whenever. You know I was under extreme stress before. You and I were really pissed. That's when it worked."

Hawk stared at the closed elevator door. "Whatever we decide, we had better do it soon. These guys will be on their way up soon. They could open the door at any moment."

They retreated into the desert. The ship was there in front of them. They turned and looked at each other.

"We could sneak aboard the ship," Joe said.

"Then what? Wouldn't that be the same as them capturing us? We would be exactly where they want us. Besides, we have no weapons, really. We can't point our fingers and play pretend gun."

"Let's at least sneak into the ship and take our own orbs back."

"What makes you think that our orbs are on board?"

"Hawk, why would they take them into the storage area? Doesn't make sense. I'll bet they have the orbs. They haven't had time to do anything with them yet."

Joe ran up to the spacecraft and stood for a moment looking at the fuselage. He cocked his head slightly to one side, and then placed his hand against the side of the ship. There was a dramatic pause as the craft ran a triangular ID check with all nearby ships and found Joe's identification on the ship a mile away. The portal opened.

Hawk was amazed that the door had opened. Joe led the way without hesitation.

Hawk followed Joe down the corridors, his eyes darting from side to side. This ship seemed to be identical to theirs in every respect. Before long they found themselves in front of the same wall that their father had shown them. Joe touched the wall. Nothing. With his hand splayed out, he made a wider circular sweeping motion. Suddenly the opening appeared. Joe saw a tray inside and reached for the contents.

"That's enough, fellas. Step away from there."

The twins spun around to see a figure standing with a pistol in his hand. A plume of green force field burst from Joe's hands, splaying outward like a spider's web and covering Joe and Hawk with a shield. The wavering transparent-green force field was like half a giant egg, covering the boys on their exposed side.

The twins didn't recognize the man. They showed no fear because they were emboldened by their prior success in the abandoned hanger. The agents had retreated when they encountered their powers.

"Are you one of Stell's zombies?" Joe asked.

The man bristled. His human Being did not like the insult. His alien Being didn't fully appreciate the sarcasm.

"You boys can come along with me. We all need to talk," he said. "The others will be topside any time now." He waved the gun toward the rear portal. "Come on. Get going."

"Screw you! You can't harm us!" Joe said.

Without missing a beat, the man fired four rounds at the boys. The bullets fell to the floor at the boys' feet, with the floor absorbing the sound.

The boys ducked instinctively, recovering themselves in one fluid motion.

"Just checking to see if your shield was really working," the man said with a lopsided grin. "Say, have you seen this one?" He reached behind his back and pulled out a different pistol-like weapon. He fired at point-blank range.

Joe and Hawk fell back as the energy arched from the nozzle of the weapon toward them. It struck the shield like lightning, and for an instant the shield wavered and turned pale. Joe groaned in pain. He had felt the thrust of this unknown weapon.

"What is it, Joe?" Hawk asked. He had felt nothing.

The man nodded knowingly. "So it's *you* who has the Aura power." He addressed Joe. "Protecting your brother with your aura force is exhausting, especially if you are young and inexperienced. You are doing the work of two people. Protecting two people with energy intended to protect only one can be very taxing indeed. Time is not a friend."

The man fired the weapon again and Joe groaned again. Sweat began to form on his brow. The shield was beginning to weaken. Joe was losing control.

Hawk held up his hand. "No more! We will follow you." He gestured to Joe. "Come on. Let's take a break."

The man waved his weapon and the brothers filed along the corridors and out of the portal into the desert. They stood outside, their backs to the spaceship. It may have been the light, but Joe's shield was looking weak. The man walked toward the entrance, talking into a device. A group of people began to emerge from the doorway of the underground facility into the desert sun.

One of them swaggered toward them. He was carrying a box. "Well, well. We meet again, my young sleuths." It was Stell. He held up the somewhat-battered box. "Looking for this? Well, you're too late. We beat you to it! This was your father's last chance. Now we have all the crews and you have none." He looked about him. "Where is he? He can't be close by, because I can't sense his Signature."

Cringen suddenly appeared at Stell's side. "He's left you all alone," he said to the twins. "All alone to die." He pulled out a pistol and fired several rounds at the boys. The bullets fell uselessly to the ground, but the boys' shield was clearly continuing to weaken.

Cringen gestured to the others, who also pulled out their weapons and began to rain bullets down on the boys. The two of them were cornered and surrounded. Joe felt his knees give way under the strain of maintaining the shield. Hawk reached for him and held him up.

Stell turned his back and began to approach the spacecraft.

"Help me, Hawk," Joe said with a strained voice.

"Let's make a run for it," Hawk said.

"I can't cover our back if we run. It will take too much of my energy," Joe said weakly. "I don't know how much longer I can hold against these guys. Try something, anything."

Hawk stood beside his brother. He concentrated hard. The force field strengthened marginally for a few seconds, then weakened again.

Joe reached out his hand. "Here. Hold on to me."

Immediately the shield brightened, soared, and roared, holding strong.

Meanwhile the group was switching weapons. They substituted bullets with some kind of energy pulse weaponry.

The twins slowly backed away from the onslaught attempting to put some distance between them and their attackers. To no avail. The boys' shield began to flutter. There was an odor of ozone in the air like the smell after a lightning strike.

Hawk turned Joe. "It's no good. I can't do the green shield thing as well as you can. I'm not much help!"

"Hawk, you must have other powers. I know it. Try something else."

Hawk tried to *push* but couldn't focus properly. Both boys were on their knees. The shield had shrunk around them, protecting them like a tortise shell.

"Don't worry! It will all be over soon," Stell said with a sneer.

Just then, the other assailants stopped firing and looked around. There was silence.

"I can feel him!" someone yelled. "Prince Kor lives!"

"I thought he was gone from my life!" Stell said.

"How could he have lived through the helicopter attack?" another voice moaned. "How? Only a true prince could have survived."

"Shut up!" Cringen said. "We can take him! Let's fight, my Liege!"

Stell seemed disoriented—yet somehow uplifted—to know that Kor was still alive. "I know Kor. We are not up to the task, especially if he has these two to help him."

"But Prince Stell —"

"To the ship," Stell said. "We have what we want. We have every-thing—both crews, intact. We have an army! We will have to deal with these puppies another time."

The halt in the onslaught helped clear Hawk's mind. He focused on Stell and the package he carried. Hawk slowly raised his arms from his sides, palms up. A mysterious breeze appeared from nowhere and the hair on Hawk's head began to rustle. The hair on his arms stood on end.

"That's it, Hawk. Use your power against them!" Joe's breathing was labored. His hair also stood on end. He could feel the air crackle with static-electric charge.

Hawk glared at Stell, focusing hard. Stell warily gripped the side of the ship to enter. Then, as he was about to go through the portal, he was thrown back, and landed abruptly on his rear, throwing up a small clump of dust. He looked wildly at Hawk, then at Joe.

"How did they do that?" he yelled. "They can't do that!"

The others scurried past Stell like rats heading for higher ground. He was the last one still outside. The desert sun was causing him to breathe hard. His body was sweating with strain and frustration. He got up, clutching his precious package of crypt-orbs, and moved toward the ship's portal opening. He was stopped at the threshold by some invisible force.

Realizing that the package was somehow being repelled at the doorway, Stell maneuvered himself so that only the package was outside the ship. Teeth clenched, he gripped it hard with both hands and tried to heave it inside with him. Sweat trickled down his forehead and into his eyes but the package was going nowhere.

If Stell wanted to leave, he could do so. The package, however, would have to stay behind.

Hawk stood, gazing evenly at Stell and the package, with both his arms stretched outwards, palms up. Stell appeared indecisive—confused and frustrated all at once.

Suddenly they all sensed movement.

Joe's ship, with Grayer at the helm, was approaching fast. It started as a dot, then quickly filled the sky. In an instant it had zeroed in on them, stopping abruptly a few yards away. Stell pulled frantically at the package. His crewmates were trying to pull him inside, unaware of the problem. He fought them off while trying desperately to pull the package aboard. "Don't pull me! Shoot at them!" he roared at his men. "Get them to release me."

Three men drew their weapons and fired at the boys. Once again, Joe jumped in beside Hawk and threw up the green shield.

The portal door to their spaceship flew open and their father jumped out, firing a pair of weapons. Plumes of white light and thin smoke burst around Stell's head. He threw up his strong green shield in time to deflect Grayer's shots. The protective shield prevented him and his crew from firing back, so the attack was one-sided and vicious.

The firepower that Grayer threw at Stell was staggering. Quickly the shield was ablaze in energy. Stell was no longer visible. Clouds of energized smoke billowed from the portal door. Hawk held on to the package with his mind. He willed that it not accompany Stell on board.

Then, without warning, it flew across the desert floor and skidded to a stop at Hawk's feet. As Hawk looked back up, Stell's spacecraft lifted from the ground.

Grayer rounded the twins up and pushed them toward the ship. "Get aboard fast!" he screamed.

Hawk scooped up the package and dashed toward the ship.

The other craft banked, turned around, and came at the trio. The three covered the few yards to the portal opening in seconds. Joe dove inside headfirst, followed immediately by Hawk and the precious package.

Joe looked back in horror. "Hawk, Dad's not going to make it!"

It was true. The silver wing of Stell's ship was on top of their father. It struck him on the shoulder. Grayer tumbled to the ground in a cloud of dust.

An instant later, Stell's ship smashed into their craft, bouncing it hard against the ground. Joe and Hawk were thrown down the corridor and slammed against the walls.

The two ships recoiled in a cloud of dust. Stell's craft reversed. Just as the enemy ship was gaining momentum to strike again, Grayer jumped through the portal door. At his voice command, the door instantly shut behind him. Grayer raced down the corridor, yelling, "To the bridge, boys."

A voice warned of an energy attack and raised the appropriate magnetic shields to deflect the force. There was a slight shaking, like an earth tremor, as the bursts hit. Their ship was under the giant dome of a near-invisible force field. It wavered like heat above the desert floor with each energy hit.

Just inches above the fuselage, great bursts of lightning ricocheted off the protective field. Grayer gained control of the panel and activated all of the screens at once. While the enemy's ship was airborne, theirs was still exposed, flat on the desert floor. A distinct advantage to the enemy craft.

Grayer commanded a liftoff and the ship leapt almost vertically from the desert floor into the air. The other craft swooped in for another attack. The trio's ship repelled the onslaught with a fireworks display of sparks.

Grayer lined up the craft for a retaliatory shot. He fired, and a burst of energy struck like lightning against the silver fuselage of the enemy ship. The air seemed to wiggle at the strike-point as the enemy shield held off the attack.

That was only the beginning. Both ships lined up for attack after attack. Since both crafts were of the same type and had healthy shields, neither sustained any damage.

Stell withdrew first. One moment he was there, and then the sky was empty.

The three Grayers searched the sky in anticipation of the next attack, but there was nothing. In the meantime Grayer requested a damage assessment. The ship self-diagnosed and provided a status report. All was well. Bio-recharging was ongoing.

"Let's chase them," Joe said, baring his teeth.

"Joe's right, Dad. We can't just let them get away. Not now."

The Grayers' spectacular silver spacecraft stood frozen above the desert floor, poised for battle.

"Getting away?" Grayer asked. "Away where? There is no place he can hide for long. Now Stell is the fugitive, and we are the hunters."

He communicated with the computer and then turned to his sons. "They're gone. Out of range. We could spend time trying to find them, as I have done for many years. Or we can prepare for the battle that is ultimately to come."

He looked at his sons. "Now is the time for healing, for mending. Think of David. He will mend. Think of our small family—we have found each other again. We have fought hard to overcome the fracture that Stell has brought into our lives."

Grayer could see he still had some convincing to do. "The time to learn your mixed heritage and hone your extraordinary skills has come. There is much training ahead. I need you strong. I need you prepared. I need you enlightened."

Hawk reached out with his right hand. "One family," he said.

"The Grayers," Joe added, reaching out with his hand and crossing it on top of Hawk's.

"The House of Narok," Grayer/Kor finished, placing his hand above both of his sons'.

Grayer voiced a soft command to the screen, and the ship eased into a flight path toward a safe destination—the place where Grayer had grown up: a place where the twins would train, unhindered, for the turbulent times ahead.

In the blink of an eye, they were gone.

Printed in the United States
132641LV00006B/53/P